"I'm a private investigator, pal. People pay me for information."

He reached in his hip pocket and produced a leather wallet. Taking some bills from inside, he laid them on the desk and stared at me with a questioning lift of his brows.

"You don't have enough money. Get out of here."

He reached into his wallet once more. This time he handed me a small white business card.

"You're Brandon Kirkpatrick?"

"You weren't what I expected, either," he admitted. "I assumed D.B. Hayes was a man. What does the D.B. stand for anyhow?"

"Dangerous when bothered." I was still angry.

He grinned. The man was gorgeous even when he was angry, but when he smiled he was downright lethal.

Dear Harlequin Intrigue Reader,

It might be warm outside, but our June lineup will thrill and chill you!

* This month, we have a couple of great miniseries. *Man of Her Dreams* is the spine-tingling conclusion to Debra Webb's trilogy THE ENFORCERS. And there are just two installments left in B.J. Daniels's McCALLS' MONTANA series—*High-Caliber Cowboy* is out now, and *Shotgun Surrender* will be available next month.

* We also have two fantastic special promotions. First is our Gothic ECLIPSE title, *Mystique*, by Charlotte Douglas. And Dani Sinclair brings you *D.B. Hayes, Detective,* the second installment in our LIPSTICK LTD. promotion featuring sexy sleuths.

* Last, but definitely not least, is Jessica Andersen's *The Sheriff's Daughter*. Sparks fly between a medical investigator and a vet in this exciting medical thriller.

* Also, keep your eyes peeled for Joanna Wayne's THE GENTLEMAN'S CLUB, available from Signature Spotlight.

This month, and every month, we promise to deliver six of the best romantic suspense titles around. Don't miss a single one!

Sincerely,

Denise O'Sullivan
Senior Editor
Harlequin Intrigue

Dani Sinclair

D.B. HAYES, detective

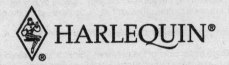

HARLEQUIN®

TORONTO • NEW YORK • LONDON
AMSTERDAM • PARIS • SYDNEY • HAMBURG
STOCKHOLM • ATHENS • TOKYO • MILAN • MADRID
PRAGUE • WARSAW • BUDAPEST • AUCKLAND

For all the caring volunteers who work with strays
and abandoned and abused animals every day.
You understand that the world is a richer place
when we open our hearts and our lives to
these intelligent beings covered in fur.
And to Roger, Chip, Dan and Barb, as always.

ISBN 0-373-88628-4

D.B. HAYES, DETECTIVE

Copyright © 2005 by Patricia A. Gagne

ABOUT THE AUTHOR

An avid reader, Dani Sinclair didn't discover romance novels until her mother lent her one when she'd come for a visit. Dani's been hooked on the genre ever since. But she didn't take up writing seriously until her two sons were grown. With the premiere of *Mystery Baby* for Harlequin Intrigue in 1996, Dani's kept her computer busy ever since. Her third novel, *Better Watch Out,* was a RITA® Award finalist in 1998. Dani lives outside Washington, D.C., a place she's found to be a great source for both intrigue and humor!

CAST OF CHARACTERS

D.B. Hayes—At age twenty-four, Diana Barbara "Dee" Hayes has a lot to prove as a woman and as a private investigator. She hopes not to get killed in the process....

Brandon Kirkpatrick—The former-cop-turned-investigator has a knack for getting into Dee's business...and under her skin.

Hogan Delvecchi—He looks like a boulder and is known to do all Albert Russo's dirty work. How dirty is he willing to get?

Lacy Dunning and Trudy Hoffsteader—Dee's aunt and her business partner have owned and operated Flower World ever since Dee can remember. Luckily they're willing to share their space with Dee's detective agency.

Brenda Keene—Dee's father's next-door neighbor insists that Dee find her mysterious stalker.

Mickey—The desperate ten-year-old comes in to hire D.B. Hayes—to find Mr. Sam, a geriatric cat....

Mr. Sam—The cat eludes D. B., but his look-alikes are taking over her apartment!

Albert Russo—The business entrepreneur and possible mobster is willing to give Dee her first big case, but does he have ulterior motives?

Elaine Russo—Is she simply tired of being a trophy wife, or is she playing a far more deadly game?

Nicole Wickley—The actress bears a striking resemblance to Elaine Russo—so striking there's some question as to whether they're really the same person.

Chapter One

Okay, so maybe my father was right. Being a private investigator can be a little dangerous.

I stared up at the mountain of flesh in front of me—six feet four, three hundred seventy pounds of masculine flab, and all of it quivering in a drunken rage. Another time I might have been fascinated by that rippling effect, but at the moment I was mesmerized by the enormous knife he was waving in one meaty hand. The only thing standing between the two of us was a rusting old porch swing, and that was one wicked-looking knife.

Lyle Arrensky was his name, and he wasn't dressed unless you count a pair of grungy boxer shorts with—so help me God—blue and green rabbits against an angry orange background. I did not want to count those shorts. Heck, I didn't even want to think about those shorts.

"I tole that bitch once," he slurred, his glazed piggy eyes unblinking, "I tole that bitch twice. She ain't gonna get that bowl back unless she comes here and asks me nice. You got that?"

Oh, yeah. I got that. I couldn't miss that. The words came accompanied by beer fumes mixed with the sour odor of unwashed flesh. And to reinforce the smell, Lake Erie sent a tepid puff of wind blowing in my direction.

It wasn't a real breeze but enough to stir the stench of traffic fumes, stale food and a whole host of other smells best not specifically identified. I began breathing through my mouth while urging the contents of my stomach to stay with me a little longer. This was not the time for a rebellion.

Keeping the porch swing between him and me, I edged closer to the steps and freedom.

"I promise. I'll pass on your message, Mr. Arrensky."

My tennis shoe found the top step, and I backed down as quickly as humanly possible without taking my eyes off the hand waving the knife. It was broad daylight. Where were all the nosy neighbors? People around here called the cops over dogs pooping on their browned-out lawns.

Not that I was anxious to deal with the police right now, but I did want out of here without bloodshed—especially mine. Susan Arrensky had hired me to obtain proof that her soon-to-be-ex-husband had physical possession of a hideously large silver-plated loving cup that had once belonged to her late grandmother. I'd managed to snap several photographs of said loving cup through the open living room window before Mr. Arrensky realized I was standing on his porch. If I hadn't gotten greedy and tried for that final photo, he'd have never noticed my hand sticking in through his window.

Someone else had put that large hole in his screen, not me. Given the way it was ripped and the knife he was holding, I'd hazard a guess that Mr. Arrensky himself had something to do with the torn screen. He seemed to like the idea of putting holes in things— or people.

"You do that," he yelled, menacing me with the long, hairy arm clutching the knife. "You tell that worthless little bitch she can crawl back here on her hands and knees if she wants the damn thing. You tell her that."

He swayed dangerously in my direction.

"Yes, sir. I'll be sure and tell her that."

I felt the cracked and broken sidewalk under my foot. Turning, I sprinted across the yellowed grass with more speed than I would have thought possible in this heat. The August sun was blistering more than just the city streets around Cleveland, Ohio, this afternoon.

Binky, my ancient VW Bug, started with a grinding noise I'm certain he wasn't supposed to make. For once I wasn't concerned about his health. *My* health was far more important. I left four feet of precious tire tread pealing away from the curb, but at least I made my escape without any new body piercings.

In the rearview mirror I saw Mr. Arrensky standing on the sidewalk scratching his considerably rounded belly while shouting curses in my wake. A scruffy-looking white poodle trotting down that same sidewalk prudently crossed the street to avoid him.

It was sort of sad to think that poodle was a whole lot smarter than I was.

The one good thing about returning to my office was that it was blessedly air-conditioned. Sadly Binky wasn't, and I couldn't afford a car that was. Sitting back carefully, I gazed around the converted closet and sighed with relief.

Okay, it wasn't really a closet. The space had always been a tiny office, just not my office. It was actually the office that came with my aunt Lacy's flower shop. I work for her and her partner when I'm not on a case. Unfortunately that's a little too often for comfort.

Aunt Lacy and Trudy Hoffsteder have owned and operated Flower World for longer than I've been alive, which is to say more than twenty-four years. Their shop is in a building on the corner of Detroit Avenue, down the street from the hospital.

Not exactly the high-rent district, but as Aunt Lacy is fond of pointing out, it's a perfect location for a flower shop. It's not a bad location for me, either. The price is certainly right.

I tried living in New York City after I got out of college and earned my investigator's license, but working for an established firm meant I spent most of my time in front of a computer screen running background checks and fetching coffee for the senior partners. Of course, I do a lot of that here, as well, but Trudy and my aunt are much nicer, and the background checks are for *my* clients.

Not that I'm exactly buried in cases in this quiet Cleveland suburb, but I grew up in this area. I know people here, and word of mouth is important for a private investigator starting out. Overall I've been doing fine—or I was until Brandon Kirkpatrick set up shop across the bridge in Rocky River a few weeks ago.

He's a male, so naturally he's getting all the really good cases. Already his name has made the local papers—twice! The first time was when he unfairly got credit for breaking up a stolen-car ring. The second time was when he located the mayor's missing sculpture. That one really ticked me off.

The car ring had been a fluke. Kirkpatrick caught the guy trying to steal *his* car, and because the little twerp wanted to cut a deal with the district attorney, he talked his head off, cracking the ring wide open.

As for the missing sculpture, that turned out to be nothing more than a high school prank. I could have figured that one out in half the time. Aunt Lacy and Trudy have a communications network that would make Homeland Security envious, and I mean, who else in their right mind would take such an ugly piece of glass and metal?

What really stuck in my craw was that the mayor hired Kirkpatrick when she lives three doors down from my brother and his family!

Brandon Kirkpatrick isn't even a native Ohioan. He grew up in Pittsburgh, for crying out loud! I know it's petty, but I couldn't help wishing he'd stayed there. Why did he have to come and set up shop on my turf?

I finished downloading the pictures of Mr. Arrensky in his oversize recliner watching a wrestling match while tossing peanuts at the loving cup, and sent them to print. Susan Arrensky would be happy, and I was comforted knowing she was good for my fee. After all, her dad is a vice president with the local bank where my family has done business for years.

"Excuse me, Dee," Aunt Lacy interrupted from the doorway. "Would you have time to finish the Martak arrangement for me? I have a dentist appointment in thirty minutes, and Trudy went home to check on Clem."

Clem is the parrot Trudy inherited from her mother. I suspect her mother inherited it from her grandmother, who probably got it from *her* mother. No one seems willing to guess exactly how old that bird is, but from some of the phrases he knows, I suspect he once traveled with pirates. He's mean and he knows more swearwords than a drunken sailor.

"No problem, Aunt Lacy. I can finish the arrangement right now." Leaning forward carefully, I stood up. There were times when the swivel chair seemed to have a mind of its own. "I'm finished working until tonight."

"Oh. You took Mr. Russo's case then?"

Aunt Lacy could convey a lot of emotion in a few short words. She was in accord with the rest of my family when it came to my career choice.

"Really, Dee, I don't see why a beautiful young woman like you wants to spend your nights outside some sleazy motel room taking pictures."

"I'm not fond of divorce work either, Aunt Lacy, but it pays the bills."

Tonight wouldn't be the first time I'd been asked to follow someone around and take pictures of the people they met. However it was the first time I was working for a client who made me nervous.

Albert Russo is considered by many to be a successful business entrepreneur. He's well connected down at city hall, but according to one of Trudy's sources, if Russo doesn't work for organized crime, he has all the right connections. Tall, thin, balding, he looks more like an accountant than someone who owns a string of nightclubs and pricey restaurants and he has the coldest, most disturbing blue eyes I've ever seen.

I tried to shrug nonchalantly at the worry underscoring my aunt's tone. "I can't afford to turn down a paying client."

A frown creased her forehead. Aunt Lacy has delicate features and gorgeous peaches-and-cream skin. Her short hair is a pretty shade of brown a bit darker than my own. Our features look quite a bit alike over-all, which gives me hope that I'll age as gracefully as her. At fifty-five, Aunt Lacy can easily pass for forty.

"I don't know what your mother would think of you skulking about in bushes and associating with known criminals," she said with a genteel scowl.

"First of all, I do not skulk in bushes." At least, not very often. "And second, no one has ever proved Mr. Russo is a criminal."

Pink tinted her cheeks a becoming shade.

"Perhaps, but my sister is probably rolling in her grave at the very idea of you being in the same room with some of these people you call clients."

Fortunately Aunt Lacy was in too big a hurry to pursue the topic any further. She patted her pockets, located her keys and settled for shaking her head.

"All right, Dee. You're a grown woman and you have to follow your own path. Trudy will be back in about fifteen minutes. I have to run."

And of course she meant that literally. Aunt Lacy is big on running. She enters races. She practically lives in jogging outfits. What she lacks in speed she makes up for in determination and endurance. I waved her off and headed for the workroom, where a partially assembled arrangement sat waiting on the counter.

The shop is always slow at this time of day, so I changed the radio station until I found one that suited me better and started singing along. I was doing a little dance around the table in time to a classic rock song when a young voice penetrated both the radio and my off-key singing.

"Hey! Lady, do you work here?"

I stopped moving and looked up from the fern I was tucking into place. Only I had to look down to find the originator of the question. A kid of about seven or eight stood there. He was a skinny little boy in a bright red T-shirt, navy shorts and dirty tennis shoes. His sandy brown hair needed combing and there were beads of sweat on his shiny red face. He had the most gorgeous chocolate-brown eyes I've ever seen. I would have killed for the thick black lashes that framed them. This kid was going to be a real heartbreaker in a few years.

At the moment those expressive eyes were regarding me with an extremely adult expression.

"Sorry," I apologized, snapping off the music. "I didn't hear you come in."

"I'm not surprised."

That made me blink. "You're kind of young for sarcasm, aren't you?"

"I'm ten."

I'd guessed younger, but then I haven't had a lot of dealings with kids other than my infant niece since I'd stopped babysitting and started dating around age fifteen. The boy was watching me closely, so I tried for a sage nod.

"Ten's a good age. Can I help you with something?"

His expression said he doubted it, but his head bobbed.

"I'm looking for D.B. Hayes."

Not what I'd expected. My mouth fell open, so I filled it with a question. "Why?"

"I want to hire him," the kid explained as if I were a moron. "There's a little sign out front that says he works here. The phone book listed this address, but this place is filled with flowers. Did he move?"

Now, the sign out front next to the door *is* on the small side, but do you know how much a sign costs? Besides, this is my aunt's shop and that means she gets the big billing. But geesh. Who needs to be patronized by a ten-year-old?

"D.B. Hayes is a private investigator," I explained to him.

"I know. That's why I want to hire him."

"You want to hire a private investigator?" I couldn't keep the skepticism out of my voice.

He shuffled his feet and looked down at his scuffed tennis shoes. His body was so tense, it made *my* muscles ache to look at him.

"I have to find Mr. Sam," the boy said. "See, he's old and I was supposed to keep an eye on him so he didn't get out and wander away, like he does sometimes, but I was playing a game and I forgot to check the screen door after my mom left."

He got it all out in one long breath, and I wondered what sort of people would make a little kid like this responsible for some old man with Alzheimer's. The boy was far too young for that sort of responsibility.

"If he gets hit by a car or attacked by dogs, it'll be all my fault."

I put down the fern and tried frantically to think of something comforting to offer. "I don't think you have to worry about him getting attacked by dogs."

He looked up at me, then gave a nod as if that wasn't a perfectly stupid thing to say.

"I guess so. He chases old man Roble's Doberman all the time. But if I don't find Mr. Sam before my mom gets home, she's going to be awful upset."

"I'll tell you what, why don't we call the police and..."

"No!" Panic filled his expression. "I want to hire D.B. Hayes! I can pay him."

He reached in his pocket and pulled out a crumpled wad of grungy dollar bills.

"I've got forty-two dollars saved to buy the Glimmer Man game. It's coming out next month, but this is more important. Do you think it's enough to find Mr. Sam?"

The kid was so pathetically earnest, I wanted to hug him and promise everything would be all right. "Look, I'll tell you what we..."

"I mean, he's just a cat. Anything could happen to him."

My mouth dropped open again. "A cat?"

The kid nodded solemnly. "D.B. Hayes has to help me find him. My uncle says that's one of the things detectives do. They find things for people."

Faced with that adorable, earnest expression, I swallowed several inappropriate responses while he waited in silence for me to say something.

"Let me get this straight," I stalled. "You want to hire me to find your cat?"

"Not you," he scoffed. "D.B. Hayes. And it isn't *my* cat, he's my uncle's cat. I was just watching him."

Why me?

"Look, I hate to tell you this kid, but I'm D.B. Hayes."

"No, you aren't. You work in the flower shop."

The tone and his assumption stung my pride. I tugged my identification folder from my hip pocket and flipped it open, holding it out for his inspection.

"See," I told him. "D.B. Hayes. Diana Barbara Hayes."

The little squirt actually took the folder and examined it, comparing me to my picture. While it wasn't a particularly flattering picture and my hair was shorter back then, my features were clear enough to satisfy him.

"You don't look like a private investigator."

"I get that a lot." Unfortunately it was true. "That's what makes me good at my job," I added, giving him my stock response. "Look, kid...what's your name anyhow?"

"Mickey."

"Okay, Mickey," I said, replacing the folder. "I'd really like to help you out, but I don't know anything about cats. Your best bet..."

But the kid had come prepared for a brush-off. He whipped out a bent photograph of himself holding an indistinguishable blob of gray fur. He thrust it in my hand before I could finish my suggestion.

"Here's his picture," Mickey said in a rush. "His name is Mr. Sam and he's seventeen. That's old for a cat. The screen door doesn't latch so good, so he musta got out between nine and ten this morning. I searched the whole neighborhood, but I can't find him. We live right near the park, so I bet he went there to chase birds or something, but I can't search the whole park by myself. And I have to get home before my mom finds out I'm not at the pool with Ray and his mom. See, my mom's kinda nervous on account of my dad getting killed. Mom's been under a lot of stress."

That put the brakes on my objections and captured my full and complete attention. "Your dad was killed?"

He nodded gravely. "That's why you have to find Mr. Sam. I don't want my mom to cry anymore. She'll be real upset when she finds out he's gone. I was supposed to watch him."

I had so many questions jamming my brain, I couldn't decide what to ask first. Unfortunately the kid moved a lot faster than my thought processes. He plopped the wad of crumpled bills on the work counter and sprinted for the front of the shop before I could blink.

"Hey! Wait!"

"You can keep the picture," Mickey tossed over his shoulder.

"Wait! Mickey! Wait! What's your last name?"

I chased him out the front door, but he was already astride a fancy red bike.

"Where do you live? I need more information!"

"I gotta go!" he shouted. "I'm late! Keep Mr. Sam when you find him. I'll come back tomorrow to get him."

The bike turned the corner and sped off down the sidewalk.

I started to run after him before I remembered that I was alone in the store. I couldn't leave until Trudy returned.

Blast! How humiliating to be caught flat by a ten-year-old kid. Since standing there wasn't going to do much good and the afternoon heat was sucking my lungs dry, I returned to the chill air inside the store. I stared at the grungy heap of crumpled dollar bills sitting on the counter in the back room. Now what was I supposed to do?

I'm a dog person. I don't even like cats.

Chapter Two

Finding a gray cat is not like looking for a needle in a haystack. It *is* the haystack. The world is full of gray cats—at least, Lakewood Park was on this particular day.

There were dozens of small parks in and around town, not to mention the valley, a system of parks that twisted around a good portion of Cuyahoga County. But using my deductive abilities, I took the direction the kid had headed and his comment about the pool and chose Lakewood over Madison Park, since they were the only two that had pools nearby.

Searching for a cat is a job for Animal Control, not a private investigator, but the kid had hooked me with those sad eyes. And I admit the whole bit about his father being killed had dangled a carrot I couldn't resist. It could have been a traffic accident. Heck, it probably had been a traffic accident. But I wanted more information.

Besides, the kid had given up a Glimmer Man game—whatever that was—to hire a detective to find his uncle's old cat so his mom wouldn't cry anymore. Heck. I didn't have any choice. Not when he'd paid up front.

I had no intention of keeping his money, of course. I'd locked it away in my aunt's desk drawer and I'd give it back to him as soon as he picked up his cat. And hopefully one of the two beasts I'd managed to catch would turn out to be Mr. Sam.

Not being totally stupid, I'd stopped by a pet store on my way to the park to pick up a few things I figured I was going to need to trap and hold Mr. Sam. Silly me. I should have added bandages, iodine, even tourniquets, to my list of necessities. Blood still trickled down my hand, squishing between my fingers and smearing the steering wheel with sticky residue. I should have remembered that cats come with claws. Nevertheless I had two mostly gray cats that sort of matched the picture Mickey had given me. One of them had better be Mr. Sam.

As far as I'm concerned, one gray cat looks pretty much like another. Even though the first one was a darker gray and had white under his chin and the second one had a patch of white on his belly, either one could be the cat in the picture as far as I could tell. The two nasty-tempered little monsters were in my car yowling at the top of their considerable lungs. They'd been friendly enough when I was petting them and offering them treats, but once I'd put them inside, all hell broke loose.

Sam One was inside the box a stock boy had given

me. Since I hadn't planned on finding more than one cat, I didn't have a second box, but Sam Two had come willingly into my arms until I'd tried to add him to the same box. Hence all the blood. Sam Two was now crouched on the floorboard in the narrow backseat after tearing strips of skin off my hand.

Driving with a cat loose in the car made me nervous, but I wasn't about to try picking the beast up a second time. And short of putting him in the trunk, there was no other option. To make matters worse, I'd spotted a third gray cat right before leaving the park. By then my need to help the kid was waning big-time. It was growing late and my stomach was grumbling over the small salad I'd had for lunch, and where would I have put a third cat anyhow? As it was, I was going to have to smuggle the two beasts into my apartment without being seen and I doubted they were going to cooperate.

I debated blowing my diet by stopping for a fast-food hamburger on my way home, but given my luck, Sam Two would prefer fast food to the kitty tuna I'd bought. He'd probably have it eaten before I got it out of the car. He'd certainly eaten the treats I'd offered him as if he'd been starving—which, from the paunch on that cat, was a big, fat lie.

I figured my best bet was to go straight home and change into something more appropriate for tailing someone who lives in the Shaker Heights area. I could get fast food on my way to the assignment. Besides, I needed to call Aunt Lacy and remind her I wanted to borrow her car tonight. I could hardly drive around on the east side of town in an antique VW Beetle painted mostly in primer-gray.

My cell phone rang as I pulled onto Lake Avenue coming out of the park. I dripped a splotch of blood on the seat cover while reaching over to answer the summons. I wouldn't have bothered except that my cell phone is listed on my business cards and I can't afford to ignore a possible client.

"D.B. Hayes," I snapped out, hoping for a red light so I could use a tissue to mop the blood before it stained. Between the rivulets of sweat dripping down my body, the throbbing gouges on my hand and the noise emanating from both cats, I was not in the best of moods.

There was a pause on the other end that made me regret my tone. Then a familiar voice—one that sounded as if the speaker had swallowed gravel shards—spoke in my ear.

"Ms. Hayes, this is Albert Russo."

I cringed. Clenching the cell phone against my ear, I prayed he wasn't calling to cancel tonight's job. The rent was due next week and I'd counted on that money.

"Mr. Russo!" I exclaimed, trying to infuse my voice with enthusiasm. "What can I do for you?"

This time the pause was enough to send my heart in my throat.

"Have I called at a bad time, Ms. Hayes?"

"Of course not."

Sam Two contradicted me with a plaintive yowl. The sound filled the interior of the car. I grimaced.

"Sorry about the noise, Mr. Russo. I'm transporting a pair of unhappy cats, uh…for a friend."

What else could I say?

He sniffed. "Nasty creatures, cats."

I wasn't about to argue the point. At the moment they didn't rank high in my esteem either. I only hoped they had all their shots. And why hadn't I thought of that before I'd gone and picked them up with my bare hands?

"Ms. Hayes, I'm wondering if you could see your way clear to start the assignment a bit earlier this evening than we agreed?" he went on. "It seems my wife made dinner plans with some acquaintances and just communicated this information to me. I'm sorry for the short notice, but she intends to leave the house a little past six. You will need to be in position before then."

I glanced at the dashboard clock. It was a few minutes past five already. Rush hour. And his address was clear across town in an area I wasn't familiar with. There was no way I could go home and change clothes and still make it to Shaker Heights before six. I glanced down at my shorts and stained blouse and bit my bottom lip.

"Is your wife going somewhere fancy for dinner?" I asked. If so, I was doomed.

"I believe she mentioned Bergan's in Legacy Village. Is that a problem, Ms. Hayes?"

His cold tone indicated it had better not be a problem.

"Of course not," I lied. "I'm on my way."

"Excellent. I'll send someone by your office tomorrow morning for a copy of the pictures and your report."

"Ah, that'll be fine, Mr. Russo, but, well, there isn't anyone at the shop before nine. If you like, I can bring everything by your office earlier than that."

"Nine o'clock will suffice, Ms. Hayes. My associate will call on you then."

"Okay, if that's your preference."

"It is. Good evening, Ms. Hayes."

"Too late for that," I muttered at the sound of the click on his end.

Actually I could have gotten to the shop earlier than nine, but I'm not a morning person. Besides, I didn't want to risk any flower shop customers coming in when I was there alone with a client. Or in this case, a client's representative.

The cat in the box on the seat beside me was scrabbling furiously at the cardboard and swearing at me in cat. The one in the back had settled for piteous mews of unhappiness. I wasn't sure which was worse.

"Look, guys, let's just make the best of this, all right? Whichever one of you is Mr. Sam is going back home tomorrow. The other one gets to go to the animal shelter to find a nice new home, so let's be quiet and let me drive, okay?"

Not a chance. Time stretched unbearably between the cats and rush-hour traffic. All in all I made decent time to Shaker Heights, but then I got lost on the side streets trying to find the address.

I was sweating profusely by the time I stumbled on it through sheer dumb luck. The sweat was only partly due to frustration. Mostly it was a result of the lack of cool air in the small car. I didn't dare open the windows, even the wings, more than a crack, for fear Sam Two might prove suicidal.

The east side of Cleveland is different from my part of town. Binky wouldn't raise eyebrows on the west side, but here he stood out like hot pink at a funeral. Somehow I was pretty sure no one in this neighborhood was apt to mistake him for one of the trendy reissued Bugs that had come out a couple of years ago. Binky made no pretenses about what he was. His numerous rust spots had been sanded, filled in and painted with primer, but I'd broken things off with Ted Osher again before the mechanic got around to putting any paint on Binky for me. Bad timing on my part.

I've known Ted since high school. We graduated together. He's a nice enough guy when he isn't being a jerk, but our relationship is not exactly the romance of the century. More like a comfortable habit when we're both at loose ends. Ted's happiest when he's covered in grease, with auto guts spread all around him. Whatever our relationship at any given moment, I have to give him credit for keeping the important parts of Binky running all these years past their prime.

As I drove past the address I'd been given, I wondered what it would be like to live in a place this fancy. Somehow I didn't think I'd be comfortable behind an ornate fence in a neighborhood where even the houses managed to look snobbish.

Since there was nowhere I could park and look inconspicuous, I pulled to the side of the road a few houses down and spread out the map I'd been trying to read when I'd gotten lost. I had the perfect cover story ready in case someone came along demanding to know what I was doing here. I'd tell the curious that I was trying to deliver a pair of lost cats to their owner. I've found it always pays to use what you have to hand.

Besides, I wasn't the only car parked along the street, even if the other vehicle was a burgundy Honda that looked far more presentable in this neighborhood than Binky. Tough cookies, as Trudy liked to say. I was here and I was staying here until my quarry appeared. I had her picture, her license plate number and a description of her car. All I had to do was wait and pray Elaine Russo hadn't left before I'd found her house.

My hand had stopped bleeding, so I used tissues and spit to clean up as best I could. I was running out of saliva when I realized the car had grown ominously silent. No sound came from inside the box. Worse, there was nothing from the backseat.

My shoulders tensed. My neck prickled. Was Sam Two preparing to spring over the seat and attack me? Or worse, had he died of asphyxiation back there? The last thing I needed was a pair of dead cats. I hadn't thought to poke any air holes in the box since I hadn't expected him to be in there for any length of time. But cats like heat, right? They were always pictured curled up in front of a roaring fire.

I lowered the windows as far as I dared and opened the wings to the extent where I was pretty sure the cat's head wouldn't fit through. Then I debated lifting a flap to check on Sam One. Except things would be worse if he got loose in the car with the other one. I was twisting to peer over the backseat to check on Sam Two when movement over near the burgundy Honda caught my attention.

A man appeared between some tall hedges. Not just any man. This was a delicious hunk of serious eye candy. He strode toward the car with the assurance of someone who knew where he was going. A sporty white shirt, open at the neck, over neatly tailored black dress slacks gave him a suave, debonair look that captured my full attention—and my imagination.

Yum. He was gorgeous. Even his dark hair, curled slightly against the nape of his neck and in need of a trim, didn't diminish his appeal. He carried his tall, lean frame with comfortable authority. His features carried a trace of ruggedness that kept him from being too pretty, but it was a face no sane woman would mind waking up beside. The man exuded raw sex appeal.

I sighed wistfully and decided I needed to get out more. My love life was nonexistent. Since moving back to Ohio, the only guys I'd dated on a regular basis had been Ted Osher and Billy Nugent. Billy was my aunt's accountant. A freckle-faced strawberry-blond, he was another nice guy, but he saved his passion for neat little rows of numbers and football. Put him in a crowded stadium with a group of men wearing shoulder pads and the transformation was downright scary. The meek accountant turned into a raging maniac.

Now, I like football as well as the next armchair quarterback, but it's a game! Billy took every bad play as a personal affront. He'd actually thrown a ledger through his mother's television set one time when the Browns missed a field goal. With the season about to begin again, I knew it was time to start looking around for someone else to date.

Ted and Billy are okay to look at, steadily employed, good to their mothers and…well, frankly, boring. The man sliding into the Honda did not look the least bit boring. I couldn't speak to the rest, but it was too bad I hadn't been hired to tail him.

I looked back toward the driveway just in time to see a gleaming white Jaguar glide through the open gate of the Russo's driveway. Elaine Russo was leaving.

Her car turned right onto the street. The opposite

direction I was facing, naturally. The handsome stranger's car fell in several car lengths behind her while I had to shoo Sam Two back over the backseat and start Binky.

Putting him into gear, I made a tight U-turn on the narrow street as the burgundy car disappeared around the corner at the end of the street. Both animals protested loudly as I hurried to close the distance. Sam One went back to desperately clawing the insides of the box while Sam Two tried to drown him out with sheer volume right behind my seat.

I turned on the radio in self-defense and hung back as far as I dared as soon as I spotted the white Jaguar some distance up ahead. There was no way I was inconspicuous if she was watching for a tail. I blessed the burgundy Honda's presence in between us until it turned off onto a side street and left me the only car on the road behind her.

Apparently Elaine wasn't paying attention to her rearview mirror. While she might not be concerned if she did notice me back here, that would change if she continued to see my car everywhere she went. If only there'd been time to borrow my aunt's light gray Buick.

Fortunately Elaine didn't seem to be in a hurry. Everyone had heard of Legacy Village, but I'm a west-side girl. The east side of Cleveland isn't my territory, so I wasn't sure how to get there from here. My map was so old, it didn't even show the development. That meant I had to stay close enough to the Jag that Elaine didn't lose me.

I was concentrating on maintaining the proper distance when it suddenly occurred to me to wonder why Albert Russo had selected me to tail his wife. I mean, there had to be other female private investigators he could have hired. Ones that lived on his side of town. They would have been more familiar with the area and no doubt would have blended in far better than I was doing.

When Russo had called and asked for a meeting, I'd simply been grateful for the work. Now I started wondering. They say you shouldn't look a gift horse in the mouth, but, as Trudy liked to point out, how else are you going to determine how sharp the teeth are?

Both cats continued making a ruckus as I pulled into the shopping center two cars behind the Jag. The village concept for housing tracts is all the rage right now, even though I'm pretty sure I read somewhere that Walt Disney pioneered the concept long before I was born. The problem is, with land being at such a premium, the builders make their money on retail spaces, not parking spaces, so they don't bother planning for adequate parking.

The Jaguar had no problem, of course. Cars couldn't get out of its way fast enough. Those same cars sneered at Binky. I lost two parking places to vehicles that cost more than the contents of my entire apartment before I got lucky. A Lexus started pulling out four cars down from me. I had to beat out a jerk with a dark-tinted SUV to claim the spot.

but Binky's tight turn radius outmaneuvered him, and I zipped in with ease. Not only that, but it was one of the few spots completely in the shade. I thanked the fates as I climbed out of the car, taking care that I was the only one who got out.

Fortunately my camera was in the trunk. The last thing I wanted to do was dispute territory with the angry animal on the backseat. The box on the front seat gave me pause. I was pretty sure Sam One couldn't eat his way through the heavy cardboard, but it sounded as if he was giving it a valiant try.

There was no time to worry about that now. I grabbed my camera and set off after Elaine Russo before I lost her in the crowd. A tall, leggy blonde with short swingy hair and an aristocratic bearing, she strolled along as if she owned the place, looking neither left nor right.

If her husband had thought this dinner was a cover for an assignation with a lover, he was going to be sadly disappointed. I was in a good position to watch her meet with three women close to her age—twenty-eight, according to what her husband had told me. Elaine was obviously a trophy wife. Albert was close to seventy if he was a day.

I snapped several good shots of the women while I pretended to photograph the area. Elaine had her back to me the whole time. I willed her to turn around to no avail. I figured it didn't matter since Russo knew what she looked like. It was the people she met with he wanted pictures of.

The restaurant was surprisingly crowded for a Monday evening. People stood inside and outside talking in clusters. The four women were standing outside. I was pretty sure I wasn't going to be able to get inside with them, but I decided it didn't matter as long as I didn't miss Elaine when she left. Besides, I felt self-conscious dressed the way I was. There were plenty of other people wearing shorts and T-shirts, but theirs hadn't come from a discount store, nor were they stained with blood and smudged with dirt and cat hairs.

At least the crowds offered plenty of cover for me. I stood wilting in the sun, trying to appear as though I belonged there and was waiting to meet someone. And as I was looking around for a place with a view to wait while they ate dinner, I glimpsed a dark-haired man moving away from me. Something about him reminded me of the sexy stranger with the Honda. To my profound disappointment, he stepped inside a store before I could get an unobstructed view of him.

I shouldn't really be wasting time ogling sexy strangers anyhow. My job was to keep my eye on Elaine, and it was a good thing I did. We'd only been standing there a matter of minutes when she did the unexpected. She left.

With a wave and a smile she sauntered back to the parking lot, nearly catching me flat. Maybe Albert Russo hadn't misread his wife after all. It appeared that this dinner with friends was nothing more than a setup for her real assignation.

I felt a hum of excitement. I had no idea where she was going next, but this was bound to be the reason Russo had hired me. If she lost me now, my client would be most unhappy.

The idea of a man with possible mobster ties being unhappy with me started a thread of tension mingling with my excitement. Tension quickly turned to panic when I nearly lost her coming out of the parking area. There was some sort of fender bender two rows over that caused enough confusion that she made the traffic light and I didn't.

I spent several minutes sweating buckets and muttering incoherently before I was able to charge down the road in the direction she had taken. I didn't slow down until I came up on the white Jag driving at a leisurely pace a short distance in front of me. Breathing a considerable sigh of relief, I noted Elaine was talking to someone on her cell phone as she drove. The boyfriend to tell him she was on her way?

Elaine was a careful driver. That came as something of a shock because the perky blonde didn't strike me as the slow and methodical type. Still, I was deeply grateful as she all but led me by the hand, using her turn signals well ahead of time as we headed into downtown Cleveland near the Rock and Roll Hall of Fame. I was on more familiar territory now, but my relief was short lived. I was seriously underdressed for her next stop.

Scarpanelli's is a new Italian restaurant with a commanding view overlooking Lake Erie near the Burke

Lakefront Airport. I wasn't sure, but I thought it might be one of the places my client, Albert Russo, owns. I'd heard the food was superb if you didn't mind dropping close to a hundred dollars on a meal. I minded. I didn't even date guys with that sort of money.

Assuming I could get the hostess to let me inside dressed in shorts, I still had a problem. I couldn't afford an appetizer, let alone a meal in there. The restaurant was busy but not yet crowded. That would come later. Right now it was mostly wealthy families and the blue-rinse walker-and-cane crowd. Elaine would stand out in that mix. Too bad I wouldn't be able to see who she was standing out to meet. This was not good. In fact, this was very bad.

I debated calling Russo on the number he'd given me to explain the problem, but I couldn't see him being particularly sympathetic. He was attending some important business dinner tonight and he'd hired me to do a job. He wouldn't want excuses as to why I couldn't do said job.

From now on, I vowed, I'd keep a couple of outfits in the trunk for emergencies like this one. In the meantime I was stuck. I couldn't follow her inside, so I'd have to see if I could find a place outside where I could peer in.

No such luck. The entire back wall was elevated and composed of tinted glass. Patrons could see out over the lake, but I couldn't see in.

I was making my way around the building when

I surprised a young man near the kitchen entrance. He was puffing a joint in a secluded nook near the trash bins. His body jerked, sharply startled when I appeared around the corner.

"Hey. What are you doing here? You aren't allowed back here."

At a guess, he was about seventeen. Based on his dark pants and white shirt I figured him for a busboy. I offered him a friendly smile.

"You aren't allowed to smoke weed either, but that doesn't seem to be stopping you. Look, I'm not interested in your drug habits, I'm a private investigator," I told him before he could get bent out of shape.

"Yeah, right."

Whipping out my ID folder, I offered him proof. He studied it almost as carefully as Mickey had.

"Hey, cool. You want a hit?"

"No, thanks, but I could use your help."

"Yeah?"

"There's a woman inside the restaurant. Tall blonde, short hair with bangs. She's wearing a pale blue skirt and a matching silk blouse." I pulled out the picture of Elaine Russo and gave him a look. "She went in alone a few minutes ago. I need to know who she's meeting in there. There's a twenty in it for you if you can help me out."

Which would leave me exactly three dollars in cash until I found an ATM. But, hey, I'd get the money back under expenses.

The kid smirked. He looked me up and down curiously. I could see he was intrigued.

"How come you want to know about her?"

I shrugged, trying for blasé. "It's my job. Her husband hired me to see if she's meeting another man."

"I thought P.I.'s were guys like they show on television."

"Lots of them are," I agreed, trying not to grit my teeth. "Haven't you ever heard of *Charlie's Angels?*"

His eyes lit. "Like the movies?"

"Less death-defying action but the same concept."

"Yeah? That's cool. You carry a gun?"

He seemed to be trying to decide where I was hiding one under my snug white shorts and thin pink T-shirt.

"Not at the moment. This is a simple tail job. No guns required. Think you can help me out?"

He finished his joint and nodded. I could see the questions bubbling up inside him, so I was surprised when he glanced at his watch and straightened.

"I'll check for you, but you'd better wait around the corner over there. Benny'll be dumping trash pretty soon and he won't like you hanging here."

"Thanks. That's fine."

"I'll be back, but it might be a while."

"I'm not going anywhere."

Unless Elaine decided to leave here all of a sudden, too.

I tried not to feel conspicuous as I moved to stand near the corner of the restaurant where I could keep an eye on the parking lot. The day's heat was finally melting away. There was even a welcome breeze coming in off the lake. Unfortunately I was too nervous to be properly appreciative. The luscious smells wafting from the kitchen were making me drool. I wondered if they fed strays at the kitchen door. I'd willingly sit up and beg for a taste of what I was sniffing. The longer I stood there, the louder my stomach complained. I fervently wished my busboy would return and tell me what was going on inside.

After what felt like I'd been standing there for hours, he scooted out the back door and rushed over to where I was waiting.

"I can't stay," he told me breathlessly. "Your woman's in there, all right. Table thirty-two. She ordered the French onion soup with tonight's special, the lobster fettuccine—"

"Did she meet anyone?" I interrupted before he could give me any more details. Visualizing food when my stomach was knocking against the back of my ribs was sheer torture. "Has anyone approached her table?"

"Nope. As far as I can tell, she's completely alone. Kinda surprising. I mean, she's not bad looking for an older woman, you know? She just ordered coffee and the white-chocolate-mousse cake, so she'll probably be in there for another half hour or so. She doesn't seem to be in any hurry."

I fished out my twenty and watched it disappear into his hip pocket. "Thanks. I appreciate your help."

"No problem. Want me to bring you something from the kitchen while you're waiting?"

More than anything in the world. With extreme reluctance I shook my head, reminding myself I was supposed to be on a diet anyhow.

"Thanks, but I have to be ready to roll when she is. What's your name, anyhow?"

"Rob. Rob Deluth."

I stuck out my hand. "Dee Hayes," I told him as we shook. "Thanks again for your help, Rob. If you ever need a P.I., look me up. I'm in the phone book. I don't have any cards on me at the moment." The new ones I'd printed were still sitting on my desk in the office back at the flower shop. I'd forgotten to stick them in my folder again.

"Cool. Thanks. I gotta get back before they miss me."

As he ran back to the kitchen entrance, I hurried across the parking lot to the Jaguar. There were a lot of people moving about now, but no one gave me a second glance. I'm not sure why I went over to her car, really. I wasn't looking for anything specific, but since I had time to kill, checking out her car seemed like the natural thing to do.

Elaine hadn't struck me as a careless person. She certainly didn't drive like one, yet she'd left her driver's door unlocked. The temptation was irresistible. This was probably the only opportunity I'd ever have to sit in a Jaguar. Besides, there was a sheet of paper lying on the passenger's seat. I needed to check it out. It could be a clue.

The plush leather seat cocooned me the moment I sank down. The opulent interior still retained a trace of coolness from the air conditioner. Reaching for the paper, I saw it was a set of hand-printed directions to a piano lounge downtown called Victor's. I'd never heard of the place, but the directions were straightforward and it wasn't far from here. Tuesday, 8:00 p.m., and a phone number had been printed across the top like an afterthought.

This was almost too easy. Fate seemed to be nurturing me for once. I blew it a mental kiss and made a note of the phone number. I wondered if the number went with the lounge or the person she was supposed to meet. Since it looked like a cell phone number, odds were it was the latter, but I wouldn't know for sure unless I gave the number a try.

The car itself was so pristine, it could have just come from a car wash. Heck, it probably had. Binky hadn't seen the inside of a car wash since…come to think of it, he may never have seen the inside of a car wash. I decided to make it up to him first chance I got while I continued to search the interior of the Jag. I didn't expect to find a thing.

Certainly not the .38 revolver she had tucked up under the driver's seat.

That gave me serious pause. Why was someone like Elaine Russo carrying concealed? I guess it made sense if her husband was a mobster. And I suppose it was possible she had a permit. Still, that heavy lump of metal made me very nervous. It implied a whole lot of things and none of them were good. People with guns have a bad habit of firing them.

I own a gun, but I've only ever used it on a firing range. It isn't something I carry around, even though I have a permit. I replaced the weapon carefully back under the front seat. A strand of blond hair on the carpeting caught my attention.

Interesting. Either Elaine had extremely dry, coarse hair or she liked wigs. Wearing one in this heat didn't seem likely unless she had some sort of a physical problem requiring one.

Tucking the hair in my pocket, I stepped from the car and crossed the lot to where I'd parked Binky. Sam Two sat on the driver's seat scratching at the box on the passenger side. The minute he saw me, he leaped onto the box and over the seat into the back once more.

Binky was warmer inside than the Jag had been, but the temperature wasn't too bad anymore. That breeze coming in off the lake through the windows had cooled things down considerably, and it probably helped that I was parked in the shade. Still, I was worried about the cats.

"Sorry, guys. I should have asked Rob for some water. I could use a drink myself, but we'll have to wait until I get you home."

Neither of them made a sound as I reached for my cell phone and punched in the number printed on the paper I'd found.

"Hello?" A decidedly delicious voice answered.

Deep, rich, sexy and male, the sound washed over me. Definitely not Victor's Lounge unless this was Victor himself.

"Sorry," I told the voice. "I must have the wrong number."

"Who were you trying to reach?"

There was a sudden edge to the voice. It was still a great voice.

"Sharon Armstrong," I told him. I pulled a friend's name off the top of my head and read him back his number, transposing the last two digits. He corrected me immediately.

I could have listened to his voice forever, but my quarry chose that moment to leave the restaurant, so I apologized and hung up. I wondered if the man matched his voice. Then I wondered if I was about to find out. Was she on her way to meet the man behind that voice?

There was enough traffic on the street that I didn't have to worry about being spotted now. When I felt certain Elaine's destination was the address on the paper, I decided to take a chance. I turned off, took a shortcut that would bring me up on the street behind Victor's and parked the car where I'd have no trouble getting out in a hurry. I walked around the block and stood across the street in the doorway of a closed shop. It afforded me a good view of the parking lot as well as the front door of the lounge while keeping me relatively concealed.

Elaine pulled in even as I slipped into position. She stepped from the Jag and flashed a look around as if she was expecting someone. After a few seconds, she frowned and headed for the entrance.

I decided to give her ten minutes to get settled before going inside myself. I was regretting my generosity with Rob. Since I only had three dollars left, I couldn't go sit at the bar. The best I could do was have a quick peek inside to see who she met. I might be able to snap a picture unobserved, but it wasn't likely. I'd have to try for the man's picture when they came back outside.

And I was fairly sure it would be a he. A woman doesn't go to a place like Victor's alone unless she's meeting someone or trolling. Either way I needed to capture the moment on my digital camera.

Since I couldn't read my watch in the growing darkness, I had to guess at the time. I was about to make my move when there was a movement near the back of the lounge's parking lot. Someone had stepped out of a car that was already parked back there. The car was a burgundy Honda. It must have been sitting there before Elaine arrived or I would have noticed it pulling in. Given that I don't believe in coincidence, I knew who the driver would turn out to be even before he came into view.

My heart skipped a beat, then started thumping

like a wild thing. I almost forgot to bring up the camera. I was right. The zoom lens wasn't necessary to tell me that this was the same man who'd been parked on Elaine's street earlier this evening.

Chapter Three

Didn't it just figure? The first interesting man I've seen since moving back home turned out to be the lover of the woman I'd been hired to follow. I shrugged philosophically. If he was the sort who had affairs with married women, he wasn't my type anyhow.

I let some time elapse before crossing the street. Instead of following him inside, I headed straight for the burgundy Honda. Unfortunately Elaine's boyfriend wasn't as accommodating as she'd been. He'd locked his car and its insides were anything but pristine. I couldn't see much besides fast-food wrappers, empty paper cups, CD cases and a paperback whose title I couldn't make out. Somehow that the handsome man was a bit of a slob made me feel a little better.

As I moved around the car I discovered the Honda had a broken taillight and a dent in back on the left-hand side. Since I'd followed that car when we'd left the Russos' place, I knew that dent hadn't been there earlier. Though I hadn't noticed his car there, I was guessing he'd been part of the accident in the parking lot at Legacy Village that had nearly caused me to lose Elaine. That meant he'd been following her, too, which didn't make a bit of sense. What was the point if they'd been scheduled to meet here anyhow?

I didn't like this, not even a little. I was feeling very edgy as I noted the time and took down the plate number before heading for the main entrance. Victor's was nothing more than an upscale bar that showcased a baby-grand piano. This being a Monday night, there was no one at the keyboard. A player piano along the far wall was belting out an old rock-and-roll tune.

There were only a handful of customers inside and most of them were sitting at the bar itself. I nodded to the bartender, ignored the other stares and strode toward the back as if I knew where I was going. Turned out I did. The restrooms were back there and so was my quarry. They were sitting in a booth conveniently close to the ladies' room. The man glanced my way as I strode past, but I didn't look in their direction. I didn't think he would recognize me. How could he?

Setting my camera down on a shelf, I washed my cuts in the cracked but surprisingly clean sink. I wanted to give the couple time to forget about me. The scratches were red and angry looking, not to mention painful, but they didn't look infected and I figured they were my own fault. The cats had only been fighting for their freedom. I couldn't blame them. After all, I was a stranger and only one of them was Mr. Sam.

By cracking open the bathroom door, I had an unobstructed view of the couple's table. I was glad now that I'd gone to the expense of an infrared lens for my camera. A flash would have been a noticeable problem. As it was, I snapped several pictures of them with their heads together before striding back past them. It was probably my imagination, but I felt his eyes on my back all the way to the door.

There was an ATM on the corner of the building next door. I figured I had time to use it if I hurried. As it turned out, I hadn't even needed to hurry. They took their time inside. I got several good shots of them coming out, still looking extremely cozy. The hunk helped her inside his car while I sprinted back to Binky.

Sam Two was sitting on top of Sam One's box. I think he'd been trying to let the other cat out. Fortunately he hadn't succeeded. He jumped over the backseat the minute he saw me coming. I scrambled inside and started the engine.

"Okay, guys, I'm really, really sorry. Honest. We're on our way to a motel unless I miss my guess. Once I get there, I'll see what I can do to make things better for you. I'll scrounge up some water and give you something to eat, okay?"

From the grumbling, it was less than satisfactory. Guilt gnawed on me as we made our way onto the highway. I like animals—sometimes more than people. I didn't want anything to happen to these little guys, even if I wasn't a cat person.

Since I was worried about the hunk spotting a tail, I hung back as far as I dared. Once seen, Binky was somewhat unforgettable. I really was going to have to get him painted one of these days, even if I had to buy a spray can and do it myself.

It wasn't until the Honda headed for the Ohio Turnpike that I got worried. Were they running away together? Not that I blamed Elaine, mind you. Sexy young hunk versus balding old man with scary eyes wasn't even a toss-up in my book. Heck, I'd be tempted to take off with the hunk, too, and I didn't even have to go home to someone like Albert Russo. The problem was I couldn't follow them forever. Binky wasn't used to traveling any distance or at speeds over forty miles per hour. I had no idea what his top speed was, but I knew it wouldn't be much before he blew something critical.

Not so the Honda. I got on the turnpike with extreme misgivings and had all I could do to keep the other car in sight. The hunk drove as if he didn't have a second to spare.

Sweat was dribbling down my face and it had little to do with the temperature, which was cooling off even more as night claimed the sky. Getting on the turnpike for a simple tryst seemed a bit extreme.

Where the devil were they going?

If they were running away together, I was in deep trouble. After a while Binky's oil light began flashing intermittently. Binky craves oil the way I crave diet soda, and I was pretty sure I didn't have a can of either one in the trunk. If he broke down out here, I was in for it. Time to turn around.

Unfortunately I'd run out of exits by the time I firmly came to that decision. We'd come to the end of the Ohio Turnpike and I spotted the Honda near the head of the line to pay their toll.

I snapped a couple of quick pictures as I waited to one side of them, much farther back in my own line. As they went through, heading into Pennsylvania, I debated my options. The next exit was Beaver Falls. I had no choice. I'd have to turn around there and stop for oil so I could make it home. Even Albert Russo couldn't expect me to follow them clear across Pennsylvania.

Could he?

Probably, I decided fatalistically, but that was too bad. He should have hired someone else. I had Binky and two cats to think about—not to mention forty-three dollars minus the toll left in my wallet.

To my surprise, the Honda turned off at Beaver Falls. I urged Binky to close the distance, hoping he wouldn't blow a gasket or something even worse. My curiosity was going nuts, especially when they pulled into a jazzy-looking motel unit right off the highway. This was just too bizarre. They'd driven all the way into Pennsylvania for a quickie? What was wrong with the motels in Ohio? Admittedly this place looked brand new, but even so, traveling all this way for a little slap and tickle made no sense.

The hunk was inside getting registered when I pulled up with my camera and found a strategic place to park. I got some quality shots of the two of them in front of the motel, then going inside a room. Mr. Russo was going to be extremely pleased with the pictures, if not their content. He'd probably like a few more intimate shots, but I draw the line at voyeurism, even if I could have seen in around the heavy drape they pulled across the window.

It was a safe bet they'd be busy for the next half hour or so. I made a note of the time, left the car and the now silent cats and walked to the gas station on the corner for a can of oil for Binky, some water for the cats and a candy bar and a can of diet soda for me. I ate the candy on my way back and wished I'd bought more than one. I was starving.

Having dated a mechanic off and on, I'd learned more than I ever wanted to know about car engines. Replenishing the oil was child's play. Except that sometime during my ministrations apparently my quarry split.

I couldn't believe it. When I closed the hood and glanced over at their parking space, the Honda was gone and the room was dark. I looked at my watch and blinked. Good grief. He might look like a hunk, but he was definitely no stud.

Maybe they'd gone out for something to eat to recharge. Except that Elaine had just finished a full-course meal including dessert. As I hurried to the driver's side and got in, I wondered if they'd had a fight and changed their minds. That's when I realized I had a second problem. Sam One had escaped.

Oh, he was still in the car—unless he'd been able

to squeeze himself through one of the side vent windows. And I sincerely doubted that, even if he was the thinner of the two cats. I peered over the seat and four green eyes peered back at me from the floor.

"You helped him get out, didn't you?"

Neither of them so much as blinked.

"Okay, fine. If you want company that bad, you can have it. As long as you both stay back there and out from under my feet, we'll get along fine. I've got some water for you, but I guess it had better wait until we stop again. We're going home, so hang on."

Binky started with a grinding noise I knew he shouldn't be making. But he did start and that was what counted. So, unfortunately, did the cries from the backseat.

"Knock it off, you're giving me a headache."

Obviously they didn't care.

Since there was no sign of the Honda in either direction, I decided there was little point in driving around aimlessly looking for it. I should have enough pictures to satisfy Mr. Russo for one night.

It was an uneventful trip back to Ohio if you didn't count the ruckus the cats made. I counted it. Particularly when they started hissing and snarling at each other. One of the Sams nearly gave me a heart attack when he leaped back over the passenger seat, bounced off the box and landed on the floor beside me.

"Hey! Beat it! I'm trying to drive here."

He hunkered down on the floor and hissed at me.

It was a fun trip. Mickey had given me forty-two dollars to find the cat, but there wasn't enough money in the world to put up with this. At least they stayed out from under my feet while I drove, but I lived in fear the whole way home.

I'd never been so grateful to park in my life—until I remembered I was going to have to find some way to smuggle the two cats inside without being seen. My apartment doesn't allow pets. They barely allow humans.

When I reached for the nearest cat, it drew back and took a swipe at me. Since my hand was still throbbing, I decided not to argue without protection. I hurried inside the building, dug out my winter leather gloves and a jacket and went back to the parking lot to play big-game hunter.

I'm sure it looked vastly entertaining to anyone watching—as long as that anyone wasn't the super. I hoped that nosy woman was absorbed in her television at this hour, because she and her husband lived in the building and they didn't miss much.

Sam One was actually a pretty easy catch. He struggled briefly but almost seemed to welcome being dumped back inside the box. Maybe Sam Two had scared him. As long as he wasn't hurt, that was fine with me.

I carried the box inside and set it on the living room floor while I went back outside for the litter, litter pan and food I'd purchased and put in the trunk. Sam One seized the opportunity to escape the box and disappeared behind a chair. Fine with me. It's a small apartment. There weren't too many other places he could go.

I got a dish of water and set everything on the bathroom floor before I went back out to try and catch Sam Two. He had no interest in letting me near him again, treats or not. He didn't intend to be taken without a fight. The little beast put a hole in my jacket and ruined my gloves before I got him out of the backseat and into the box.

If there had been anyone in the lobby or on the steps as I ran upstairs with my yowling prize, I'd have been given an eviction notice on the spot.

The moment I plopped the box on the living room floor, the ungrateful little beast pushed up the flap and took off down the hall to disappear inside my bedroom. Not good. I did not want that cat in my bedroom. But after peering under the bed and being stared down by a pair of defiant green eyes, I decided he could stay. I wasn't up for another battle.

After zapping a frozen dinner to fill my stomach, I decided I'd better download the photos before calling it a night. There was an especially good one of the hunk. I framed out the face and blew it up for a closer look. Despite the grainy texture his features were clear. He had light-colored eyes, probably blue, and rugged, sharply defined features.

I traced the square face on the screen with a fingertip. It was a strong face and very symmetrical—the face of a man who took charge and got things done.

"In a hurry," I added aloud with a snicker as I remembered how short a time he'd spent in the motel room. "So much for gorgeous hunks. You really should get a haircut, you know."

But instead of deleting the picture, I printed it out along with the others and set it to one side before I carefully marked and stored the memory stick. By the time I'd typed up my notes into a report, I was yawning. There hadn't been a sound from either of my unwanted guests, so I went in search of them.

One was still under my bed. The other was squished behind the blue hand-me-down sofa in the living room. I worried that he might be stuck back there, but when I would have moved it out from the wall, he proved me wrong by wriggling even farther back from the end.

"Fine. You want to spend the night back there, be my guest."

I wasn't quite as happy about the one under my bed, but as long as he stayed put, we'd be fine. I set my alarm so I wouldn't oversleep and got ready for bed.

I needn't have bothered with the alarm. The cat-fight woke me before eight. Even I'm not enough of a zombie to sleep through noises like those, especially when the sounds were coming from the foot of my bed.

"Knock it off!"

The sudden silence was almost as loud as the fight had been. I swung my legs off the bed and one of the

Sams streaked out of the room. The other one must have gone back under the bed because there was no sign of it.

Great. It wasn't even eight o'clock in the morning and I was wide awake. My body clock doesn't normally start until midmorning, after a couple of diet colas. Obviously this was not going to be a normal day. I'd be very happy when Mickey claimed Mr. Sam so I could take the other cat to the animal shelter.

By the time I was dressed and ready to leave, I decided I was risking all-out war by leaving the two of them together unattended. I made a second makeshift litter box out of the cardboard box by cutting it down and lining it with aluminum foil. I left it in my bedroom with Sam Two and a second bowl of food and water.

I actually got to the shop ahead of my aunt and Trudy and utilized the time by setting up for the morning. I had coffee brewing and had started on the first of the day's arrangements by the time the pair arrived.

"Well, you're here bright and early this morning," Trudy greeted in surprise.

"How did your evening go, dear? I thought you wanted to borrow my car last night," Aunt Lacy added.

"The evening was…interesting," I told them, "and it turned out I didn't have time to borrow the car, but it worked out okay. Mr. Russo is sending someone over to pick up his report first thing this morning. And if a young boy named Mickey shows up looking for me while I'm busy, keep him here at all costs."

"A young boy?" Trudy said, raising one eyebrow in question.

I hated when she did that. I'd been trying to do it ever since I can remember, but my face just isn't built right.

"He's ten," I said to head off the direction her thoughts were taking.

It was part of a grand conspiracy, of course. My entire family figured if I got married, I'd give up this silly nonsense of being a private investigator. And what their matchmaking lacked in subtlety, it made up for in sheer volume. Any male in the right age bracket was considered fair game.

"Dee," Aunt Lacy said in an urgent whisper. "There's a man standing at the front door. I think it may be Mr. Russo's, uh, person."

Her alarmed expression brought me around the counter in a hurry. The man standing on the other side of the glass door didn't move. I had the sense he was prepared to stand there indefinitely, like the boulder he resembled. Solid, unmovable, timeworn yet sinister in a way I didn't want to define.

A craggy gray face perched over a gray silk tie on a gray silk shirt under a light gray pinstripe suit. If he had a neck, it wasn't obvious, but then boulders rarely have necks. Central casting would have loved this guy. Even his hair was turning gray at the edges.

The only part that looked alive was a pair of incongruous light brown eyes, and they didn't miss a thing.

He'd seen me, so there was nothing for it but to open the door and let all that sinister gray inside the colorful shop. He was going to look out of place. If that man had ever been inside a flower shop in his life, I'd eat the daisy in my hand.

"Ms. Hayes," he said when I unlocked the door, "I'm Hogan Delvecchi. Mr. Russo sent me."

A nervous giggle tried to break free. I suppressed the urge—barely. This was too much like some bad television show—a softly spoken gangster with an Italian last name. And Hogan? Was he kidding? No, I could see he wasn't. There was certainly nothing humorous in his expression. And he seemed to have only the one—a blank stare that absorbed the details of everything around him without revealing his thoughts. I was pretty sure his face was incapable of smiling. Human boulders don't have a sense of humor.

Everything about the man gave me the creeping willies. I worked hard not to let it show.

"Come in, Mr. Delvecchi. I've been expecting you."

Well, not him. No one in their right mind would expect him. And the thing was I wanted him gone as fast as possible. I would never doubt Trudy or my aunt's sources again. If this guy didn't have underworld connections, no one did.

"I'll just get my report."

My heart hammered its way up my throat when he followed me back to the office. He closed the door as I reached for the folder on the end of the desk. I caught him staring at the scratches on my hand.

"Did you have any problems?" he asked.

"N-no."

I was not going to explain about the cats, nor would I think about how the couple had left the motel when I wasn't looking. It was all in the report. I knew it made me look bad, but what could I do? I wasn't about to lie to a mobster. On the other hand, I wasn't going to mention my failings to this guy if I didn't have to.

"Good. Mr. Russo would like to have the picture of his wife back."

That surprised me, but I pulled it from her file. Hogan Delvecchi reached a broad hand inside his suit jacket. My breath caught in the back of my throat. With slow deliberation he pulled out a slim piece of paper and extended it to me. A check, I realized in relief.

I tried not to shake as I took it from his hand, but my legs were emulating gelatin just like my insides. He knew it, I was sure. It probably gave him some sort of salacious thrill to go around scaring people by being polite. Let it. I just wanted him gone.

Less than a minute later he was.

"Well," Trudy said, coming to stand in the open doorway. "He wasn't much for conversation, was he?"

I sank down in the swivel chair and it tilted precariously until I readjusted my weight.

"Is everything all right, dear?" Aunt Lacy asked, coming into view, as well.

"Terrific. He even paid me."

Except, how had he known what to pay? For the first time I really looked at the check in my sweaty palm. Once again my heart began to pound.

"He overpaid."

"That's nice, dear."

"No it isn't. It's terrible. Now I have to call Mr. Russo and return the extra three hundred forty-seven dollars he overpaid."

"Oh, I wouldn't do that, dear. A man like Mr. Russo can afford to tip generously."

"Tip? You think it's a tip?" When he read my report and saw I'd lost them at the motel, he'd want more than his "tip" back.

"At least he didn't shoot anyone," Trudy said glibly as the two of them moved out into the workroom.

No. That would come after Mr. Russo read the report. I'd placed an itemized bill right on top. He'd know exactly how much he'd overpaid. I closed my eyes and groaned.

"Dee?" Trudy called out. "There's a young man up front to see you."

Now what? I wasn't sure I could put on a friendly, professional face right now. I felt sick. It wasn't wise to mess with gangsters. I should have listened to

Aunt Lacy and Trudy right from the start and turned the job down.

I stuffed the check inside the desk drawer and squared my shoulders before going out to meet the newcomer. Once again I had to look down before I spotted him.

"Mickey!"

He was dressed in green shorts and a striped top today, but other than that he looked exactly the same. The same amazing chocolate-brown eyes looked up at me with an expression of hope mixed with fear.

"Did you find him?"

"I think so," I told him. "Actually I found two cats. I'm not sure which one is Mr. Sam."

"I gave you a picture," he said, sounding disgusted.

"Yeah," I said trying not to be defensive, "but he's gray. So are these two guys."

He looked around the shop and started toward the back. "Where are they?"

"At my place. Come on, I'll give you a ride over and take you home afterward."

Doubt filled his expression.

"I'm not allowed to ride in cars with strangers."

Great. A kid who actually listened to his parents.

"You'll have to bring them here," he told me, sounding extremely adult.

I didn't even have to think about that. The back of my hand was still smarting from the last set of scratches.

"How old did you say you are?"

"Ten."

Going on thirty, I decided uncharitably.

"If you're ten then you're old enough to understand the difference between getting in a car with a stranger and getting in a car with me. I work for you, remember?"

He thought about that before standing a little straighter.

"Okay, but what about my bike?"

"Trudy, would it be okay if I take the van over to my apartment for a few minutes? My client and I need to pick up a cat."

"No problem. We don't have any deliveries until later this afternoon."

"Thanks. This will only take a few minutes." To the boy I asked, "How were you going to get him home on your bike?" If those cats had seemed frantic in a car, I could just imagine their reaction to a bicycle.

"I attached a basket to my handlebars and brought the cat carrier with me," he explained.

Reaching down, he picked up a small carrier that had been on the floor at his feet, out of my line of sight. Based on its size, Sam One was the missing cat. Sam Two would have needed a shoehorn.

I secured the bike in the back of the van and drove the short distance to my apartment. I'd be glad to have those animals gone before the super realized they were inside the building.

"What happened to your hand?" Mickey asked.

"Mr. Sam. He doesn't like cars."

"Most cats don't," the kid said philosophically. "I hope you put something on that. Cat scratches can be dangerous."

"Dangerous how?" I asked nervously.

"You know, germs and stuff."

"Right." Germs and stuff. No good deed goes unpunished, as Trudy is fond of saying. In this case, I devoutly hoped she was wrong. If I got an infection because of that stupid cat, I was not going to be happy.

Mickey tensed a little as we started walking into my building a few minutes later. I hated to go against the smart conditioning his parents had put on him, but I was not going to go up there and try to cage that little monster by myself. He'd had all the skin he was going to get off my body.

I unlocked the deadbolt and opened the door carefully. No blur of gray came running out to greet us.

"Where is he?" Mickey demanded.

"I'm not sure. One of them is in my bedroom. The other one was hiding behind the couch the last time I saw him."

The kid whipped out a bag of treats. I wouldn't have thought he could have stuffed something that size into the pocket of those shorts.

"Here, Sam. Here, Sammy."

He got down on the floor and rattled the bag. Nothing happened.

"He always comes out for treats," Mickey said plaintively.

"He's probably nervous. This is a strange place for him."

I walked over and tugged the couch out from the wall. A gray streak whipped past me to cower behind the potted palm frond near the window.

"It's okay, Sammy, it's me." Mickey walked over toward the plant, and the cat scooted around the chair and took off toward the kitchen.

"That's not Mr. Sam," Mickey said.

"How can you tell?"

He gave me another of those disturbingly adult looks that said plainly what he thought of my inability to distinguish the difference between the picture he had given me and the cat now hiding somewhere in my kitchen.

"Okay," I said, "then it must be the one in the bedroom."

Mickey had to crawl under the bed with a flashlight to see Sam Two. He crawled back out in disgust.

"That's not Mr. Sam either."

My stomach churned. "Are you sure?"

"Of course I am."

Of course he was. I remembered the other gray cat I'd seen as I was leaving the park and my heart plunged to meet my roiling stomach. I was going to have to go back to the park.

"We've gotta find him. My uncle's coming for dinner this week. We hav'ta find him before then."

Of course we did. The kid looked ready to cry. I had no idea what to do if he started crying. He looked so upset, I heard myself telling him about the other cat I'd seen and agreeing to help him try and find it.

It was those darn eyes of his, I told myself half an hour later as we scoured the park for gray cats. I'm a sucker for soft eyes like those. But the word had gone out. Avoid the crazy lady at all costs. We didn't even see a cat, let alone a gray one.

"I hav'ta go home," Mickey told me, looking pathetically discouraged. "My mom's picking me up to go shopping."

He made it sound like a surgical ordeal.

"All right. I'll run you home and come back. I can keep looking for a little while longer."

Hope replaced his despair.

"Thanks! You can keep the carrier. I'll take my bike and come to the store as soon as I get back."

Wondering when my brain had turned to fuzz, I agreed and got his bike from the back of the van. "Where do you live, Mickey?"

"On Broadhurst."

Two streets away.

"Maybe I should concentrate on some of the side streets between here and there. He's probably hiding in someone's bushes."

"Okay. Just find him."

"I'll do my best."

Only, after walking four blocks in both directions, I decided to call it quits. The cat could be anywhere.

He was probably up some tree laughing at me as I trudged past making kissy noises at the bushes. The day was heating up in an effort to top yesterday, and I was wilting faster than cut flowers left out of water.

As I crossed to my car, I spotted a little gray cat trotting across the parking lot. This one had four white paws. Looking at the picture Mickey had given me, I realized the paws didn't show. I'd forgotten to ask the kid if the cat was all gray. How could I have forgotten something so basic?

The little guy came willingly when I called him Mr. Sam. He was much smaller than the other two cats and his hair wasn't as long, but he was mostly gray and that was good enough for me. He even went into the carrier without a fuss. Elated, I headed back to the shop with my prize.

Trudy and Aunt Lacy had to hear the entire tale once I got back. They fussed over the small cat like a pair of broody hens. Mr. Sam seemed to enjoy all the attention—a refreshing change from the first two.

Trudy and my aunt sent me down the street to pick up more cat food and litter, even though I explained we wouldn't have him more than a few hours, but when I got back, they were looking at me with the same sort of expression I'd come to expect from Mickey.

"Didn't you say this cat was called Mr. Sam?" Aunt Lacy asked.

"Wrong sex," Trudy said.

"What?"

"She's a she, and if she's over a year old, it can't be by much."

I groaned. "Are you sure?"

"Positive," my aunt told me. "You'll need to make signs."

"Signs?"

"Well, you can't turn the poor little thing loose on the street," she objected.

"But that's where I found her."

"Use your camera to take her picture and make some Found signs so we can find her owner," Aunt Lacy insisted.

There was no arguing with that tone of voice. I went and got my digital camera. I was printing the Found Cat signs when I heard a commotion out front.

"I said you can't go back there! Sir! You can't go back there!"

I didn't even have time to get up before a large shape filled the office doorway. Elaine Russo's lover stood framed there. His eyes were a brilliant blue, I discovered, and they could shoot invisible flames. Those flames ignited a heat that started low in my belly and spread outward at an alarming rate.

"What did you do with her?" he demanded.

Chapter Four

Okay, my hormones were thrilled to have such a fantastic-looking man standing in my office, but no one is *that* good looking, and I'm not such a wimp that I cave to my body's hormones. I put on an indignant face and started to get up. The stupid chair seized the moment of inattention and rolled backward. My head met the wall with an audible thunk.

I lunged forward out of the miserable piece of junk to avoid falling flat on my back along with the chair. Somehow I managed to land on my feet and, with great restraint, kept my hand from rubbing the sore spot on the back of my head. Thank God he didn't laugh.

"Aunt Lacy, call the police."

He turned to give Aunt Lacy a cold look. "I wouldn't do that if I were you," he said with a quiet firmness that sort of scared even me.

"Fine," I said with false bravado. "I'll call them."

His hand covered mine as I reached for the old black rotary-dial phone on my desk. Sexual chemistry was all well and good, but this was the sort of man

I'd feel a whole lot safer adoring from afar. With that warm, firm hand swallowing mine, I felt the surge of attraction clear to my toes. A tingle worked its way up my arm from the point of contact and short-circuited my brain.

"You followed us last night," he stated.

The closet-size office shrank away until there was nothing but him and me. My stomach did one of those quick roller-coaster dips, and somehow I found my voice even as I pulled my hand out from under his.

"That's quite an ego you carry around," I managed. "But as a pickup line, it's original."

I wouldn't have thought his eyes could harden any further. I would have been wrong. Adrenaline was sending me all sorts of mixed messages. Chief among them was the urge to run.

He rocked back on his heels to study me. I was suddenly all too conscious that my hair was in its usual disarray and both my navy linen slacks and my light blue blouse could have used the help of an iron this morning.

Not that I own an iron or would have been inclined to use it if I had one, but this man made me abruptly, stunningly aware that I was a woman facing the most fascinating man I'd ever seen.

"You told Russo where she was," he added without inflection.

I wanted to deny that charge, but of course I couldn't—any more than I could admit that I was both drawn to and intimidated by this gorgeous male.

"Go away."

"How does it feel to know you conspired to murder someone?"

That sent a punch of a whole new sort to my insides.

"Whoa! What do you mean murder? Who's been murdered?" My intestines did a quick roll while my heart rhythm went staccato.

"That's what I'm trying to find out."

Maybe the bump on my head had scrambled my hearing. I shook my head and focused on his lips.

"Okay, I think we need to back up here," I told him. "Who are you?"

He looked genuinely surprised. "You don't even know that?"

Now that really stung. "I didn't bother to run your plate," I admitted. "And that really is some ego you've got."

He might be great eye candy, but I'd about had it with him and his gibes. He shook his head.

"Russo must have loved your report if you left my name out. Unless… Of course. You took her, didn't you? Convinced her to go back with you as soon as I left."

He'd pushed all the right buttons. Now I was angry, as well.

"Get out!"

He placed his hands flat on the desk and leaned in toward me. "Not going to happen *Ms.* Hayes. You're going to tell me exactly what you said to Elaine."

I came around the desk to get in his face. Unfortunately I hadn't taken into consideration the difference in our height. He straightened up. At six feet, he towered over my five-foot-one-inch frame, giving him the advantage. Unfortunately I was angry enough now not to care. I jabbed a finger in his chest, taking him by surprise.

"You don't come waltzing into my office throwing your weight around. I'm not afraid of you," I lied. "You want to have sex with a married woman, you take the consequences, buster."

"Sex? You think we were…" He swore.

"Right back at you."

I was quaking inside, but I'd die before admitting it. Though I'm licensed to carry a gun, I never do. Guns scare me—but not nearly as much as he did.

He looked down at my hand, and I realized my finger was still pressed against his crisp white linen shirt. Aware of the scratches, I dropped my hand and fought an urge to take a quick step back. Instead I opened my mouth and more words came tumbling out.

"Why would I think the two of you were getting it on?" I asked to cover the flush I could feel stealing up my neck. "Oh, wait. Could it be because you drove the very married Elaine Russo across the state line to some sleazy motel? So sorry. I'm sure it was for an innocent, if illegal, poker game."

His eyes went flat. There was something very scary about the banked anger I read in his expression.

I found myself taking that step back after all until my posterior came up against the edge of the desk.

In an instant all that scary anger disappeared. He regarded me with something that looked suspiciously like grudging respect mingled with humor.

"My cousin will not be happy to hear you think his motel is sleazy."

My knees felt disturbingly wobbly.

"Your cousin?"

"Vinnie and his wife just sank their life's savings into building that 'sleazy' motel."

Oh, boy.

"You're not the least bit afraid of me, are you?"

If he only knew. I swallowed, grateful for the acting classes I'd taken in high school, and tried for a sneer.

"I didn't know fear was a requirement."

More of his tension eased. He tipped his head to regard me. It was all I could do to keep my hand from straying to my hair in a vain attempt to control the loose curls. If only I'd gotten up when the alarm clock went off so I could have worn it up, like I usually do when I'm working. It makes me look older.

He definitely seemed amused now, and I didn't like that reaction any better than his anger. Having a gorgeous man regard me with humor is not my idea of a compliment.

"We've strayed from the point," I told him in annoyance. "I'd like you to leave."

"Yeah. I got that. *Did* you talk to Elaine and convince her to leave or did Russo send someone after her?"

"I'm a private investigator, pal. People pay me for information."

He reached in his hip pocket and produced a leather wallet. Taking some bills from inside, he laid them on the desk and stared at me with a questioning lift of his brows.

That fanned the flames of more anger. "You arrogant—"

"Not enough?" He started to take out another twenty.

I was so furious, I was starting to shake.

"You don't have enough money. Get out of here. I'll see you in divorce court. I'll be the one pointing a finger at you and telling the judge you're the man who was having the affair with Elaine Russo."

"Then you'll be lying," he said calmly. "Elaine isn't my lover, she's my client."

That pricked my anger and filled me with confusion.

"Client?"

He reached into his wallet once more. This time he handed me a small white business card. Not the type I pull off my printer—this one was embossed in bold script. Heat, then cold, swept me as I stared at the name on the card.

"*You're* Brandon Kirkpatrick?"

"You aren't what I expected either," he admitted. "I assumed D.B. Hayes was a man."

We stared at each other.

"What's the D.B. stand for anyhow?"

"Dangerous when Bothered." I was still angry despite the hollow feeling in my belly.

He grinned. The man was gorgeous even when he was angry, but when he smiled, he was downright lethal.

"Beats Dumb Blonde," he said.

My teeth came together with a snap. "I'm not a blonde. I have brown hair."

He stared at my hair. "Looks more like burnished teak to me."

My tummy quivered. The desire to melt was incredibly strong. Sternly I took control. This man had taken my client's wife to a motel room only the night before.

"I'll bet you get far with that puppy-dog look, don't you, Mr. Kirkpatrick?"

His smile invited me to share the humor.

"Generally speaking, yes. Doesn't seem to be working on you though."

If he only knew.

"Everything all right, Dee?" my aunt asked.

I'd forgotten all about Aunt Lacy and Trudy. Apparently they'd decided I could handle the man and were just checking to be sure their assumption had been correct.

"Fine, Aunt Lacy. Mr. Kirkpatrick was just leaving."

"Dee and I are just getting to know each other," he said at the same time.

"We are not," I said sharply. "I have no desire to get to know you."

"Why not? I'm a nice person and we have a lot in common."

"We have nothing in common."

"We're both in the same profession, and this is a small community, after all."

"That's right, so stay on your side of the river and we'll get along just fine."

"Can't do that. It appears we're on opposite sides of more than the river at the moment."

"There are no sides. I was hired to do a job and—"

"So was I," he interjected quickly. His features grew serious. "Elaine hired me to protect her from her husband. She has reason to believe he plans to kill her."

The matter-of-fact way he said that sent an icy chill straight up my spine.

"Look, Dee, you seem like a nice kid. I doubt you want something like that on your conscience."

Kid? He thought I was a kid?

"Did you talk to her after I left or did Russo send someone after her?"

I pictured Hogan Delvecchi and tried not to shudder. Was it possible? Had I been used to set the woman up to be killed?

"She wasn't at the motel when I went to pick her up this morning," Brandon continued. "No one saw her leave and she isn't answering her cell phone. What happened?"

"Look, Mr. Kirkpatrick—"

"Brandon."

"Mr. Kirkpatrick," I said firmly, "I don't know what sort of ethics you have, but my job demands client confidentiality."

His expression hardened once more.

"I hope your ethics give you comfort when they find her body."

"You aren't laying that at my door. I'm not the one she hired for protection, pal. You're the one who left her alone in the middle of nowhere without a car."

He turned without a word and strode through the door.

"I will tell you this much," I called after his back. "I never spoke with Elaine Russo."

He didn't break stride or say a word, but I gave him points for inclining his head to acknowledge Aunt Lacy and Trudy as he passed. Trudy gaped, standing there holding a tulip in one veined hand. Neither of them spoke as he strode out of the shop.

"Well," Trudy said after a minute, sticking the flower into the arrangement in front of her. "Who's the stud?"

I leaned back against the door frame. My knees threatened to buckle at any moment.

"Brandon Kirkpatrick."

"Oh, my," Aunt Lacy murmured.

Trudy grinned. "Cool. I didn't realize he was such a looker. That one is definitely a keeper. Much better than your usual sort."

"Are you out of your mind?" I demanded. "I don't even like him."

She raised a single eyebrow. "Honey, all those sparks flying around in that itty-bitty office practially blinded me."

"What you saw was sheer rage on his part," I told her.

"I wouldn't be so sure of that, and certainly not on our part," she said provocatively.

"Trudy," my aunt chastised.

Trudy looked unrepentant. "Lacy, even you have to admit that man could inspire sparks in a female corpse."

"If he wasn't such a jerk," I inserted. "Emphasis on the *jerk,* Trudy. He has an ego the size of Colorado. Besides, pretty boys aren't my type."

"Honey, that was no boy, and I'd say he's every breathing heterosexual woman's type."

"Trudy!" Aunt Lacy protested. "Leave the girl alone. We need to get this arrangement finished. Dee, we have five orders that have to go out this afternoon—are you free to make deliveries?"

"Sure," I said absently, still fretting over my conversation with Brandon. "I'm not in the mood to hunt cats again in this heat."

"Now, dear, you mustn't give up. You'll find him," she replied. "I have faith. And I wouldn't worry about what that Mr. Kirkpatrick told you. I'm sure Mr. Russo isn't going to kill his wife."

No, he'd probably have Delvecchi take care of that detail for him, I thought sourly.

"Are you kidding?" Trudy exclaimed. "I keep telling you that man has mob ties. If he wants her dead, she's dead."

"No one's going to die," I said with more force than I felt.

"Of course not," my aunt agreed. "And anyhow, it wouldn't be your fault. Like you told Mr. Kirkpatrick, if anyone screwed up, it was him. He's the one she hired for protection."

That did not make me feel any better.

I knew when I'd decided to use the flower shop as my base that privacy was something I'd have little of, but while my aunt and Trudy loved to gossip, we had an agreement that my cases were to stay private. I sincerely hoped they'd honor that promise.

I stewed over the scene with the sexy Brandon Kirkpatrick all afternoon as I delivered flowers to business offices and happy homemakers. Normally I enjoy seeing a person's reaction to receiving flowers, but today was hardly normal.

Once I finished my deliveries, I drove up and down the side streets near Mickey's looking for cats. They, however, weren't stupid enough to be wandering around in this heat. I didn't blame them, but I was starting to worry about Mr. Sam. Mickey had said the cat was old. It was really, really hot outside and we hadn't had rain in weeks. Would the poor little thing be able to find water? Would he be able to find food? I know hunting is supposed to be a natural instinct, but if the poor old feline was used to humans providing everything in a dish, how would he manage? Do cats get Alzheimer's? While I was heartily sick of looking for the little beast, I'd feel awful if something bad happened before I found him.

Reluctantly I stopped at the park and got out for a quick look around. The only animals in sight was the flock of geese that had taken over the ball field. As they were bigger than most cats, I figured wandering in that direction was a waste of time and a pair of good shoes. Other than some small children playing on the playground under the weary eyes of their mothers, the rest of Lakewood was crammed into the sun-baked pool, noisily trying to cool off.

By the time I got back to the shop, my blouse clung like an unpleasant additional layer of skin and my forehead was dripping sweat. For some stupid reason I couldn't stop thinking about a pair of flashing blue eyes and the gorgeous face that went with them. Why couldn't Brandon Kirkpatrick have been some seedy middle-aged man with a receding hairline and love handles?

Trudy was waiting on a customer. Aunt Lacy was in the office, on the telephone, with the shop ledger spread in front of her. I scooped up my portable computer and wiggled my fingers to let her know I was leaving when my cell phone rang. Setting the computer on the workstation, I answered the summons, half hoping it wouldn't be another job. I was tired. But at the same time, for the sake of my bank account, I half hoped it *would* be a new client. Even an old one.

"D.B. Hayes."

"Ms. Hayes, this is Albert Russo. I wanted to thank you personally for a job well done."

"Uh—"

"You may be called on to testify on my behalf in the divorce settlement. If that happens, suitable recompense will, of course, be given. I was foolish not to insist on a prenuptial agreement. I'm afraid it's going to be an ugly divorce. My wife appeared in my office this afternoon and created a most embarrassing scene in front of my staff over those photographs you took."

"She did?"

Elaine Russo wasn't dead. She wasn't even hurt. And instead of sounding angry, her husband sounded genuinely embarrassed. My relief was amazing.

"She claims she's been trying to break off her relationship with Mr. Kirkpatrick for weeks now," he went on.

Shocked, I stared at an African violet sitting out on the counter in the back room for some reason. Russo knew who Brandon was. And Elaine Russo had admitted to having an affair with him. I pushed aside a pang of regret. The pretty boy had lied to me.

"Elaine claims Kirkpatrick threatened her," Russo continued. "I don't believe that, of course, but it makes no difference. The point is, thanks to you, I have sufficient physical proof to meet with my lawyer this evening. I want you to know I appreciate your diligence. I will be happy to pass your name along to my colleagues, should they ever require the services of an investigator."

"Thank—"

"And, of course, there will be an additional bonus for you once the divorce goes through. Again thank you."

"Oh, it was my…pleasure," I added to the dead line.

Mr. Russo had said his piece and disconnected. Okay by me. His wife was alive. He was pleased with my work. He'd offered to pass along my name to his wealthy friends. Life was good.

Something brushed against my leg. Startled, I yelped out loud as I looked down to find the small gray cat rubbing up against me. I was in such a good mood, I even bent down to stroke her furry head. Instantly she began to purr.

"You have a loud purr for such a little thing, you know that, cat?"

"Oh, Dee, I'm glad you're still here," Aunt Lacy said. "Did you remember to hang the Found signs for Annabelle?"

I blinked at my aunt in surprise. "You named the cat Annabelle?"

"Well, we can't just call her 'cat.'"

"Why not?"

My aunt gave me one of those speaking looks, and I managed a meek shrug.

"You could keep her," I suggested.

"Absolutely not. Clem would not take kindly to a

cat. Besides, someone must be missing this sweet little girl, right, Belle?"

Annabelle immediately left my side to rub against my aunt. Aunt Lacy opened the workstation drawer and pulled out a bag of kitty treats. Annabelle scarfed down the offering as if she was starving.

"Your young man was in again while you were out."

"Brandon came back?"

Aunt Lacy got a peculiar look on her face.

"No, dear. I believe his name is Mickey. A very bright, polite young man, but he's quite discouraged. I do hope you'll find his cat soon."

I did not like the newly speculative look on my aunt's face. I'd just made a big blunder and I knew it. What on earth had made me think she was talking about Brandon? It was understandable that the stupid man would be on my mind after the way he'd scared me with that drivel about being responsible for the woman's death but nevertheless...

"I'm trying to find Mickey's cat, Aunt Lacy. I just came back from looking at the park some more. You'd think one of these miserable animals would be the right one. I mean, how many gray cats can be running around loose in Lakewood? The place isn't that big."

She handed me the leaflets with Annabelle's picture. "Here, dear."

One does not argue with Aunt Lacy when she gets that expression. I was hot and sweaty all over again by the time I finished hanging the signs around the neighborhood where I'd picked up Annabelle. When I finished, I thought about stopping by my dad's place and sharing a meal with him, but frankly I was too hot to eat. I decided to go home, pop some microwave popcorn, open a cola and try to figure out how to remove the other two animals from my apartment without getting caught.

Since I was pretty sure the animal shelter closed by six, that meant they'd have to spend another night in my apartment. The thought was depressing. Maybe that's why my subconscious decided I should drop by Brandon Kirkpatrick's office on my way home.

I found myself crossing the bridge into Rocky River before I could really think things through. Still, why not? Turnabout only seemed fair. If he could burst into my office, I could reciprocate to let him know his client wasn't dead and I knew him for a fast-talking liar. Besides, I was dying to see his office.

I hate to admit I'm so mean spirited, but I was glad I made the decision. His office was a small hole-in-the-wall squished between storefronts—much smaller than Aunt Lacy's flower shop. On the other hand, he didn't have to share space with anyone, so his name was prominently displayed on the front door.

No one sat at the scuffed teak desk in what proved be an outer office. A phone, a pad of paper, some pens and an older-model computer were the desk's only adornment. There were four mismatched chairs scattered around, but no plants, no photographs—nothing to break up the plain, bare, institutional white walls.

Brandon emerged from the inner office almost immediately and filled the doorway between the two rooms. Seeing him again, my stomach took on a funny fluttery feeling I haven't had since the first time a boy asked me out.

"You could use a decorator," I told him.

He didn't smile. "My sister-in-law agrees with you."

So much for small talk. "She's not dead," I told him without further preamble.

He leaned back against the door frame and crossed his legs at the ankle. The casual pose should not have troubled me in any way at all.

"And you know this because…?"

"Albert Russo phoned to thank me. Your client made a big scene in his office this afternoon. She claims you threatened her when she tried to break off your affair."

"What!"

He came off the door frame so fast, I didn't have time to do more than flinch. Fear sent my heart slamming against my rib cage as he spanned the distance between us to loom over me with a ferocious look that left me quaking inside. Why had I thought coming here to gloat was a good idea?

"Tell me exactly what he said," Brandon demanded from between clenched teeth.

I took a step back and wondered if I could reach the door before he did.

"Every word, Dee."

I tried not to let him see I was intimidated even as I proceeded to tell him what Russo had said. Because I was watching him the way a mouse watches a bird of prey, I saw the shock and anger in his expression before his face turned impassive.

"He lied," Brandon said flatly.

At least he hadn't said *I* was lying.

"I don't think so."

His eyes narrowed.

"Look, he sounded pretty embarrassed by the whole thing."

"Then why would he tell you about it?"

"He was upset. I think he was sort of thinking out loud. Maybe he was trying to warn me."

"About what?"

I shrugged and shifted, trying to inch my way toward the door without being obvious. "That it's going to be a messy divorce?" I replied, not liking the uncertain tone in my voice.

Brandon shook his head. "No way. A man like Russo doesn't marry a much younger woman like Elaine without a prenup. He's setting you up."

I blinked at his flat tone. "How?" I asked, truly curious.

Brandon rubbed a hand across his jaw. "I don't know. This makes no sense. Why would Elaine lie?"

"Did she?"

The green in his eyes flashed dangerously. "I did not sleep with Elaine Russo," he enunciated carefully.

Maybe it was naive, but I wanted to believe him.

"In that case, you're the one who's being set up. Has it occurred to you that maybe there is a boyfriend? Maybe Elaine wanted her husband to go after someone else in his place?"

He exhaled through his nose as he thought about that.

"According to you," he said slowly, "Russo isn't coming after me. He's filing for divorce."

"And if she's using you to obtain it, there must be a reason."

We both fell silent. He looked tired, I realized, as he rubbed absently at his left shoulder. Those striking blue eyes were clouded in thought. Frown lines marred his forehead. And why was I noticing he had the sort of long, curling eyelashes I'd kill for?

"Have you eaten dinner yet?"

His question caught me unprepared. My heart stuttered with a flash of instant excitement that I quickly suppressed.

"No."

"The Tambor is only a couple doors away. The place has decent food. I missed lunch and breakfast and I think we need to talk."

I had to quell a surge of inappropriate disappointment. He wasn't asking me on a date. He just wanted to pump me for information while he ate.

So what? Sitting across from Brandon Kirkpatrick beat eating popcorn in front of the television set, no matter what questions he wanted to ask. Nothing said I had to answer those questions.

"All right."

"Let me shut down my computer."

I followed him into his inner sanctum without an invitation. Like the outer office, the room was starkly impersonal but a whole lot messier. Papers and files covered his desk. Empty Styrofoam cups that had once held coffee were interspersed with fast-food wrappers and an old pizza box.

As if embarrassed, he gathered up the trash quickly and tossed it out of sight in a wastebasket next to his desk. I knew he'd been here seven months at least, but the room felt so bare other than the clutter that it looked as if he had just moved in.

His desk was twin to the one in the outer office and looked well used. A pair of slightly battered, matching teak filing cabinets rested against a blank wall while one of those all-in-one printer-fax-copier machines perched on a bookcase beside them. Another older-model computer sat on a stand beside his desk, but it wasn't even plugged in. He had a slim portable computer open on his desk. I had the exact same model out in my car.

From my angle I couldn't see what was on the screen, so I scanned the papers spread across his desk. When he saw me craning to look, he immediately scooped them into a folder. But not before I saw that they were official police reports.

What was Brandon Kirkpatrick doing with official reports on what appeared to be a murder investigation?

"Big case?" I asked, trying for nonchalance.

"No, it's personal."

Yeah. Right. Hadn't I known he'd get all the good cases because he was a man? Life wasn't fair.

Not surprisingly, they knew him at the restaurant. He flirted easily with the pretty black hostess and greeted the young waiter by name. Brandon ordered a beer and a steak dinner. Since this wasn't a date and whatever I ate I'd have to pay for, I settled for a glass of water and a grilled chicken salad.

Walking to the restaurant with him, I'd had time to think. Despite his assertions, Brandon and Elaine had seemed pretty cozy inside that piano bar. They'd also been inside that motel room long enough to be a lot closer than a client and her protector, even if it had been a quickie. Still, somehow it didn't add up.

"I wasn't, you know," he said as he raised his glass to take a sip of the foamy brew.

I had no trouble following that statement. "Reading minds now? In a way, that's too bad. If you're going to have to face the consequences, you should at least have had the fun of an affair."

He set the glass down carefully. I could see I'd shocked him. That made me feel better and I settled back into the booth more comfortably.

"She's an attractive woman," I added.

"So are you, but I don't sleep with a woman just because she's attractive."

My stomach leaped into free fall. He thought I was attractive?

"Your business," I said, trying to sound blasé, "but if I were you, I'd start watching over my shoulder. Based on the rumors I've heard, Albert Russo isn't the type to sit back and let the world know he's been cuckolded without getting a little of his own back. It doesn't matter if you're innocent if he believes you're guilty. There's a man who works for him that looks like he could break you in half without even working up a sweat."

"Hogan Delvecchi," he said with a scowl.

"You've met him?"

"Not yet."

"Trust me, you don't want to. The way I figure it, if you two weren't having a go, the only reason Mrs. Russo would name you her lover is so her husband won't damage the real one."

"Cheery thought."

A slight tic near his left temple was the only sign he was actually worried.

"Whose idea was it to drive all the way into Pennsylvania?" I asked.

"Mine. Elaine told me she was afraid of her husband. She wanted a place to hide where he wouldn't find her. How sure are you that Russo told you the truth?"

I had time to mull that over as our food arrived. I waited for the waiter to leave before I answered him.

"Why would Russo lie to me? His story would be easy enough to check out. He said his staff heard the whole thing. Be pretty hard to get an entire group of people to lie about something like that, don't you think?"

He cut into his steak. The aroma made me drool, so I plunged my fork into my generous salad.

"You said you tried calling her?" I added.

"She's not answering her phones and she hasn't returned any of my messages."

"Big surprise there," I said, forking up a large piece of lightly breaded chicken. "If I was setting some guy up to take a pounding, I wouldn't be answering his calls either."

The round of dark rye bread they'd brought with the meal was fresh and warm and perfect, I discovered after cutting off a generous hunk. I'm a confirmed carbohydrate junkie, and that bread was worth every calorie.

As I chewed blissfully, I realized Brandon was watching me with the sort of fascination that made me aware of just how much I savored every bite. I set the bread down self-consciously.

"Would you like to try a bite of my steak?" he offered.

There was nothing sensual in the question, but the low-voiced delivery left me quivering on the inside.

"No, thanks." I could feel the pink staining my cheeks. "I enjoy fresh bread."

"Yes, you do. I'll have to remember that."

I tamped down a rolling surge of lust, wishing I could control my blush as easily.

"What are you doing here, Brandon?"

"Having dinner with a beautiful woman."

So much for warm fuzzies.

"You can't help yourself, can you? You have to flirt with every woman you meet."

"Not every woman."

I set down my fork with more of a clatter than was really necessary.

"Stick a sock in it, Kirkpatrick. I'm not interested in being part of a crowd. Did you ever think maybe that's why Elaine chose you?"

All hint of humor fled those brilliant blue eyes. I'll give him credit—Brandon didn't let a little thing like hurt pride stop him from thinking through what I'd said. He set his own knife and fork down more carefully and regarded me.

"You could be right."

Okay, so maybe the words didn't give me warm fuzzies, but his response wasn't what I would have expected and I found myself warming to him all over again.

"One of them was lying to us," he said.

"Gee, you think?"

He ignored the sarcasm. "I'll check it out—see if that scene really did take place in his office."

"And you'll watch your back?"

"Unless you're offering to do it for me."

I sucked in a breath as another wave of instant lust hit me. Watching his back or any other part of him would be no hardship at all.

"Sure. For a fee," I said primly. "I don't normally take on bodyguard cases, but it never hurts to diversify."

His grin melted my socks.

"Your looks really are deceiving, aren't they?"

I bristled. "How am I supposed to take that comment?"

"As a compliment, Dee. You look about seventeen. Bright, cheerful—"

"If you say *bubbly* I'm going to have to stab you with your steak knife."

I felt his laughter like warm brandy sliding across my skin. Two women turned to look our way. I tried not to appear self-satisfied, but I did want to preen a bit. After all, it wasn't every day I sat down with a man who looked as gorgeous as Brandon.

"Look," he said turning serious. "You've lived around here most of your life, right? If you'll nose around, I'll do the same and we'll pool our information before one of us ends up in deep kimchi."

"Is that a real word?"

"Kimchi? Yeah. Actually it's a Korean dish of cabbage, onions, garlic and a bunch of other stuff I couldn't identify. They ferment—"

"Hold it. That's more than I want to know. You've actually eaten it?"

He shrugged lightly. "A Korean family lived next door to us a number of years ago."

I picked up my fork and plowed back into my salad wondering who the "us" referred to and whether I'd look too interested in him personally if I asked.

"I'm not a big fan of cabbage," I said around a mouthful of raw lettuce.

He lifted his fork and steak knife and smiled. "Something else we have in common. Do we have a deal?"

I couldn't see how asking Aunt Lacy and Trudy a few questions about Russo and his wife and relaying their answers to Brandon could hurt, so I nodded and reached for another slice of bread.

We finished the meal in companionable silence and both opted to pass on dessert and coffee. When the check came, I pulled out my wallet.

"I'll get it," Brandon offered.

Given the current state of my bank balance, I was sorely tempted, but this hadn't been a date and I really didn't want to find myself in debt to him, even over something as simple as a meal. I handed him a twenty, and after a second, he took it, checked the bill and made change from a wallet a whole lot thicker than mine.

"Come on, I'll walk you to your car," he offered.

"I can make it across the parking lot."

"You're a prickly little thing, aren't you?"

"I'm not little. You're just supersized. What I am

is careful," I corrected. "If I'm right, Delvecchi or someone like him is out there somewhere just waiting for a chance to beat you to a pulp."

"Then maybe you should walk me to my car—for a fee, of course."

My stomach took a quick dip at the intense way he was looking at me.

"How much?" he demanded.

"What?"

"How much would you charge to walk me to my car?"

My heart started hammering way too fast. He was teasing, of course, but there was an intensity in his expression that was making it hard to think of anything beyond the fact that I'd give quite a lot to find out what it was like to kiss that tempting mouth.

"What are you doing a week from Saturday?"

I heard the question tumbling past my lips too late to call the words back. His eyes sort of darkened before humor set them to sparkling again.

"What's a week from Saturday?"

There was no way out now. I had to tell him the rest.

"A friend of mine's getting married."

"*You* need a date?"

The way he phrased it went a long way toward salving my pride. Not *You need a date because you're too unattractive to get one?* but *Why on earth would someone like you need a date?* He was good. Better than good.

"I'd prefer not spending the entire evening listening to a discourse on the Browns' chances for next season."

I'd put off asking Billy Nugent to take me for that very reason. Brandon laughed out loud. Someone should bottle that laugh. They'd make a fortune selling that rich sound.

"You'd rather hear about the Pittsburgh Steelers' chances?"

"Only if you have a death wish," I told him smartly.

His chuckle was almost as good as his laugh.

"Look, there's another reason I brought it up. A lot of people will be there. It's an opportunity for us to ask some discreet questions. People in this town talk, and the Russos generate a lot of gossip. One of the bride's sisters knows a clerk in the mayor's office. Russo's got connections there."

It sounded weak even to me, but Brandon nodded seriously.

"Then it's a deal. Come guard my back," he invited. "My car's over here."

I managed to keep pace with his much longer legs only because he shortened his stride to accommodate me. I found myself actually peering around the parking lot as evening stole across the sky. His burgundy Honda was only a few rows away from where I'd left my car.

"Thank you," he said seriously.

"I should probably follow you home."

What was I saying?

His smile did warm, disturbing things to my nerve endings.

"I don't think that'll be necessary. I'll give you a call later."

"You don't have my number."

His easy grin warmed my insides.

"I'm a detective. I'll find it."

For one very brief second I thought he was going to lean down and kiss me. The bump to my heart rate and the roll in my abdomen left me breathless, but he just squeezed my upper arm gently and climbed into his car.

I'm not sure, but I think I floated the rest of the way home. The most gorgeous man in Ohio was taking me to Lorna's wedding. My friends would die.

I was practically giddy—until I saw what was waiting for me inside my apartment.

Chapter Five

When I opened the door, my first thought was I'd
been burglarized. The place was trashed.

My pretty, sheer drapes hung from the broken rod
in shreds. The turquoise vase I loved was a shattered
memory. The artificial flowers it had held were scattered across the carpeting. My potted palm plant lay
on its side, dirt spilled in all directions. Every knick-
knack and loose item had been knocked to the floor.
Two were broken. The blue-and-green table runner
was still partly on the table, but only because my
grandmother's crystal bowl was heavy enough to anchor it there. And Sam One shot out from under one
of the dining room chairs to dart behind the couch.

"*You?* You did all this?"

As hard as it was to believe, I could see that the
vicious little feline had indeed caused all the damage. Under the table was a pile of cat puke filled with
leaves from my poor plant. Tiny black paw prints had
left a trail in the dirt leading away from the mangled
greenery.

If I hadn't been in such a good mood from my dinner with Brandon, I might have retrieved my gun and shot the beast. As it was, I settled for yelling at him.

"What did you do? Throw a party?"

The bedroom door was still shut, so he hadn't had help. Nothing had been disturbed in the kitchen except the bowl I'd used for his water. He'd turned that over completely. I wondered if he'd done that before or after he'd scattered the used litter over the bathroom floor and walked in it with wet paws.

"You are a bad, evil cat. No wonder you were wandering the streets. Who would keep you?"

A quick peek in my bedroom gave me some relief. Everything in there appeared just as I had left it this morning. There was no sign of Sam Two, but I figured he was still under the bed.

"You are a bad cat," I scolded Sam One again as I began to pick up broken bits of glass. "A very, very, very bad cat. First thing tomorrow morning you are going to the pound, you hear me? Do you know how much drapes cost, you little fiend? I can't afford new drapes. These are ruined! I can't salvage them. And you broke the rod. How could you break the rod? Were you playing Tarzan on my drapes? I don't believe this. And my favorite vase. Do you know how much I loved this vase? You are a bad cat. A *really* bad cat."

There wasn't a sound from the bad cat as I continued to berate him while I set the rooms back in some semblance of order. I decided then and there that I really did not like cats. I especially didn't like cat puke. And cleaning a litter box had just moved to number one on my list of things I never, ever wanted to do again.

I mopped the floors and replenished the water dish, grudgingly adding a bowl of food. It was a good thing I was getting rid of the little monsters, because this was the last of the cat food I'd bought to trap them with.

I was still fuming when I finally stepped into my bedroom and closed the door so the two animals couldn't join forces. I pulled off my clothes, piled them on the dresser and padded naked to the closet for my nightgown. I'd been in a hurry this morning and I hadn't closed it tightly. That proved to be the worst mistake I'd made all day.

Clothes, many of which were stained in blood and ick, had been pulled from hangers, including my brand-new, never-worn formal for Lorna's wedding. It lay on the floor beside the matching shoes. Curled in the middle of the skirt was Sam Two nursing six tiny, writhing, wormlike kittens.

"No. Oh, no. Not my dress!"

Sam Two gazed up at me with tired, watchful eyes.

This wasn't happening. It couldn't be happening. It had taken me weeks to find the perfect dress. And the shoes! The shoes had been even harder to find— shoes that were now stained with ick.

I backed out of the closet and reached for the telephone.

When they arrived, Aunt Lacy and Trudy were not the least bit sympathetic. They were much too busy oohing and aahing over the colorful array of kittens. They'd brought stuff. A whole lot of stuff, including a large, round cat bed.

"We'll just clear this space in the corner of the closet and set the bed there," Aunt Lacy said. "I'm sure Mama will move the kittens as soon as we let her alone."

"But my dress," I wailed.

"Toast," Trudy declared.

"Maybe a good dry cleaner can get most of the stains out," my aunt offered doubtfully.

"Most? What about my shoes?"

Aunt Lacy eyed them with a dubious shake of her head. "Perhaps if they were dyed?"

I groaned and sat on the edge of my bed.

"Good thing she has four sisters, so she didn't need you to be a bridesmaid," Trudy said. "If I were you, I'd buy myself a new outfit."

"If you were me, you'd know I can't afford a whole new outfit. Or new drapes, or a new vase—"

"Maybe we can help you," Aunt Lacy said.

"Thanks, but I don't want to take money from you."

"Oh, I wasn't thinking in terms of money, dear, but I do have some old drapes that should fit. And don't you still have that dress you wore for your cousin's wedding, Trudy?"

I eyed the older, chunky woman and shook my

head. I was doomed. I had a date with the most gorgeous man in Ohio and nothing to wear. Not to mention eight cats in an apartment that didn't allow pets.

"Doomed," I muttered under my breath.

"Now dear, it's not so bad. The kittens are adorable."

"Take them home with you," I begged.

"No, it's best if we don't move them right now. We got to the pet store right before it closed, and the young man was so helpful. I think we have everything you need."

I'D NO IDEA THINGS THAT SMALL could be so much work. By morning Sam Two had indeed moved her kittens to the bed Trudy had set up. But by the time I cleaned two litter pans, fed and watered all the animals and wasted fifteen minutes trying to catch Sam One and put him in Mickey's carrier to no avail, I was running late.

I stopped by the dry cleaner's down the street from the shop. Mr. Choy was not hopeful when I showed him the stain I needed removed. As a result, it was quite late when I reached Flower World. Six people had called about the Found posters I'd put up. Mickey had come by, disappointed to learn I didn't have Mr. Sam yet, but he wanted to know if he could come and see the kittens. And Brandon had called for me twice—which would have increased my heart rate if Mrs. Keene hadn't arrived seconds after I did.

The widow Keene is my father's worst nightmare.

She lives next door to my dad and she's decided in the past year and a half that it's silly for the two of them to maintain separate households. To her consternation, my father doesn't see it that way. In fact, he'd like to maintain separate houses in separate states, but she refuses to follow her children back to Michigan. I suspect she's the reason they chose to move back there in the first place.

As a result, she'll do anything—enlist anyone— in her plots to trap my father into marriage. Dad's learned the creative art of barricades. Recently he's taken to pretending that he's going deaf.

"Dee! Thank goodness you're here."

"Uh—" I looked around frantically. Aunt Lacy and Trudy had both vanished with a speed Houdini would have admired.

"I need to hire you."

I blinked and stared foolishly at the wide-brimmed floppy denim hat she wore perched on top of her tightly permed head of steel gray. My mind was a complete blank.

"I'm being stalked."

It took several tries before I could close my mouth to lock in the snicker of disbelief.

"Who—" I had to swallow a couple of times before I could finish "—who's stalking you?"

"I'm not sure. I think it's that terrible Mr. Farnim. You know, the man who runs the convenience store on the corner? He's always leering at me when I go in to buy milk."

Mr. Farnim doesn't leer. He grimaces, like most people when they first catch sight of Mrs. Keene. Her taste in clothing tends to make small children point and stare and ask their mothers if she works for the circus and can they go see the other clowns.

Poor Mr. Farnim is a businessman. Since Mrs. Keene is a regular customer, he feels compelled to paste a phony smile over his grimace. I've seen him do it. I can see why she thinks he's leering, I guess. Mrs. Keene has a vibrant imagination. Look how she chases after my father.

"Uh, Mrs. Keene, I don't think you have to worry. I'm certain Mr. Farnim—"

"I'll pay you a hundred dollars if you'll make him stop."

She opened her yellow-and-pink-plaid handbag and fished out a hundred-dollar bill.

"Mrs. Keene—"

"Maybe it's not Mr. Farnim. It could be that Henry Palmer over at the post office. He's always flirting with me when I go in."

"Mr. Palmer flirts with everyone. That's just his way."

"I know. That's why it could be him."

I wasn't about to argue with that logic.

"Someone has been sneaking around my house the past few nights. I want you to catch them and make them stop. Unless it's your father. You don't think—"

"No," I said quickly. "My father wouldn't sneak around your house at night. Why would he?"

"Well, someone has and they've been following me around. There's a red car I've seen more than once. It's got dark windows, so I can't tell who's driving."

"What sort of a red car?" I asked.

I could see she was truly upset about this. I told myself I was not being sympathetic simply because she was waving a hundred-dollar bill under my nose when I desperately needed money to replace my shoes and maybe my dress, as well, but hey, I'm only human.

"A small one," she answered proudly.

I swallowed a groan. "Right."

"So, you'll come over tonight? I'll make lasagna. I know how much you love my lasagna."

I hate her lasagna. My father keeps trying to palm it off on me every time she brings one over for him because she knows he doesn't get enough to eat now that I've moved out.

"Uh, wait, Mrs. Keene. I'm not sure—"

"Such a good girl. And bring your gun."

"Gun? No! No guns. I don't use a gun."

"But he might be armed. What if he's—" she lowered her voice to a shrill whisper "—a rapist?"

"I'll hit him with a baseball bat. No guns."

"All right, Dee," she said doubtfully. "You know best. I'll see you tonight."

My half-formed protest died as she laid the hundred-dollar bill down on the counter. I watched her leave with a sinking heart. What was I doing?

"What are you doing?" my aunt demanded.

"You're not really going to take that wacko's made-up case, are you?" Trudy asked. "Brenda Keene made up that story to use you to get to your father."

That thought had occurred to me. I fingered the hundred-dollar bill. It was crisp and new.

"Look at it this way, If I go over there, dad will be safe for another night and I'll make the easiest hundred dollars I'll ever earn."

Aunt Lacy gave me a look that shrank me down at least four inches.

"You are not going to keep her money, Dee."

"I'm not?"

The look intensified.

"Well, if I have to eat her lasagna, I'll have earned at least fifty of it. It'll cost that much to have my stomach pumped afterward."

Trudy chuckled. Aunt Lacy pursed her lips and said no more, but I knew I wasn't going to keep Mrs. Keene's money. Going over there to humor the lonely woman would be my good deed for the week—maybe the month. I was definitely making it a year if I had to eat her lasagna.

Remembering my promise to Brandon, I quizzed my aunts about rumors on the Russos as we worked on table arrangements for a banquet at the Regal Hotel downtown. They were one of our regular clients, so we always gave their orders priority. Of course, Aunt Lacy demanded to know why I wanted the information, so I swore them to secrecy and told them what Brandon and I had discussed over dinner.

"You had dinner together?" Trudy said with an excited gleam in her eye.

"We had to eat," I explained, trying not to sound defensive. "We just killed two birds with one meeting."

"Uh-huh. Did he pay?"

"No! It wasn't a date, Trudy. I insisted on paying for my own meal."

"But he offered, right?" Trudy persisted.

"Are you going to stick that fern in or hold it there all night?" I looked to Aunt Lacy for help. She in turn gave Trudy one of her looks and Trudy subsided.

"Elaine Russo isn't particularly well liked," my aunt said thoughtfully. "Helen Brighton's daughter does her hair every month. She works over at that fancy salon in Legacy Village. Do you know what they charge for a cut and blow-dry?"

It took me a while to redirect that conversation, but all I learned was that Elaine wasn't the friendly sort and was a lousy tipper.

"Shameful, when everyone knows the Russos have scads of money." Trudy put in. "And her pretending to do all that charity work. I hear it's only for show so she can get her name in the paper and make everyone think her husband's just a regular businessman."

"What about affairs?" I asked, desperate not to let Trudy wander down that path.

"I don't think so, dear," Aunt Lacy said. "If she's been having an affair with anyone, she's been extremely discreet."

"Albert, on the other hand, isn't so careful," Trudy put in. "Betty Sue's mother said her neighbor's son has seen him hanging around that actress—you know, the one who does those awful commercials for Jerry's Cars?"

Jerry Striker is a local car dealer whose commercials are loud, stupid and annoying. I went to school with his son, Jerry Junior. I always turn the channel whenever one of the commercials airs, so I couldn't picture the woman they were talking about, but I vaguely recalled seeing an attractive brunette sitting in one of the convertible commercials once.

Aunt Lacy paused, a daisy poised in the air over her arrangement. "Do you mean Nicole Wickley? Is she still doing those? I thought she was appearing in a local production of some Shakespearean play at The Palace downtown."

"She is. They film those commercials months ahead of time. I heard she was trying to get a program on channel eight by sleeping with somebody important there. What was his name, Lacy?"

And they were off once more. But at least I had something to tell Brandon when he came striding through the front door unexpectedly a few minutes later. Or I would as soon as I could get my brain jump-started again.

What was it about seeing him that threw my syn apses into neutral? It's not like I'm some innocen who has never been kissed before. I've even let Ted grope me once or twice before calling a halt—which, of course, is one of the reasons we are on the outs again. Somehow I was pretty sure being groped by Brandon would be nothing at all like being groped by Ted Osher.

Only too aware of Trudy's and my aunt's interest in his arrival, I greeted Brandon lightly. "I wasn't ex pecting to see you today."

"I was in the neighborhood. Do you have time to talk?"

"Go ahead, dear. Trudy and I can finish up here. We'll deliver them on our way home."

"Are you sure?"

"Absolutely. Go ahead."

"Uh—"

My aunt smiled.

"We'll swing by your place and feed the cats, as well."

"You have cats?" Brandon asked, glancing at my hand.

"Don't ask. Thanks, Aunt Lacy. And thank you both for the information."

"Our pleasure," Trudy piped up. "Good luck to night."

Brandon looked the question at me as I practically shoved him out the door. I don't think he saw her wink.

"I have a job tonight," I said by way of explanation for her parting remark.

"That's too bad. I thought maybe we could grab a sandwich and compare notes."

I thought about lasagna and antacids with Mrs. Keene versus a sandwich with Brandon. I admit it. I caved.

"Give me a minute, will you? I need to make a quick phone call."

Brandon walked around the corner to stand beside his car. Wouldn't you know it was parked only two spots from the front of the flower shop? Binky was in the farthest, darkest corner of the lot out back.

I called information, got the phone number for Mrs. Keene and prayed she was home. She was, but she was not happy that I wanted to come after dinner.

"I have the lasagna all ready to bake," she protested.

I looked at Brandon leaning against his car. Tall, dark, sexy enough to be on television, he was the sort of man young women fantasize about and he wanted to have dinner with *me*. So I stretched the truth to the breaking point.

"Mrs. Keene, I have a lead on a small red car." Well burgundy was sort of red wasn't it? "I really think I should check it and the driver out before I come over. You said the prowler doesn't come around until after dark anyhow. I'll be there before then."

"But what if he comes early this time?"

I knew I was going to live to regret this, but I gave her my cell phone number. "If you see or hear anything that upsets you, give me a call right away."

"All right, Dee. I'll make us some snickerdoodles for later."

"That would be great. Thanks, Mrs. Keene."

I hoped she remembered to put sugar in them this time. My conscience only pinched a little as I disconnected and walked to where Brandon lounged against his burgundy red car—which did not have dark-tinted windows. He straightened up as I approached and I took firm command of my hormones.

"Okay, I've got the situation covered. I don't have to be there until dusk. My car's out back. Where should I meet you?"

"Hop in. We'll come back for your car after we eat. And, Dee, this is my treat since you're helping me out."

I could have protested. I should have protested. But when I cave, I go all the way. I got in the car, regretting the decision a few minutes later when we drove past the store window and Trudy waved to us, beaming broadly. By tomorrow I'd be hearing what a terrific couple we made. I'd worry about that tomorrow.

Larry's Place is an unpretentious restaurant with the best home-style meals you could ask for. They make all their breads, soups and desserts from scratch and they have a varied menu of entrées. I started salivating the minute we pulled into the parking lot.

"I hope this is okay," he said.

"It's fine." Terrific. Better than terrific.

He grinned and I was sure he was reading my mind. I hoped it was that and that I wasn't drooling.

"So, what did you learn?" I asked after we ordered. He watched me slather butter on a generous serving of corn bread, still warm from the oven.

"Russo's story checks out," he admitted, taking a cinnamon-apple muffin for himself. "There was quite a scene in his front office, according to the assistant I talked to. Elaine came storming in, furious over those pictures you took. Fortunately no one else actually saw the pictures, so the woman I spoke with didn't know who I was."

But that didn't stop her from talking freely with a complete stranger. Not when he looked like Brandon.

"And she said Elaine admitted to having an affair with you?" I asked.

"Yes."

His expression was as dark as his tone, the fire in those blue eyes banked tight. "I think you may be right about Elaine using me to cover for her real boyfriend."

Over perfectly fried chicken, mashed potatoes and freshly grilled mixed vegetables I learned he'd spent a large portion of the day trying to track down Elaine Russo, without success.

"If she's at the house, she isn't answering her phone or the door," he told me. "Her car's not there and it isn't in the parking lot where we left it the other night."

"Maybe she went to stay with friends. I mean, if she made a big scene, it makes sense. And I know for a fact she has friends in the area. She met three women the other night before she went to meet you."

"I don't suppose you got any of their names?"

I scowled at him. "I told you, collecting names wasn't part of what I was hired to do. All Russo wanted was photographs, locations and times. That's what I gave him." I knew I sounded defensive, but I couldn't help it.

"All right. Did you learn anything from your aunt?"

I told him what Trudy and my aunt had divulged, but I couldn't see how it would be of much help and said so.

"You never know."

"Instead of going into all these theatrics, Elaine should have just hired you to get evidence on him. Then she would have had something to fight him with in the divorce settlement."

Brandon looked thoughtful. I had the distinct feeling there was more going on here than he was saying.

Over coffee and slices of banana-cream pie that melted on the tongue he turned the talk to general conversation, mostly about the Cleveland area and its suburbs.

"How is it you came to set up shop here instead of Pittsburgh?" I asked when I found an opening.

"My brother moved here with his family a little

while ago. His wife is from this area. My parents recently moved to North Ridgeview to be closer to their grandson. When my brother…died, I decided to move closer to the rest of my family."

"Oh." Somehow I hadn't pictured him with family. Before I could ask any more questions, he signaled for the check and changed the subject.

"What's this job you're doing tonight?"

I squirmed uncomfortably—and only partly at the question. I wondered if he'd notice if I undid the button on my slacks. Yeah, he'd notice. Those sharp eyes of his didn't seem to miss a thing. I shouldn't have eaten so much.

"I've got a stakeout," I exaggerated slightly. "My client thinks someone has been stalking her. She wants me to make them stop."

Brandon leaned forward, his expression turning earnest. "A stalker is nothing to fool around with, Dee. You should let the police handle something like that."

I almost told him he didn't know Mrs. Keene, but his intent stare and the phrasing he'd chosen irritated the heck out of me.

"Is that what you'd do?" I asked sweetly. "Call the police?"

He was smart enough to see the trap before stepping into it, but the answer he didn't say out loud was written plainly on his expression.

"Or is that what you think I should do because I'm a woman?"

"You are a woman."

"Who happens to be a licensed private investigator. Just like you."

"Not like me, Dee. You're how old—twenty-one, twenty-two?"

He'd definitely pressed my hot button.

"What does my age have to do with anything?"

"I'm twenty-nine, Dee. I spent almost five years as a police officer in Pittsburgh. I've had a lot more training and experience than you've had."

"Is that right?"

"Yes, it is. You're just a—"

"If you call me a kid, I'm going to seriously hurt you. I'm twenty-four and I spent almost two years working for Hunter and Barnett Investigations in New York City. Good. I see you've heard of them. Now maybe that experience doesn't equal being a street cop in Pittsburgh, but it does take me out of the novice category, wouldn't you say?"

"Look—"

"No, you look, Mr. Kirkpatrick. I like being a detective. I'm good at my job. I'm not the one who was set up to be someone's patsy, remember? And I don't need some condescending pretty boy trying to tell me what to do."

I didn't realize how much my voice had risen until a hush fell around us. My face flamed as I stood and dropped my napkin on my half-finished pie.

"Be a good little detective and pay the waitress, won't you? I'll wait for you outside. I believe you did hire me to guard your body, so I'll just make sure no one is lurking out there waiting to murder you—besides me."

I stalked past the other tables with my head held high. A little old lady who had to be at least eighty if she was a day beamed up at me as I came abreast of her.

"You go, girl," she said.

I offered her a weak smile, already feeling foolish. After all, I still had to ride back to the flower shop with Brandon and I didn't figure he was going to be in the best of moods.

Outside it was still muggy and hot. I hoped Lake Erie would send some rain our way soon to cool things off, but it didn't look promising. I was the one starting to cool off. I admit I have a quick temper. Fortunately it tends to cool almost as quickly as it flares. I was already cringing over what I'd said as I hurried to where he had parked. Since I wasn't paying attention to my surroundings, I never saw the man until Hogan Delvecchi stepped directly in front of me.

All that rich, wonderful food I'd just eaten threatened to backpedal. My mouth went dry and I stared up at him, tongue-tied.

"Mr. Russo doesn't think you should be consorting with Brandon Kirkpatrick," he said without preamble. "Mr. Russo says you might get hurt that way. Mr. Russo says to remind you that he paid for a confidential investigation."

I swallowed hard. The man was threatening me!

Maybe it was because Brandon thought I was incompetent. Maybe I was PMSing. Whatever the case, I swallowed my fear and met his little piggy eyes with a hard stare of my own.

"Please assure Mr. Russo he has nothing to worry about. Mr. Kirkpatrick and I are merely acquaintances in the same line of work. I have no intention of betraying any confidences to Mr. Kirkpatrick or anyone else."

I could feel a trickle of sweat sliding down my back as Delvecchi regarded me. It was not a pleasant sensation.

"That's good," he said after a long pause. "Mr. Russo would be very upset if anything was to happen to you."

Oh, help. It wouldn't do for my knees to buckle now. I tried for a smile, but it felt more like a grimace instead.

"I'd be pretty upset, as well."

He gave a curt nod.

"Stay away from Kirkpatrick."

I watched him stride over to a late-model Lexus, of all things—silver gray, naturally—that was double-parked. I noted the license plate number as he slid behind the wheel and pulled out of the parking lot without a backward glance. Relief vied with quivering excitement. I'd faced down a gangster who had threatened me. An edge of fear slipped into the mix. He'd actually threatened me.

"Dee, I owe you an apology."

Dazed, I saw Brandon approaching, his expression contrite.

"Is something wrong?" he asked quickly.

I shook my head, still trying to sort out my emotions. "Not anymore."

"What do you mean?"

"You just missed Hogan Delvecchi."

His head swiveled about the lot. "Delvecchi was here? He approached you? What did he want?"

"To warn me to stay away from you. Mr. Russo doesn't like you. He doesn't want to see anything happen to me."

Brandon's jaw dropped.

"I'm thinking maybe we could both use a bodyguard."

Chapter Six

I nibbled at the cookie with all the eagerness of a condemned person. Mrs. Keene had not forgotten the sugar this time. She'd doubled it. If I'd been a diabetic, a single cookie would have sent me into insulin shock. There is no kind way to tell the woman she shouldn't cook—ever—so I suffered through stoically and continued to explain why it would be better for me to watch the house from the outside.

"But what if he sneaks in the back while you're out front, or vice versa?"

"You call me at the first sound of anything."

"But what if I don't hear anything? I'm old, you know. My hearing isn't what it used to be."

I wasn't going to win this battle. I could tell.

"You've only seen him twice after all the lights were out, right?"

"Yes."

"Then we need to pretend you're going up to bed early. If he's watching the house, he won't come if he knows you have company."

"Oh. I didn't think of that."

"I'll move my car next door and go and visit with my father for a while."

"I should go with you. I haven't talked to your father in ages."

He'd kill me.

"No. You can socialize with him another time. Right now we need to deal with this first." Her face dropped. "You make it appear that you're getting ready for bed. We'll let things quiet down and then I'll come back over and patrol."

She didn't like it, but she finally agreed to the plan. I left Mrs. Keene to go over and say hello to my father. I found him in the basement, as usual.

Dad works for the sanitation department by day. For some unfathomable reason, he'd recently decided to take up woodworking in his spare time. To that end, he'd cleaned out the basement and purchased all sorts of power tools that scare the heck out of me. So far all he's made is a stool. It's a very nice stool, if a little wobbly, but he's pleased with the results, and as long as he doesn't give it to me, I'm happy if he is.

We conducted our chat over the sound of the circular saw, with me standing a respectful distance away hoping I wouldn't witness anything being mangled beyond the wood. He finished sawing a board in half, lifted his goggles and stared at me.

"Why'd you say you're going to be next door?"

"Mrs. Keene thinks someone has been…prowling around her house at night."

"Woman's a nutcase."

"Yes, well, she's paying me to make them go away. You haven't seen a red car in the neighborhood, have you?"

"Fred Lyons down the street has a red Jeep. What sort of car?"

I grimaced. "Small."

Dad snorted and pulled his goggles back into place.

"You need to find a good man and settle down like your brothers."

I decided that was my cue to leave. "Have fun, Dad. And be careful."

He grunted as he lifted another board for slicing. I was starting across the backyard when my cell phone rang. Mentally I groaned as I saw Mrs. Keene's name flash on the screen.

"Dee! The car's here."

That stopped me in my tracks. "Where?"

"At the end of the block. He's parked near the corner."

I hesitated. "How can you possibly see that from your house?"

"With my night-vision binoculars, of course."

Of course.

"I'm on my way. Is he in the car?"

"I think so, but I can't tell."

"I'll check it out."

She had night-vision binoculars. Even I didn't have night-vision binoculars.

I saw no reason for subterfuge. I mean, even if someone was in the car and was for some inexplicable reason watching her house, they wouldn't expect me to come strolling down the sidewalk right up to them.

I expected it to be some kid and his date looking for a dark place to park, but as it turned out there were two burgundy red cars parked near the corner. A large, dark shape emerged from the one nearest to me to stand there waiting as I approached.

Nervously I reached into my purse and fingered the can of pepper spray I always carry. Except there was something familiar about the man. The car was familiar, too, and as I drew closer, I knew why. I'd last seen it driving away from the front of the flower shop where I'd demanded to be dropped off only a short while ago.

"Brandon?"

Shoulders lifted and fell in a rueful shrug.

"What are you doing here?"

It wasn't as if we had exactly parted on good terms. We'd argued all the way back to the shop. He'd wanted to come with me tonight. I'd pointed out that I'd be safest wherever he wasn't. In the end I'd gotten mad and told him exactly how little use I had for his help.

"I can't believe you followed me!"

"I didn't. I called your aunt."

"Aunt Lacy told you where I was?" I asked, outraged.

"No, Trudy told me."

"I don't believe this. You actually called my aunt! After all the things I told you—"

"You don't even carry a gun, Dee."

"Trudy told you that, too?" I'd kill her.

"I figured you might need backup if things got sticky."

"Sticky? Sticky!"

"Uh, Dee, you might want to keep your voice down."

"Don't you dare tell me what to do! Who do you think you are?"

"A friend."

"A friend?"

"You're starting to sound like a parrot, Dee. I just thought it might be a good idea to—"

My cell phone trilled. I was so mad, I pressed the button to answer it without thinking.

"Dee! He's here! He's on my back porch. I think he's trying to get in through the kitchen window!"

"What?"

Her shrill, terrified voice carried easily in the still night air. Brandon began to pound down the street. His much longer legs ate up the ground ahead of me as we raced back toward Mrs. Keene's house.

I am not a runner like Aunt Lacy. My idea of exercise is a comfortable stroll through the shopping center—or a frantic dash, if the sale is spectacular— so I was slightly winded before we reached her yard. Brandon had no such problem. He disappeared into her backyard before I reached the front. His backside was just disappearing over the neighbor's privacy fence as I came around the side of the house.

I don't do fences. I especially don't do fences behind which dogs are barking. Brandon was welcome to play hero. Dog bites are much worse than cat scratches. I lightly rubbed my offended hand.

Lights were coming on around me at the commotion. This is generally a quiet neighborhood with mostly older residents. As I moved onto the back porch, I saw the screen had been removed from the window over the kitchen sink. The window itself had been pried halfway up. I stuck my head inside and yelled to Mrs. Keene.

"Are you okay?"

"Yes! He ran toward Clarence."

The intersection we had just left. Didn't it figure?

"Come and lock this window."

I trotted back the way I had come. Maybe I should reconsider joining a gym. Except I hadn't liked PE even in school. Swimming? I could take up swimming. It was good exercise, cool, refreshing, not sweaty. But swimming involved water and the whole wet-hair issue. Besides, I'd seen Lakewood Park with its wall-to-wall bodies. No, thank you. Maybe yoga.

A car came whipping down the street going at least fifty miles an hour. It was hard to tell the exact shade of the vehicle given the dim streetlights, but I thought the color might have been red. The windows were darkly tinted, but there appeared to be only the driver inside. I was guessing a young male based on his speed and the fact that the car was a sporty-looking model. The car went past so fast, I only thought to look at the tag as an afterthought, much too late.

I reached Brandon's car and glanced inside. He had a pair of night-vision binoculars lying in plain sight on the front seat. The other burgundy car that had been parked behind his was gone. I had a sinking feeling I'd just seen it whiz past.

I was feeling very foolish as I waited for Brandon to show up.

And waited.

And waited some more.

When he didn't arrive after several minutes went by, I started to worry. That had sounded like a very big dog on the other side of that fence. He could be lying there bleeding to death, with his jugular ripped out, for all I knew. I headed back to Mrs. Keene's house at a respectable jog.

Brandon met me in the side yard holding a bouquet of long-stemmed yellow roses.

"Nice touch," I panted, more relieved than I wanted him to know, "but I don't think I've known you long enough for you to give me flowers."

"Funny lady. He dropped these going over the fence."

My jaw sagged. "Do you know what yellow roses cost?"

"Nineteen ninety-nine, according to the sticker."

"Only at a discount store. Let me see those."

The sticker at the bottom of the cellophane did indeed say nineteen ninety-nine.

"These aren't good-quality roses."

He looked at me like I'd lost my mind.

"Well, they aren't. Your arm's bleeding. And your pants are torn."

"I scratched the arm going over the fence. The terrier ripped the pants."

"That was a terrier?"

"Mixed breed with a deep voice."

I shook my head. "Are you okay?"

"I'll live, but he got away."

"I assume you don't mean the terrier." He gave me a dirty look and I sighed. "I know. He was doing about fifty going up the street."

"I don't suppose you got the license plate?"

"I got a partial." I bristled. "It's dark, in case you hadn't noticed, and he was moving when I saw him. How come you didn't get it?"

He shrugged. "Same reason."

"Did you at least get a good look at him?"

He shook his head. "He's young, dark haired, Caucasian, early twenties or late teens. Five-ten, one-fifty-five, right-handed."

"Right-handed?"

"Primary hand he used to pull himself over the fence."

I was impressed, but I shook my head. "It doesn't make any sense."

"Why? Most people are right-handed."

"Mrs. Keene is in her sixties."

It was Brandon's turn to gape.

"Does she have a daughter?"

"In Michigan. Married with two children."

"A burglar?"

"Who planned to leave her a dozen yellow roses after casing the place for the past two nights?"

"Mind if I meet your client?"

Since I wasn't going to get a say in the matter, I simply shook my head. Mrs. Keene came bustling up to us, an impossibly colorful muumuu waving about her generous form.

"You caught him!"

"No, ma'am. This is Brandon Kirkpatrick, my... associate."

Brandon raised his eyebrows at me but smiled graciously at Mrs. Keene. He clasped her hand warmly, causing her lashes to flutter.

"Brandon was acting as my backup tonight in case things got...sticky," I said with a pointed look in his direction. Brandon only smiled.

"He brought you flowers?"

"Actually the man who attempted to enter your house dropped these."

Her eyes widened in shock. "Who was it?"

"We don't know," I told her.

"But he was young," Brandon interjected. "Early twenties."

"Oh, my." Her hand fluttered to her ample bosom. "Imagine that."

I was trying hard not to. I mean, it didn't make a lick of sense. Obviously it didn't make sense to Brandon, either. He allowed Mrs. Keene to drag him back inside and ply him with coffee and cookies. I figured he must be in shock. He actually took a second cookie.

"She's as stubborn as someone else I know," he told me when we finally left after fruitlessly trying to convince Mrs. Keene to call the police.

"I may be stubborn, but I'm not stupid," I told him. "If I had a kid almost young enough to be my grandson trying to break in to my house with a bouquet of cheap flowers, I'd call the cops, leave or get someone to stay with me. I don't feel right about leaving here tonight. You're sure she'll be okay?"

"I doubt he'll come back after all the excitement. Would you?"

"Are you kidding? I wouldn't have come in the first place."

I loved his grin. Even in the moonlight that flash of teeth was the sort of grin that makes all sorts of impossible things seem possible.

"I'll follow you home," he offered, moving closer without seeming to move at all.

My brain finally reengaged and a bubble of protest burst forth. "No!" I had a sudden image of the sort of chaos I might find when I went home tonight and I couldn't imagine taking Brandon there. The very idea of him in my apartment gave my belly serious quivers.

His hand reached out and tucked a strand of wayward hair behind my ear. "You're right. Bad idea. I wasn't followed over here, but undoubtedly Russo knows where you live."

"He probably knows where you live, too. You shouldn't go there."

That slow, easy smile curled my toes. "You're worried about me?"

"Why would I worry about you? You've got night-vision goggles."

His laughter was magic. His strong features were kissed by the moon. So when his eyes turned serious without warning, I wasn't prepared. Not for the dark probing look that held me rooted to the grass, nor the strong, warm fingers that lifted my chin to meet his descending mouth.

I have never been kissed before. Not like that. Not with such heart-pounding, soul-searching thoroughness. It was like the first time all over again, only more intense. Way more intense.

When he stopped, he had to hold me upright for a second or my legs would have let go and I'd have sprawled at his feet. Humiliating. He knew it, too. I knew he knew. But he only smiled that devastating smile of his.

"You be careful driving home."

"Right. Careful. No. That is, my dad lives next door. I'll probably just stay there tonight."

"Good idea."

"Yeah." My brain was fuzz.

"We'll talk tomorrow."

Tomorrow. Because obviously I'd be doing no more talking tonight. He'd swallowed my tongue and sucked out my intellect before melting away into the darkness of the night.

On legs that were far from steady I crossed the lawn to my father's front porch. I felt Brandon's eyes on me every step of the way and I continued to shiver.

Dad was still downstairs in his workroom, and I really didn't want to explain why I was spending the night. Besides, I had the cats to feed in the morning, so I changed my mind and headed back outside. I don't remember driving home. I remember opening my apartment door and finding lights on in my living room and new pink drapes where my simple white sheers had been.

Hard to forget that moment. It was the pink that pulled me from my sugarcoated daze. I have nothing against pink. Pink's a fine color. It even looks good on me. But in my living room, with its forest-green carpeting and blue hand-me-down couch, the color's as good as a slap in the face. Especially that particular vibrant shade of pink. Mrs. Keene would have loved the effect. In fact, my living room was starting to look entirely too much like her wardrobe.

There was something else new. It was rather hard to miss since it clashed so violently with the drapes. My bedraggled plant, looking even worse than it had before, had been moved across the room. In its place in the corner stood a six-foot cat tree—carpeted in gaudy, tattered orange.

Closing my eyes did not make either sight go away. It did, however, help me focus on the note my aunt had left on the dining room table—pinned in place under Grandma's heavy glass bowl.

Dee, sorry about the color, but we figured as long as the drapes fit, we might as well leave them until you can buy something to replace them. The cat tree was an absolute steal. Mr. Murphy down the street was going to take it to the church rummage sale, but he let us have it for only thirty-five dollars when I explained the situation.

I'd pay him forty to take it back.

Trudy and I felt so bad about your little friend, Mickey, that we drove around over near the park for you this evening. We found a cat that might be Mr. Sam! He's a male and all gray except for the tip of his tail. We had to lock him in your bathroom because he doesn't seem to like the cat that's hiding behind your sofa, but we got most of the blood off the chair.

I closed my eyes. They hadn't. Not another cat. But of course they had. I should be glad there was only one. I opened my eyes again. I didn't even want to know whose blood or on which chair.

Everyone's been fed for the night. The kittens are so dear! And we got the Barnett wedding right before closing tonight. See you in the morning. Love, Aunt Lacy

Well, that explained the new litter box on the floor in the dining room. I had another animal in my pet-free apartment.

I love Aunt Lacy and Trudy, but at the moment I would happily have choked both of them. I do not want to move back in with my dad. And I definitely do not want to move in with Aunt Lacy and Trudy and Clem—though it would serve them right if I showed up on their doorstep with nine cats in tow. If the management found out I was running a cat house out of 24B, that was exactly what was going to happen.

I headed for the bathroom with trepidation. The newest Mr. Sam regarded me from solemn green eyes from the tank on back of the commode.

"Okay, look, cat. This is temporary. Tonight and tomorrow morning only, okay? After that you're out of here. In the meantime we have to share this space, all right?"

"Meow?"

"Good. Now, I have to use this toilet, so you need to get off the back."

To my utter shock, he leaped down and immediately began to strop my legs, purring. Tentatively I reached down and touched his head. The purring went up another decibel.

"Okay. We're going to get along."

Except that as soon as I opened the bathroom door to leave, he scooted out between my legs and shot for the cat tree. No amount of talking or cajoling would convince him to get down. I was too tired to keep pleading with a cat, so I gave up. I went in the bedroom and started getting ready for bed only to find myself mesmerized by mama cat and her tiny kittens.

I sat on the floor near the closet opening and watched them nurse while she watched me watching them. Because she was such an attentive listener, I found myself telling her all about Brandon and my day.

"You cats have it easy, you know—mate, have kittens, mate again. People have to have relationships. I mean, we're rivals. How am I supposed to date the competition? And why would he want to date me anyhow? Not that there's anything wrong with me. I'm not one of those women who picks her looks apart or anything, but I'm not exactly the sort of a woman men hang posters of on their walls. And I don't want to be—that's not the point!"

I hesitated. What was the point? Oh. Yeah.

"He's gorgeous, cat, you know? No, of course you don't. But, oh, kitty, that man can kiss. I can still feel his mouth on mine. Why did he have to kiss me? How am I supposed to sleep now?"

Mama cat closed her eyes.

"Am I boring you? Forget it. You're a lousy conversationalist anyhow."

She opened her eyes as I stroked the tiny little black-and-white kitten closest to me and got to my feet under her watchful gaze.

"I'm going to bed, cat. But you do have beautiful little babies—even though I'm not a cat person."

I expected it to be a long, sleepless night, or at least a night filled with disturbing dreams, but surprisingly it wasn't. I slept deeply and well and there were no signs of mayhem when I left the bedroom to check on the other two felines. Of course, Sam One was still hiding behind the couch and could be dead for all I knew, but the newest addition—I decided to call him George just to be different—even came out to greet me, rubbing against my leg like we were long-lost buddies and diving into the fresh food as if he'd been on the street starving for months. A fact belied by his glossy coat and rounded little belly.

"You had better be Mr. Sam," I told him sternly. "If not, fake it, okay? I need to be cat free by the end of the day."

I'd decided to ask Mickey to help me trap Sam One and take him to the animal shelter when he came to pick up what I hoped and prayed was his Mr. Sam. But all that was forgotten when I got to the shop.

Chapter Seven

"Your young man's in the office. He should have stayed in the hospital," Aunt Lacy greeted me.

"Hospital? Mickey's here? He's been hurt?"

"Of course not. Brandon's been in an accident."

Brandon was sitting in the chair from hell leaning his head against the wall. Annabelle was curled in a happy lump on his lap. A bandage on his left cheek didn't begin to cover the colorful bruise forming underneath.

"Must have been some date," Trudy said, plopping a bottle of aspirins on the desk along with an unopened bottle of cold water.

"Delvecchi," I said.

Brandon opened his eyes. "Technically it was a small run-in with a large tree."

"You had a car accident?"

"After Delvecchi ran me off the road," he agreed.

Trudy and Aunt Lacy disappeared, but I noticed they left the door open so they could listen. Since my insides were feeling a little shaky, I sat down in one of the lumpy visitor's chairs without bothering to close the door.

"Are you okay?"

"I've had better starts to my day. Think you could give me a ride over to a car-rental place? The Honda's going to be out of commission for a few days."

"Are you sure you should be driving? What happened to your face?"

"A tree branch came through the windshield. I'm fine other than a scrape and a twisted knee. I'm not sure how I managed that one, but nothing's broken."

"You have to report this."

His smile held no humor. "Actually the ten or so witnesses did it for me. Of course, no one got a look at the driver, including me, so technically it could have been an accident—if some driver of a silver Lexus was badly impaired or felt inclined to force a complete stranger off the road and into a tree first thing this morning."

"That isn't funny."

"Do you see humor in my expression?"

"What are we going to do?"

He raised his eyebrows and I could feel heat stealing up my neck. I refused to look away, and before he could say anything else, his cell phone began to ring. He checked the name and excused himself to answer the call.

The polite thing to do would be get up and give him some privacy, but I was still trying to get my mind around the fact that I'd been right. Albert Russo wanted Brandon dead because of the report I'd turned in.

The booming voice on the other end of the cell phone carried clearly to where I sat, bringing me out of my guilt-laden funk.

"What the hell's going on, Kirkpatrick? I hear you were just run off the road."

Brandon shot me a rueful look.

"I'm fine, Dex."

The man called Dex swore inventively. "Isn't one dead Kirkpatrick enough? I told you to let us work it."

Something cold slithered to life inside me. I remembered the police file on Brandon's desk. He'd said he'd moved here after his brother had died. His eyes darkened, accepting that he knew I'd heard the caller.

"I have to call you back, Dex."

"Don't you dare—"

He disconnected and stared at me.

"One dead Kirkpatrick?" I asked.

"You could be polite and pretend you weren't listening."

"I'm not that polite."

He closed his eyes and leaned his head back against the wall again. He stroked Annabelle's head with the ease of someone who was quite comfortable with a cat on his lap.

Aunt Lacy appeared in the doorway, started to say something, took one look at my expression and closed her lips along with the office door.

"Seth was older than me," Brandon said in a velvety voice full of memories I could only imagine. "We were close in that friendly, rivalry, I-can-do-anything-you-can-do-better way a pair of close-knit brothers have. He was an investigative reporter."

Light dawned. I must have made a sound, because he opened his eyes. I gave an apologetic shrug.

"I don't know why I didn't make the connection before. Kirkpatrick isn't that common a name. Your brother was Seth Kirkpatrick, wasn't he? He wrote articles for *The Plain Dealer.* He was killed in a drive-by shooting while doing a story on gang violence. Or was it drug use?"

Brandon's jaw hardened.

"Not the truth?"

"Truth's a fragile thing, isn't it?"

For a long time I thought he wasn't going to say any more, then he sat up carefully. Annabelle leaped onto the desk and watched as he opened the aspirin bottle, tipped four tablets into his palm and washed them down with a third of the bottle of water.

"Not everyone, even in the police department, believes the official theory. He was a stringer, but his editor never authorized either story and he never discussed them with anyone. Strangely enough, both his work and home computers had a virus that effectively wiped out all his working files."

"It could happen," I said hesitantly.

"Yeah, it could. Except that Seth never relied on technology. Coincidentally his handwritten notes and his tape recorder disappeared, as well. No one knew exactly what he was working on, not even his wife—and he always talked about his work with her."

"Okay, I can see where you'd have believability issues. So this Dex guy that just called you is…?"

Brandon expelled a slow breath of air. "A friend. A local cop and one of the men who doesn't agree with the current theory."

"Well, why didn't you tell him about Russo and Delvecchi? Maybe he could help."

Brandon gently touched the bandage on the side of his face. The look he gave me raised goose bumps along my skin.

"I think Delvecchi murdered my brother on Russo's orders."

"You can't be serious."

He pinched the bridge of his nose. "That branch must have hit me harder than I thought. I shouldn't be telling you any of this."

Part of me was all too willing to agree with that assessment. The other part, the part that was forever curious and had led me into becoming a detective in the first place, demanded satisfaction.

"Well, you can't stop now."

He mustered a weary smile. "No. If I'm going to get myself killed, Dex needs to know what's going on."

"Whoa! Nobody's getting killed here. Got that? This is a no-kill zone. Violence is unacceptable."

He stared as if trying to decide if I was kidding or not.

"What's going on, Brandon?"

"Elaine Russo called me this morning."

"What?"

"She claims she wants to hand over the proof that her husband had my brother killed."

I thought about that for a full second and shook my head. "She's setting you up. Again."

"I did consider that, but what's the point? It's more likely that she's actually trying to get back at her husband, like she claims."

"Are you out of your mind? She set you up once already!"

"And apologized."

"Oh, she apologized. Well, then. That makes it all right."

He smiled. A real smile this time.

"I'm not totally stupid, Dee. She's working her own game. I know that. I'll take appropriate precautions. But she wants to meet with me, and if she really does have evidence to show that Seth was investigating Albert Russo—"

"I'll turn into a cat and learn how to purr," I said as Annabelle swiped playfully at my hand. I sat back out of range. "Get real, Brandon. You can't possibly trust Elaine."

"I don't, but initially when Elaine called me, she

claimed she had information on my brother's murder. She said Seth had been to their home one evening shortly before he was murdered."

"I could tell you he'd been to my place, too, but that wouldn't make it so," I scoffed.

He shook his head and winced. "I've been talking to people, tracing his movements over the last few days of his life. Elaine had met Seth, I'm sure of that. Some of what she told me tied in with information I'd already put together."

"What sort of information?"

"Remember how you mentioned Russo and his connections at city hall? Well, Seth was investigating some sort of graft at city hall. And Seth was the sort who always believed he was invincible."

There was pain in his voice and in the blue depths of his eyes. I didn't doubt for a minute that he'd loved his brother deeply.

"I can see Seth going right up to Russo and asking him questions the way she claims he did. Elaine says they argued—loudly. Russo threw him out. The next day he was shot and killed in a drive-by shooting and no one knows why. She doesn't believe it was a coincidence and neither do I."

I didn't say anything. I could see he was serious and maybe he was right. What did I know? I was out of my depth and more nervous than I'd ever been in my life.

"When she called me the first time, she said she was pulling together some documents that I'd want o see. When she called me back, we arranged to meet at Victor's Lounge downtown. Being the suspicious sort, I went over to scope out her neighborhood that afternoon. As you know, she left the house early. I decided to follow her but lost her when I had a fender bender in the parking lot after she stopped at Legacy Village. I went to Victor's to wait for her and you know the rest."

"Did she give you the files?"

"No. She claimed she had to hide them because she thought Russo was suspicious. She was sure he was going to kill her."

"Uh-huh."

"I was skeptical, too, but she did seem frightened and edgy that night. By the time we got to the motel she'd worked herself into quite a state. It took me a while to get her calmed down. I offered to stay, but she finally decided it would be best if I left. She turned off the lights and said she was going to take a shower and then try to sleep."

"Right."

"I know. I didn't handle it well, but Vinnie promised to keep an eye on her room and I figured she'd be safe enough in Pennsylvania. There was no reason for Russo to look for her there."

"Except for me."

Ruefully he nodded.

"I never spotted your tail. Elaine kept me distracted, not that that's any excuse. The fact is there was no sign that anyone followed her to the lounge, so I wasn't paying as close attention as I should have been on the way into Pennsylvania."

It was nice to know he wasn't perfect.

"She called again this morning. I'm supposed to meet her at her place this afternoon to pick up these files she claims she has. She says she's passing them to me and then she's skipping town for good before Russo does her in."

"And you believe her?"

He pinched the bridge of his nose again. "No, but I do think she has some information. She definitely has no love for her husband. And it's possible she deliberately passed off our meeting as an affair to protect both of us. Better her husband thinks we're having an affair than she's handing me information to convict him of murder."

"Better for her! Either way she gets you killed. This is *not* a nice person. You can't seriously go meet with her by yourself. Call your friend Dex back. Have him go with you. In fact, take the whole police force along!"

"If she sees a bunch of uniforms, she'll panic and run."

"Then I'll go with you. Just don't go by yourself."

He smiled and my heart started thumping irregularly. I swallowed hard as he stood carefully and somewhat painfully and rubbed his knee.

"How soon do we have to leave?"

He limped around the desk. Annabelle jumped down and ran for the door and stood there waiting for it to magically open.

"I appreciate it, Dee. Really. But you're staying here. The only reason I told you was so you could tell the police in case something goes wrong."

"Are you insane? This whole setup is wrong. Why would you go there? Why not meet her someplace else? Someplace with lots and lots of other people around."

Brandon rubbed at his jaw. "She didn't give me that option. She told me if I wanted the information she'd meet me there and hung up."

"How can you be so stupid? It's definitely a setup."

He opened the door. Annabelle scampered out into the workroom.

"I know. I'll be careful. Will you drop me off so I can rent a car?"

"You can borrow mine," Trudy offered before I could voice another protest. "I just filled the tank this morning."

"Trudy!"

"Are you sure, Ms. Hoffsteder?"

"Of course. For a special friend of Dee's…"

"Trudy!"

"I really appreciate this. I'll take good care of your car."

"It's the blue Pontiac with the Parrot Power bumper sticker on back. It's parked on the side street about four cars down."

She handed him the keys and I grabbed his arm.

"Don't be an idiot! You're going to get yourself killed!"

"No, I won't, Dee. I can handle it from here."

And then he kissed me. Right there in the shop in front of my aunt and Trudy and Mrs. Crispen, the minister's wife, who had just that moment entered the shop.

It wasn't one of those gentle, sisterly pecks on the cheek, either. No, this was a toe-curling lip-lock that left me standing there unable to breathe long after it was over while he walked calmly out the door with Trudy's car keys.

"Oh, my."

I'm not sure who said that, but it pretty well summed up the situation.

Annabelle stropped my legs and meowed.

"Sugarplum, it *is* you! You naughty girl. Where have you been? I've been looking everywhere for you."

It took me a minute to realize that Mrs. Crispen was talking about Annabelle. She'd come in response to our Found signs. Annabelle was her missing cat Sugarplum.

"Where on earth did you find her?"

I looked helplessly at Aunt Lacy. "I have to go," I told her. "He's going to get himself killed."

"Just be sure you don't," she admonished with a worried expression.

I nodded and rushed out the door, leaving Trudy and Aunt Lacy to explain Sugarplum.

Brandon was already pulling away. By the time I reached Binky I'd gone from stunned to fuming mad.

Who did he think he was? Brandon Kirkpatrick needed to be taken down a peg or two. How dare he kiss me like that? And borrowing Trudy's car that way. He had no right! He wasn't family. He wasn't even my boyfriend. Technically we hadn't even been on what I'd consider a real date yet.

I'd worked myself up to a righteous anger by the time I was on the highway pushing Binky to his limits. When my cell phone rang, I answered tersely. "Hayes."

"Dee? It's Mrs. Keene. I was wondering, are you and that nice young man going to be coming back again tonight? I was thinking I could put in a pot roast and maybe invite your father over."

"No! No dinner. I don't think I can make it this evening."

"Oh."

She sounded so forlorn, I instantly felt guilty.

"I could make some brownies to snack on. You like brownies, don't you, dear?"

"I love brownies, Mrs. Keene, but I'm on a diet," I lied. "And I'm on another case right now. I really don't know if I can make it over there this evening."

"But you must. What if he comes back? I'm here all alone."

"Mrs. Keene, you should call the police. We told you that last night."

"I couldn't do that, Dee. If you need more money—"

"No! No more money!" I thought fast. "All right.

Look, I'll try to be over tonight at dusk, but maybe you should call one of your friends to come and stay with you. You shouldn't stay there alone today."

"Oh, I won't. I'm working at the church rummage sale all afternoon. We're going to set up tables and get things organized. I'll be fine. It's just tonight I'm worried about."

"Okay. I'll try to make it."

"With that nice young man?"

"No! Brandon won't be able to make it tonight."

"Oh, that's too bad, dear. You make such a nice couple."

I winced.

"You be sure and tell him hello for me."

"Yes, I'll do that. I have to go now, Mrs. Keene."

"All right, dear. I'll see you tonight. And I'll make brownies."

"I can't wait."

Could the day get any better?

It could. I got lost again. Well, heck, I'd only been to the Russos' the one time and I didn't even have a map with me now. By the time I found the right street I was sweating profusely, and only partly from the hot summer sun.

I parked behind Trudy's car, which was parked right where Brandon had parked before. Binky still stood out in this neighborhood, but I no longer cared. And now that I was here, I wondered what the heck I thought I was going to do. I mean, I could hardly go marching up to the front door and demand to be let inside. Still, letting Brandon meet with Elaine Russo again by himself was just plain stupid, but I was hardly in a position to call the cops myself.

The neighborhood was dead quiet, raising prickles all up and down my arms despite the fact that the midday sun was turning Binky into an unpleasant sauna. The longer I sat here, the worse my sense grew that something was badly wrong. I tried to tell myself I was being fanciful, but myself wasn't listening.

As I got out of the car and stood there nervously, I vowed not to do anything stupid or rash. And as I crept along the tall hedge that divided the property lines between one house and the other, I kept reminding myself that I was no television heroine. No one was going to conveniently yell *Cut!* and send in the stunt double if things got dangerous. And if the neighbors saw me skulking in the bushes in the middle of the day, I was going to have a fine time explaining to the police that rather than casing the Russo house, I was spying on my competition. Yeah, that would go over big with everyone involved.

A wide sweep of lawn left me no choice but to leave the sheltering shrubs if I wanted a closer look inside the house. Since there was no fence, I figured the odds were good that large dogs with pointy teeth wouldn't be involved, but I sprinted across the grass and circular drive with a speed that would do Aunt Lacy proud.

A large portico with heavy white columns graced

the front of the house. I skipped that area since there were no side windows with convenient views and I'd already dismissed the idea of ringing the front doorbell. Unfortunately most of the windows up front—not to mention the well-manicured but prickly-looking shrubs—were up too high for me to get a clear view inside.

I circled around, bobbing my head up at every window I came to until I reached the shady side of the house. A cluster of large blue hydrangeas partly blocked a series of wider, lower windows.

Movement inside brought a surge of panic sliding up my throat. I pushed my way into the thick bushes and froze, praying no one had noticed me. After several seconds of pretending to be invisible, I crept even closer to the house. Moving away was unthinkable. I'd be seen for certain then.

Flattening myself against the house, I peered in through the window, prepared to duck immediately. The sight inside negated any thought of ducking. The room appeared to be a living room. Of course, in a house like this it was probably called by some fancier name. There was a curved arch opening across from me that opened into a hall. Elaine Russo looked as if she had just stepped inside the room from that hall. Brandon was partly in profile to me, as though he'd been crossing to meet her. Also in profile to me—close enough I could have reached out and tugged on his sleeve if it hadn't been for the window—was Hogan Delvecchi. He'd entered the room from a side door I could see plainly. The arm I could almost touch was holding a gun and it was aimed at Brandon.

I edged back from the window and looked around wildly. Where the heck was a rock? I had to cause a distraction before that gun went off and someone got hurt. There wasn't so much as a pebble in the pristine landscape, and I'd left my purse in the car. I patted my pocket and came up with my keys, my identification folder and the cell phone clipped to my pants. I couldn't throw that.

Oh, heck. Why not? It was an older, heavier model and I'd always wanted one of the smaller, sleeker phones—maybe one that took and sent pictures.

I threw the cell phone as hard as I could. I expected it to bounce off, maybe crack the glass, at most.

The crash was awesome. I mean, really awesome. That window shattered in a billion tiny and not-so-tiny pieces, just like some Hollywood movie or something. Delvecchi spun. Brandon tackled him brilliantly. The two of them went down with a thud I could almost feel.

There was no need to ring the doorbell now. I raced back around the side of the house to the front. Elaine Russo nearly knocked me over as she came flying out the front door.

"Hey! Wait! Stop!"

I started to go after her and hesitated. Despite a pair of three-inch-high heels and a straight skirt hiked halfway up her thighs, she was running fast enough to give my aunt Lacy some serious competition—and Brandon was alone inside with Delvecchi and a gun. The man had already tried to kill him once today, and Brandon was injured. I had absolutely no idea how I was going to prevent Delvecchi from succeeding in his goal, but I was running on adrenaline and sheer fear as I plunged inside the house.

The hall was wide and circular and contained two built-in niches with lit statuary. I started down the opening toward the back of the house on my left because I could hear the clear sounds of the struggle in progress. But backing up, I returned to the nearest niche. The sculpture was modern, twisted and tall, fashioned in some dark metal. I picked it up, discovered it was suitably but not uncomfortably heavy, and took off again in the direction of the fight—only to arrive too late. The battle was over. Brandon stood over Delvecchi breathing hard, the clear victor. He held the man's gun with a calm expertise I had to admire.

"Good work," I said letting my admiration show. I mean, Delvecchi's built like a rock and Brandon's just, well, trim and gorgeous and Brandon.

He glanced at me as I came in. "Where's Elaine?"

"The last I saw she was running down the driveway."

"You let her get away?"

"Well, gee, I thought it was a little more important to come in here and be sure you weren't getting your butt kicked."

"Thanks for the confidence."

"If I'd had confidence, I'd still be at the shop helping to plan the Barnett wedding and you'd still be looking down the barrel of that gun you're holding—that is, if he hadn't already shot you. And in case you're interested, your face is leaking some serious blood underneath that bandage."

Something flew from Delvecchi's hand, striking Brandon's left kneecap. His leg buckled. He folded before I could blink. Delvecchi scrambled up off the floor. He was through the door at his back faster than I would have thought possible for such a big man. Automatically I started to give chase.

"Dee!"

I spun. Brandon was painfully standing, bracing himself on the back of the couch. The room looked like you'd expect after a brawl had taken place. Furniture was pushed around or overturned, like the coffee table. Two lamps lay broken. Shards of glass littered the expensive-looking Oriental rug. In fact, the room reminded me of my apartment after Sam One got through with it.

"What do you think you're doing?" he demanded when I stopped and ran back to his side.

"I was going to go after him! He's getting away!"

"And what were you going to do—throw that sculpture at him when you caught up to him?"

Good point. I set the sculpture down on the nearest chair and bent to retrieve the object that had hit his leg. My cell phone!

Brandon teetered. I reached out to steady him as he tested his weight on the leg that had been injured.

"Are you all right?"

He shot me a dark look. "Wonderful. Don't I look all right?"

"No," I snapped back, "as a matter of fact, you look—"

"Never mind. We don't have much time."

"You're right. We need to get out of here."

"Help me search," he said at the same time.

"Search? Are you crazy? We've got to get out of here before the police come. Search for what? What are you doing? Where are you going? Brandon!"

He was heading down the hall at a fast limp, the opposite way from the front door, and he was tucking Delvecchi's gun into the waistband of his slacks as he went.

"What do you think you're doing?"

"We're detectives," he said gruffly. "We're going to detect."

"Detect what? The blood trail you're going to leave all over the house if you don't stop your cheek from bleeding?"

He paused, swore softly and pulled a handkerchief from his back pocket. Pressing it over the now-soaked bandage, he continued on his way down the hall.

"Do you at least know where you're going?"

"Upstairs."

"Great. What's upstairs?"

"I'm hoping the safe."

I didn't like the sound of that at all. "Next time lie to me."

I wasn't sure, but I thought he smothered a chuckle.

"Brandon, the cops could show up any minute now."

"I don't think so. Good. I knew there had to be a set of back stairs somewhere."

"But the police…"

"Who's going to call them? Elaine wants to get as far from Albert Russo as possible. Delvecchi's going to have to go back to his boss and admit he was taken out by a cell phone and a man he already tried to kill once today. That was quick thinking, by the way."

"Thanks."

"No, thank you. And the last thing any of them want to do is bring the police into this. Even if they did, this is the last place the police would look for us, don't you agree? If you were us, wouldn't you get the heck out of here?"

I stopped and watched his butt disappear around the top of the landing. Obviously he'd taken one blow too many to the head. Yet somehow his twisted logic made sense. So, what did that say about my thinking processes?

However, he did have a seriously nice-looking butt.

The first room we came to was yellow. Yellow walls, yellow drapes, yellow bedspread, yellow paintings, relieved only by white furniture and white accents.

"Yu-uck."

Brandon offered me a lopsided grin. "Not a fan of yellow?"

"I'm going to have mustard nightmares for a week!"

He opened a door that led to an enormous bathroom. Done in yellow and white, of course. The next door revealed a walk-in closet larger than my entire bedroom.

"Pay dirt first try. Obviously this is Elaine's suite. Looks like the couple doesn't share a bedroom. Funny though, she didn't strike me as the yellow type. Albert's room must be next door."

He found the connecting door and entered a room that was done in rich dark browns and tans. To my surprise, he turned around and came back into Elaine's bedroom.

"You take the dresser over there. I'll start with the armoire here."

"What am I looking for?"

Every nerve ending in my body was shouting at me to put as much distance between me and this house as humanly possible.

"Anything. Papers. Keys. Anything we can use."

I started to ask for clarification, but one look at his dark expression and I swallowed the words down. He was angry. Furious, even. And intently focused. I tried not to shiver. This side of Brandon made me just as nervous as the side that had stood there so calmly holding that gun on Delvecchi. Brandon might look like a hunky fashion model, but there was a sinister, dangerous side that lurked under that gorgeous surface that frankly scared the heck out of me.

I have to admit going through someone's dresser drawers is extremely unsettling. These were Elaine's personal belongings. She wore this underwear against her body every day. This was wrong. I turned around to tell him so and stopped to watch Brandon run his hands impersonally along the underside of the open shelf in the armoire. The contents didn't seem to concern him at all.

He opened the drawer below, barely glanced at the insides, pulled the drawer out, checked the bottom and sides of the wood and then inside where it fit. I heaved a sigh of relief. Okay. I could handle that. I followed his lead, a bit awkwardly, and pulled the drawer from its sleeve while he checked under the bed, turned the mattress and scoured the headboard and footboard. Before we were done we'd covered every single piece of furniture in the large room. Then we moved on to the closet.

Elaine Russo had more clothing than any woman could possibly wear in a year. And she had an equal number of shoes. If we'd been the same size, I probably could have found a replacement for my damaged outfit and she never would have known. Some of the outfits still had price tags on them, and those tags made my jaw sag.

"Check every pocket," Brandon admonished, as if I couldn't figure that much out for myself, "and inside every shoe."

The woman had a *lot* of shoes.

At first I wasn't sure what it was nagging at the back of my mind, but as we worked the closet, something began to bother me. It wasn't until we moved into the large bathroom and Brandon grinned in triumph that it hit me.

"Brandon, there aren't any wigs."

"What?" he asked absently.

He was down on the marble floor doing something to the set of drawers between the double sinks.

"She wore a blond wig the other night, but there aren't any wigs or any wig stands. That doesn't make sense. What are you…? Oh."

The shallow drawers swung out of the way to reveal a hidden safe.

"I don't believe it. Who puts a safe in their bathroom?"

"Can you think of a better place? No one breaks in a house to burglarize a bathroom."

"Drug addicts?"

He shot me a look and I subsided. I doubted even a drug addict would have found that safe, and how would he have gotten it open if he had found it?

"What are you doing?" I asked when Brandon began to study the dial.

"What does it look like I'm doing? I'm going to try and open it."

"Can you do that?"

"Not if you don't stop talking."

I stopped talking, but mostly because I was appalled and amazed at the same time. No one had taught me safecracking when I was learning to be a detective. I wanted to ask if this had been part of his police training, but he didn't look like he'd appreciate another question.

About the time I concluded he didn't know what he was doing, I heard an audible click. Instead of the door opening, Brandon scrambled awkwardly to his feet, grimacing as he put weight on his left leg.

"Run!"

"What's wrong?"

"I tripped an alarm. The safe was wired. The police will be here any minute."

"I don't hear anything."

"You aren't supposed to hear anything. It's a silent alarm. Come on. We have to go. Now!"

I wanted to ask how he knew, but for a man with an injured leg, Brandon could move when he needed to. We all but flew down the main staircase and out the front door, still standing wide open to the hot and by now late afternoon sun.

"Where's your car?"

"Behind Trudy's."

"Let's go."

Brandon directed our path across the yard and into the shelter of the tall hedge once more. I'd have thought haste was more important than being seen, because by now Russo already knew we were the ones who had foiled Delvecchi's plans, but Brandon insisted we not upset the neighbors. It wasn't the neighbors I was worrying about, but it was tough to argue when panic was clawing at my brain. I had visions of my license being rescinded as we raced to the cars.

We came out near the street in the same place where I had seen him emerge the first time I'd lain eyes on him, and I nearly ran into his back when he came to a dead stop.

"That's *yours?*" Brandon demanded.

Since Binky was the only thing in sight, I nodded breathlessly. "Binky," I said. "My car."

He looked at me as if I'd gone crazy. "I know Elaine was keeping me preoccupied that night, but how the devil did I miss you tailing us in that?"

"Hey, he may be small and he needs to be painted, but he runs. Most of the time."

"Glad to hear it. Where's Trudy's car?"

"Huh?"

But I didn't really need him to repeat the question. I got it the first time. Hard to miss since Binky was sitting there all by his lonesome. Trudy's bright blue Pontiac with the happy parrot bumper sticker was conspicuously missing.

Chapter Eight

"What am I going to tell Trudy?"

"I told you, I'll get the car back."

He *had* told me several times already. What he hadn't told me was how he planned to go about doing that. I glared at him over the hamburgers sitting in front of us and waved a French fry in his face.

"Do not patronize me."

"I wouldn't do that, Dee. If you hadn't shown up when you did this afternoon, things would have gotten sticky. Despite how it must seem to you at the moment, I am not stupid. I knew when Elaine called me that situation had *setup* written all over it. That's why I didn't want you coming with me. It was okay for me to take a risk, but I didn't want to put anyone else in potential jeopardy."

"The police—"

"Don't want me messing in their investigation of Seth's murder," he said flatly. "I have a few friends on some of the local forces, but even they think I'm running rogue and dangerous."

"Well, du-uh."

He managed a small smile. I was still feeling shaky from our narrow escape, and despite his best efforts to clean up in the men's room at the local restaurant where we were now having lunch—or dinner, depending on your point of view—he still looked like he'd been in a street brawl and lost. We'd gotten more than a few strange looks since we'd arrived. In fact, one couple had actually gotten up and moved after we'd sat down.

"What happened to the papers Elaine was supposed to give you?"

"She had to go upstairs to get them. She had them in her hand when she came into the room, so I'm guessing she took them with her when she ran. Delvecchi appeared almost the minute she came back inside the room. He must have been there all along waiting for her to get them."

"She didn't know he was there?"

"Not unless she's a good actress. She took one look at him and her face went white."

"Okay. If she took the papers with her, why were we searching for the safe?"

He leaned back and picked up his burger. "A woman that scared isn't going to give me originals. She made copies. Where there is one set of copies, there's probably another set as insurance. We were looking for the insurance."

"Uh-huh." But it made sense. "What made you think you could open that safe?"

"Keep your voice down," he instructed.

Suitably chastised, I bit into the burger that dripped juice satisfactorily.

I'd chosen a burger place in Rocky River that had once operated drive-in restaurants all over the area, according to my dad. After the day I'd had, my body craved a jolt of cholesterol-laden carbs, and I was in no mood to deny the craving. I took a sip from the rich chocolate shake and tried not to think about calories.

"My dad used to work the robbery division. He got pretty good with locks and safes. I picked up a lot from him. I wasn't sure I could open it, but if it proved to be a simple safe, as it did, I figured it was worth a shot."

I swallowed in surprise, nearly choking. "Your dad's a cop?"

"Retired. Look, Dee, I'll get Trudy's car back. I imagine Elaine dumped it pretty quick. I called in a couple of favors, and if it gets spotted, someone will call me."

"Whoa. You think Elaine stole Trudy's car?"

He looked at me as if I was nuts.

"You don't imagine there were two people running around that ritzy neighborhood in desperate need of a car to steal at that exact time do you?"

I set down my half-eaten burger. "How would someone like Elaine Russo know how to hot-wire a car?"

He stopped chewing and swallowed. "Good question," he said slowly.

I nodded, tamping down a swell of satisfaction.

"And why did she need to steal any car? Why didn't she use the car she came in? Come to think about it, I didn't see her Jag out front, did you?"

"No. Did she have her purse with her when she left?"

I thought back to the running figure and shook my head. All she'd been holding had been a sheaf of papers.

"We should have searched for her purse," I said.

Brandon nodded. "Want to go back?"

"Very funny."

"Sounds like it would be very informative to do some background research on Elaine Russo. Trudy and your aunt didn't happen to mention her maiden name by any chance, did they?"

He spoke as if we were a team.

"No, but I can call them."

"Go ahead. We'll finish eating and go over to my office and run her name through the computer and see what pops."

"Uh, I'm not sure that's such a good idea. Going to your office, I mean."

Brandon shook his head. "You're right. I'm not thinking straight today. Do you have a place you can stay tonight?"

"Me?" It came out a squeak.

"Delvecchi's probably not going to bother with you. It's me he wants, but let's not take any risks."

Risks. I was at risk. Was my brain stopped up or what? I'd just made a local gangster with possible mob ties mad at me. I'd broken into his house, broken his window, gone through his wife's drawers and closets and tried to break into her safe. The wonderfully greasy hamburger suddenly wasn't feeling so wonderful at all anymore. I pushed the food aside, feeling sick.

"Hey. It's going to be okay."

"Yeah? How?"

"We're going to nail the bastard."

"Could we do it before he kills us?"

Brandon grinned, making me feel marginally better.

"That's the plan, kid."

I wanted to argue that I wasn't a kid, but at the moment I felt about two and I wanted my mommy. Instead I drove us over to my dad's house.

"You really need a car with air-conditioning, Dee."

"Only a couple of months out of the year. The rest of the time I need heat and an oil job, but that's life. We'll be there in a minute, so stop complaining."

Brandon argued that he had a place to go, but I pointed out he lacked transportation and I had to be next door to pull stakeout duty on Mrs. Keene's house again. Abruptly he changed his mind and seemed anxious to come with me.

"I still think Mrs. Keene should call the police," he said.

"You're preaching to the choir," I told him. "Convince her."

"I doubt the kid'll come back. Still, it's strange."

"We're talking about Mrs. Keene, here."

"Point taken."

Dad wasn't in when we got there, so while Brandon got cleaned up in the downstairs bathroom, I got my former bedroom ready for him and readied sheets for the pullout couch—not that I figured I'd sleep a wink with Brandon in the same house all night.

Then I called Aunt Lacy. She didn't try to hide her relief at hearing from me. Mickey had come in. She'd taken him over to the apartment to see George, who had turned out not to be Mr. Sam either. Mickey had been disappointed on the verge of frantic. His uncle was supposed to come for dinner tomorrow night. He needed Mr. Sam back before then.

I closed my eyes. Finding a lost cat had never been high on my list of priorities and now it had dropped to just above zero. I felt bad for the kid, but I had real problems of my own. Aunt Lacy went on to say that Mickey had loved seeing the kittens and thought they were cool. And because George and Sam One hadn't gotten along—and the two of them had made rather a mess out of my poor plant, which Aunt Lacy had thought best to toss out completely—Mickey and Aunt Lacy had taken Sam One to the animal shelter. She hoped I didn't mind. I managed not to cheer out loud and suggested they might want to take Mama, the kittens and George there, as well.

Aunt Lacy thought I was kidding. She was already in the process of posting Lost signs for George. She'd decided it was a good idea to take George to the shop now that Annabelle, née Sugarplum, had been returned to Mrs. Crispen.

"After all, Dee, it would be best if mama cat doesn't have the stress of having other strange cats around her babies."

"Right." Not to mention my stress levels.

It was a great relief to learn I'd be down to seven cats in my cat-free apartment building. Maybe I could convince Mickey to take Mama and her kids home with him. His uncle could then have his pick of a replacement for the missing Mr. Sam if we didn't find the ancient cat.

"Look, Aunt Lacy, I'd like to help Mickey out, I really would. But I'm a little, uh, busy right now."

"Dee, is something wrong?"

"You could say that. I need to tell you about a small problem. Okay, maybe a big problem. Brandon and I sort of ticked off Hogan Delvecchi and Albert Russo."

Aunt Lacy inhaled sharply.

"I don't think they'd hurt you or Trudy, but Brandon and I think it's best to keep a low profile for a couple of days. I'm worried about you going over to my apartment again. On the other hand, we can't just leave the cats there."

I could almost hear her spine straighten.

"I'll be perfectly fine to take care of the cats, Dee. You see to it Brandon takes care of you."

My own spine straightened. "I can take care of myself, Aunt Lacy."

There was a long pause. "You remind me more and more of your mother every day. You be careful, all right?"

Surprised, I nodded, then realized she couldn't
see me and agreed out loud. I was trembling when I
hung up and I couldn't have said exactly why.

I found Brandon in the basement with my father
when I hung up. I don't know when he had come
home, but introductions were apparently unnecessary. The two of them were setting up planks and
talking saw blades like old friends when I appeared.

"Hey, Dee, everything okay?" Brandon greeted.

"Fine. I see you've met my dad?"

"Nice to see your taste has improved, Dee," my
dad said. "You really think the quarter-inch blade is
better, Brandon?"

"Yes, sir. If you use the half-inch, you'll—"

I slipped back up the stairs.

MRS. KEENE'S BROWNIES CAME as a shock. They were
edible. Except for the icing, of course. I did my best
to scrape the dark goo off into my napkin when she
wasn't looking. I could almost feel the sticky sugar
boring holes in my molars.

Brandon had been upset, but Mrs. Keene was ec-
static when I offered to spend the night on her couch.
It wasn't that I wanted to stay there, but I knew I'd
never sleep with Brandon in the same house. Besides, he'd insisted on taking the couch at my dad's
place and he didn't fit. There was no point in both of
us not sleeping.

Dad simply shook his head when I explained the
plan. He told Brandon to get used to my hard head

because he'd be butting up against it often enough if he decided to hang around.

Brandon patrolled the neighborhood on foot while I stayed close to the house itself. Neither of us really believed any more would happen after last night, but it gave me an excuse to put a little professional distance between us.

I was standing out back under the wide branches of the maple tree that all but swallowed her small yard when Brandon walked up, startling me.

"By the way, out of curiosity, what are we being paid for this job?" he asked.

"We?"

"Well, if I'm acting as consultant, like you told her, I should get half, don't you think?"

"Half?"

"Half the work, half the pay."

I wasn't in the mood to argue. "Fine. Half."

"So what are we making?"

"A hundred."

"An hour?"

"For the job."

There was a long beat of silence.

"You're joking."

My defensive hackles rose. "She's an old lady and my dad's next-door neighbor."

"Why charge anything at all then?"

"I wasn't going to, all right? I was going to give her back the money."

He regarded me for a long second in silence. "If

this is how you do business, how do you earn a living?"

"I work in my aunt's flower shop!"

Angry tears began to build and I blinked them back. Around Brandon my emotions seemed to feel free to pinwheel out of control. I was totally unprepared for him to pull me into his arms.

"You are the most amazing woman."

"Wha—"

I only had an instant to prepare for those fantastic lips to descend, but heck, I didn't need longer than that. Anger and thought both fled as he kissed me with a hunger that left me too shaken to stand unsupported.

"Amazing," he whispered against my mouth.

"Oh, yeah," I agreed. And dimly I heard a car door.

Brandon jerked his head up. Wheels squealed as a car sped off. I twisted to look back over my shoulder. I was in time to see a dark car that could have been burgundy red disappear up the street. Brandon released me so fast, I nearly fell, as he went racing toward the front of the house. My pocket was buzzing and I realized it had been for several seconds.

My cell phone. I'd put it on vibrate, not even certain it still worked after all the abuse it had suffered today. I fumbled it out of my pocket as I pelted unsteadily after Brandon.

"Dee, did you see him?" Mrs. Keene demanded shrilly in my ear.

I held the phone out away from my ear. "I saw."

"He came right up on the front porch this time!"

"Did you get a good look at him?"

"No. By the time I found my glasses he was getting back in his car. Those dratted dark windows. Why do they allow them to tint the windows so dark?"

"I don't know," I agreed.

Brandon was moving from the sidewalk to the porch. I cut across the grass and arrived on his heels. The bouquet of pink roses lay in their plastic sleeve in front of her door. Beside them sat a wrapped box of Malley's chocolate candy.

"What the devil is going on?" he asked me.

"Some kid with a grandma fetish?"

"Does she have a grandson?"

"Yeah, he's seven."

IN THE MORNING I SNUCK OUT of her house the minute I heard her in the bathroom. I know it was cowardly, but I couldn't face Mrs. Keene before coffee. I'd barely slept and I knew Brandon hadn't gotten much more sleep than I had. I'd seen the light on in my former bedroom until quite late. Perversely the thought that he couldn't sleep either had cheered me.

Dad had already left for work by the time I arrived, but to my dismay, he'd taken Brandon with him, according to the note they'd left for me. Angry but not sure exactly why I was angry, I drove over to my apartment to check on the cats.

Mama jumped off the bed and ran for the closet when I came in. Her babies were making soft baby noises as she nuzzled them into place. I figured she'd been taking a break. Having six little ones clinging to you 24-7 must get tiresome, so I didn't blame her. They were pretty cute even if they did still look more like rodents than kittens.

I marveled over how each one was different. One was black and white, one was brown and black and white, two were gray, one was orange and white and one looked to be all black. Together they were certainly a colorful array. It was surprisingly hard not to want to touch them.

Mama watched closely but offered no protest as I lifted the black one and stroked its tiny head. The eyes were still closed and its ears were flat to its head, with its fur close to its body. It made a small sound and I put it back down so it could squirm its way back into the mass of writhing bodies with its brothers and sisters.

I showered quickly, donned a fresh pair of jeans and a T-shirt and headed out the door. Since I hadn't worked the shop all day yesterday, I figured it would be nice to go in early and get things started before Aunt Lacy showed up. I owed her for getting rid of Sam One for me.

GEORGE THE CAT WAS HAPPILY batting a broken fern across the back room and I was in the middle of telling my aunt and Trudy what had happened at Mrs. Keene's house when my cell phone rang. My stomach gave a flip and my heart went into overdrive at the name on the caller ID. I'd been expecting Brandon to call all morning. He hadn't. The one name I hadn't been expecting was Albert Russo. I excused myself to take the call in the office, shutting the door for privacy.

"D.B. Hayes," I said, trying hard to sound professional.

"Albert Russo, Ms. Hayes. I am most…disappointed in you."

I swallowed air because I didn't have any saliva left.

"I'm not overly happy with you either, Mr. Russo," I managed with false bravado.

His pause nearly killed me.

"I don't like being used," I added boldly into the pause, sitting down on one of the lumpy visitor chairs before my legs gave out.

"Used? Ms. Hayes?"

"Used," I said firmly, warming to the subject. "I understand about divorce. It's always a messy situation. But before you start threatening people and pointing guns—or having your associate do it for you—check your facts, Mr. Russo. You didn't ask me for information. You asked me for photographs and a record of where your wife went the other evening. That's the information I provided. Information I did not divulge to anyone, I might add, as I consider it confidential. However, I can't speak for the other people involved. And before you make assumptions based on those photographs, my professional opinion is that you should do some in-depth checking on the facts behind your wife's professed association with the man in question. I think you'll discover the relationship is not what it appears on the surface."

I paused to draw a breath and he chuckled.

"You have moxie, Ms. Hayes. How unexpected. I trust then that you know what you are doing."

The soft click as he disconnected was the scariest sound I'd ever heard. I wasn't entirely sure, but I thought I'd just ticked off one of the most dangerous men in Cleveland. I was certifiably out of my mind.

When I finally got my nerves settled enough to leave the office with what I hoped was a serene expression in place, I lost it all over again. Brandon was standing in the workroom with his back to me, talking with Trudy and my aunt. George the cat was happily twisting himself around Brandon's legs, vying for attention.

"And I know my friend, Suzanne, has two tickets for tonight's performance and she can't go," Aunt Lacy was saying. "Her husband's back is acting up again. She offered them to Trudy and me last night, but I'm not all that fond of Shakespeare's dramas. *Macbeth*, isn't it, Trudy? Let me give Suzanne a call. You and Dee can go."

"Well, actually I had dinner plans for this evening—"

"I'll bet her son can get you a backstage pass to meet Nicole after the performance," Aunt Lacy added persuasively. "He works there. I'll just give Suzanne a quick call."

As Aunt Lacy bustled away I told myself I was not jealous. A man like Brandon is bound to have a girlfriend or ten hanging around. There was nothing wrong with him having dinner plans for the evening that didn't include me. On the other hand, if my aunt could get us in to talk to the woman who was having an affair with the man who had just threatened my life… At least, I think he had threatened my life. I wasn't real clear on that point.

"We should go," I said.

Brandon turned quickly and grimaced. Our gazes locked. My knees suddenly felt wobbly. Good thing that man couldn't bottle his powerful thrall over women, or the entire female population would be endangered.

"Knee still bothering you?" I asked, going for nonchalance.

"It's fine."

His face was shaping up to be pretty spectacular with that bruise turning interesting shades of blues and blacks. He'd given up on the bandage. The cut was scabbed over and the bruise hid most of it anyhow.

"Colorful," I told him.

He started a hand toward his cheek and let it fall back to his side. "Yeah. Ms. Hoffsteder—"

"Trudy," she corrected.

"Trudy," he acknowledged with a nod in her direction, "said you were on the phone with Russo. What did he want?"

I thought about that for a minute and shrugged. "I have no idea. He told me I had moxie and he guessed I knew what I was doing."

"He threatened you?" Trudy said, outraged.

"Who threatened her?" my aunt demanded, returning to the workroom from the office. "Russo?"

"No one," we said at the same time.

My aunt regarded me sternly. That was nothing compared to the look she turned on Brandon.

"I got you the tickets. Suzanne is going to ask her son to get you a backstage pass, as well, but I expect you to look out for my niece."

"Aunt Lacy!"

"Don't you Aunt Lacy me, not this time. That man is no one to fool around with, girl. I don't like this."

I pushed myself forward, trying to hold back the anger. I love my family, but here was the reason I couldn't live with any of them.

"*This,*" I said with quiet force, "*is* my job. I love you, Aunt Lacy, but if you can't deal, then I have to go, because it's what I do. You knew that when you agreed to let me rent space from you. I can't fight you and Russo and Brandon all at the same time."

"Hey, what did the boy do?" Trudy asked.

I spared her a glare.

"Never mind, Dee's right, Lace. She knows how to take care of herself."

Aunt Lacy's lips thinned, but the bell rang out front and she turned away and walked out to take care of the customer who'd just entered.

"Thanks, Trudy," I said.

The older woman shrugged. "It's the truth. She knows it. You just remind her of your mother is all. She was always a scrapper, too. Being the older sister, Lacy just got in the habit of worrying and fussing. Your tickets will be at the box office. If Jason is able to get you a backstage pass, it will be waiting with the tickets. But, Dee, because I like to worry, too, the both of you be careful. Lacy's right about one thing. Russo isn't someone you want to fool around with."

"I'll do my best." I gave her a quick hug and found Brandon watching the whole scene silently. It was hard to believe I'd forgotten about him for even a second, but I had.

Aunt Lacy was helping a pair of women select an arrangement for a sick friend as I walked Brandon outside, so I simply nodded to her and stepped into the early afternoon heat with Brandon at my side. I blinked and turned sideways to avoid looking into the sun.

"Sorry about that," I said uncomfortably, not sure exactly what I was apologizing for.

"Your aunt has a point, you know."

"I know. I believe that's why you spent the night in my father's guest room? Or was that solely to protect me from Mrs. Keene's mystery stalker?"

"Doesn't that chip on your shoulder get to be a drag after a while?"

I glared at him. "When you're five foot one and you look like you're still in college—"

"High school."

"When we first met, you asked me if I was twenty-one or twenty-two."

He offered me an easy grin. "Because I figured you had to be older than you looked."

"Thanks a lot."

"Hey, in ten or twenty years you'll welcome your youthful appearance."

"Come talk to me then."

"Dee—"

"Look, Brandon, I don't know if Russo was threatening me or not. He didn't say a word about the house or anything. I'm not even sure why he called me unless it was to warn me off."

"Obviously he doesn't know you very well."

"Darn right. So why'd you disappear so early this morning?"

"I had to pick up Trudy's car."

"You found it?"

"Dex called me at four this morning. Your dad dropped me off to meet him on his way in to work, and Dex drove me to the east side to pick it up. It was in a supermarket parking lot not far from Russo's place. I didn't figure she'd take it very far. She didn't want to be picked up driving a stolen car. There was no damage, so I filled the tank, had it cleaned and brought it by."

"That was nice of you. Thanks. But how are you going to get around?"

"My ride's waiting over there."

I looked in the direction he'd indicated with his nod and wished I hadn't. The car was a blue mini-van and the driver was a blonde. A very attractive blonde.

"Your dinner date?"

He started to answer and stopped. A smile played around the corners of his mouth.

"Jealous?"

"You know something, Kirkpatrick, I'll stack my chip against your ego any day. If dinner with the blonde is more important than talking to Russo's side dish, I'll see if Billy's free tonight and let you know what I learn. No sweat."

I rocked back on my heels, feeling I'd handled that pretty well. I was *not* jealous. I would not *be* jealous. I had nothing at all to be jealous about. We were business acquaintances. Nothing more.

"Which one's Billy?" he asked with a gleam in his eyes. "The mechanic or the accountant?"

I held on to my temper with mental fists. "You and my father had a nice long chat did you?"

"Let's just say it was educational."

Too bad I knew the penalty for patricide. I forced a sweet smile. "Whichever one would worry you the most."

The devil lent him that grin.

"I'll pick you up at closing," he said.

"What about your dinner date?" I inclined my head toward the van without looking directly at the blonde again.

"Julie won't mind if we postpone. You and I can grab something to eat downtown before the play."

That sounded uncomfortably like a date to me. "Your tab?" I demanded.

The grin widened.

"My tab," he agreed.

"Fine. Want to take the blonde some consolation flowers?"

"Nah. I'll just use the ole Kirkpatrick charm."

The worst part was, it would probably work.

"Huh. I'm buying garlic and charms."

I could hear him laughing as I strode off down the street toward the dry cleaner's. I did not look back.

Chapter Nine

Too bad there were no dry-cleaning charms.

"I'm sorry, Dee," Mr. Choy said. "Blood's one of those nasty stains once it sets. If the fabric had been anything but—"

"It's okay, Mr. Choy. I was hoping for a miracle, but I wasn't expecting one."

"You know my daughter, Kai?"

"Of course. Hi, Kai."

I felt foolish as soon as the words left my lips because the combination sounded so ridiculous, but his daughter merely smiled and said hello.

"Kai is studying to be a seamstress. She has a suggestion. Tell her, Kai."

"As it is only the skirt that is damaged," Kai said at her father's prodding, "you could take other material and stitch it to the bodice here. This color and fabric would not be so easy to find, but there are others that would work."

"Kai, I appreciate the thought, but not only do I not

have the time to make a whole new dress, I'm no
compatible with needles and thread. I've been known
to buy an entire new blouse rather than sew on a button."

Kai stared at me in unwinking shock. "You would
throw the dress away?"

"It's no good to me now," I said regretfully. I really had liked that dress and it had cost a small fortune.

"With your permission, I could take the dress and
use it as one of my class projects."

"Permission granted. It's totally useless to me, but
thanks for the suggestion."

And because I gave her the dress, Mr. Choy refused to let me pay for the dry cleaning. We haggled
and eventually he let me pay his cost to clean the gar-
ment. It was only fair.

Fortunately the afternoon was busy. I ran orders
all over town, stopping by my place only briefly to
pick up a dress and sandals to wear to dinner and the
play. Mama and the kittens were fine, and I wasted
several minutes watching and petting each of them
I was not turning into a cat person, but they were so
tiny and helpless, they were cute.

I discovered I'd just missed Mickey when I got
back to the shop. Aunt Lacy said he was so de-
pressed, she was worried about him. His uncle was
coming to dinner that night, and without Mr. Sam,
he was going to have to confess he'd let the cat get
out. I felt guilty, but what could I do? There wasn't

ime to find him another cat. As it was I had to call
Mrs. Keene and tell her I wasn't going to make it to
her house tonight.

It turned out at least that wasn't a problem. A
friend of hers had fallen over some boxes at the
church rummage sale and Mrs. Keene was going to
spend the night keeping her company. Mrs. Keene
was concerned about her house, however, so I promised to drive by and make sure everything was all
right when I got the chance.

BRANDON IN CASUAL SLACKS AND an open-necked shirt
is sexy. Brandon in a suit and tie stole my breath and
left me metaphorically panting. And I was pretty sure
he knew it, too, darn the man. Except for the ugly dark
bruise on his cheek, he was so good looking, I was glad
now that I'd given in to vanity and my aunt and Trudy.

"You look lovely, Dee," he told me and sounded
as if he meant it.

"I do? I mean, thank you."

I was flustered. Billy and Ted rarely compliment
me. The truth is, I seldom think about my looks. I
rarely bother to wear makeup since it tends to dis-
solve on my skin after a few hours anyhow, so why
bother? Eye makeup irritates my eyes, causing me
to rub them until it smears. Then I look like a pathetic
raccoon. My hair isn't tamable with a whip and a
chair no matter how much gel and spray I use.

Genetics can be cruel. On the other hand, I have
nice skin and even features, so I can't complain.

The shop had been quiet the last half hour or s[o] before closing, so Aunt Lacy and Trudy had de[-] cided to make me a project. I really hate when tha[t] happens, but for once I didn't fight.

It started when Aunt Lacy lent me some blush a[s] a peace offering and insisted on dabbing a hint o[f] brown eye shadow on my lids. Trudy then wanted t[o] fuss with my hair, pulling the sides up and tyin[g] them on top of my head, anchoring the spill wit[h] strands of flowers. She'd parted it in the front dow[n] the middle, leaving it to fall in soft waves over m[y] brows. It wouldn't stay that way for long, but I ha[d] to admit it looked good for the moment.

I'd stopped by the drugstore at lunch and bough[t] some new long-lasting, guaranteed-not-to-rub-or[-] wear-off lipstick in a soft peach. The color went wel[l] with the blush and eye shadow. Of course, I gave th[e] lipstick fifteen minutes tops on *my* lips, but the over[-] all effect was nice for those fifteen minutes.

Vanity had forced me to be choosy when I'd se[-] lected my dress. Brandon had given up a date wit[h] a very pretty blonde to go with me. Since I am def[-] initely no blonde, I figured the least I could do wa[s] look presentable. While the dress I'd picked wasn'[t] fancy, it was new and tailored with a wide, colorfu[l] belt that emphasized my figure. The cream colo[r] looked okay against my skin and I had pretty crys[-] tal earrings that sparkled in an array of bright color[s] reminiscent of the belt. Heels would have looke[d] better than my off-white sandals, but I draw the lin[e]

at nylons in this heat. Besides, flats were more prac-
tical, just in case. I was finding I tended to do a lot
of running since meeting Brandon. I figured it paid
to be prepared.

I knew I looked good overall, but I hadn't expected
Brandon to comment even though I was vain enough
to hope he'd notice. Still, I was flustered when he said
so out loud, and with Aunt Lacy and Trudy nodding
approval, I let him lead me outside and over to the
blue minivan. The bubble of happiness instantly
burst.

"You borrowed your girlfriend's car?"

"Mine won't be ready for another couple of days,"
he said patiently, holding the passenger door open.

"Why don't we take Binky?"

I hated that he knew exactly why I objected and
was amused. At least he was smart enough not to
show his amusement openly.

"I've been folded enough for one week," he told
me.

"Binky has plenty of head- and legroom."

"Dee, get in the car."

Before I could summon another protest, he lifted
me as if I weighed nothing at all and sat me on the
passenger's seat.

Brandon was stronger than he looked. And I had
no business enjoying that quite so much. He shut the
door with an easy smile and came around to climb
in behind the wheel.

"Where would you like to go for dinner?"

He shouldn't have asked. I was flustered but also irked that he'd borrowed his date's van to take me out. Okay, this wasn't officially a date, but he had offered to pay tonight—and I was in a mood to make sure he did.

"We could try Scarpanelli's," I suggested. "Russo owns the place."

He grinned. "You're Machiavellian, you know that?"

I sat back smugly. "You don't know the half."

I had to keep reminding myself it wasn't a date, because Brandon kept acting as though it was. He held doors for me, lightly touched my back to guide me as we walked. Little things that made me want to shiver. The sort of things lovers or would-be lovers might do. The sort of things that made me nervous.

Brandon made me nervous.

I was sure he knew all about lovers and making love. He'd just better not expect this dinner to come with that sort of price tag. But over dinner he couldn't have been more relaxing. He told me a bit about growing up in Pittsburgh with his brother and seventeen cousins. The stories made me oddly wistful.

While I love my two brothers, Tony and Russ and I aren't exactly close. They're older by nine and twelve years and they've always treated me like a baby or a pest—unless they need a babysitter or a favor. Maybe things would have been different if Mom hadn't died of pneumonia when I was young, but she did, and we never had any cousins that I knew about. Aunt Lacy never married and Dad never had any siblings. Brandon made cousins and his family life sound like such fun.

Dinner proved to be even more expensive than I'd expected. I felt guilty when I caught a glimpse of the bill since I couldn't even offer to pay my share. I didn't have that kind of money in my checking account if I wanted to make my rent payment this month. Brandon never flinched. He pulled out his credit card and continued talking. It was entirely too easy to like Brandon—a whole lot.

I'd been keeping an eye out for Rob Deluth, but I hadn't seen the busboy. Either he'd been fired or it was his night off. There was also no sign of Albert Russo or Elaine, not that I'd expected to see either one of them here tonight, but you never knew.

The tickets were waiting for us at the theater box office, as promised, but not the backstage pass. The reason became apparent when it was announced that Nicole Wickley's understudy would be going on in her place. The costumes were ornate, the staging lavish and the play bored me to tears. Since I was so conscious of Brandon at my side the entire time, I tried to sit there attentively instead of fidgeting, but I guess I made a hash of it because he turned to me at the intermission with a flat expression.

"Would you like to go?"

I debated lying and decided he'd see right through me if I tried. "Yes, please."

"Good," he said sounding genuinely relieved.

"You don't mind?"

"I prefer modern English to ye old English."

"Thank God."

He grinned and led me back out to the van. The night hadn't cooled off by so much as a single degree. It was still hot and far too muggy to come close to comfortable.

"What do you say we go find out why Nicole didn't show up tonight?" Brandon asked.

"You know where she lives?"

He grinned. "I've been doing my homework."

The apartment sat off Edgewater Drive. An older building, it was newly refurbished and pricey. Once more I was glad for my choice of outfit tonight as we parked and headed for the front lobby.

"How are we going to get inside?" I asked.

"By acting like we belong."

Brandon surprised me by taking my hand.

"We're just returning home after an evening out," he said.

"Casual."

"Uh-huh." There was nothing casual about touching Brandon and it was all too easy to imagine what the hand-holding was leading up to, but I didn't pull back and we strolled toward the entrance hand in hand. He released me abruptly and hurried forward to help an elderly couple who were struggling with the doors. The man was in a wheelchair.

Brandon grabbed the inside door for them and I

moved to hold the outside door so the wife could guide the chair. Seconds later we were in the lobby with their thanks ringing in our ears.

"Piece of cake," he whispered as he guided me over to the elevators with his hand at my back as if we did this every single day.

"And you know the apartment number?" I whispered back, trying to pretend my hormones weren't jumping at the contact with his body once more.

"Five-fifteen. It was on her mailbox."

"You had time to read the mailboxes?"

"It was right under my nose as I held the door open."

"Were you born lucky?"

His grin widened. "My father always said a person makes their own luck."

"Don't tell Aunt Lacy. She'll think I'm doomed."

The grin became a low chuckle that gave wing to butterflies in my stomach. He reached out and stroked my cheek with a knuckle. The butterflies began hosting a party. The elevator door opened before I could think of anything to say. By the time the four chattering people inside disgorged, I managed to find my equilibrium again.

"Since you're making your own luck, what exactly do you plan to say to Nicole?" I asked in what I hoped was a neutral tone of voice.

He deliberately crowded me as we stepped inside the gold-veined, mirrored elevator.

"Am I making you nervous, Dee?"

Oh, yeah. Even my reflection thought so.

"Of course not."

His lips curved. He was definitely standing much closer than was necessary since we had the entire elevator all to ourselves.

"If you're nervous, you can wait downstairs. I'll talk to her myself."

He was trying to keep me off balance on purpose, I realized. I steadied my pounding heart. Determinedly I forced my fingers to reach up and lightly caress his chin. His eyes widened. My fingers tingled, but I tried not to let that show.

"I couldn't let you do that, Brandon. If Russo's willing to kill you for running off with his wife, imagine what he'll do when he finds out you went to see his girlfriend next. You'll be the only person to have firsthand knowledge of where they buried Jimmy Hoffa. The problem is you'll be right there beside him."

I turned around as the doors opened on the fifth floor.

"Better think up a story fast," I tossed over my shoulder. "We're on."

As it turned out, our performance was canceled because there was no one home to his knock. I started to turn away but Brandon stopped me with a firm— not to say painful—grip on my arm.

"Block the view."

"Wha—"

He pulled a set of lock picks from inside his suit

coat pocket and went to work on her door. I tried to cover my shock as well as his movements by pivoting to gaze guiltily down the hall in both directions. If anyone had been around, I'm sure they would have called security at once just based on my expression. Lock picking had definitely not been part of *my* curriculum as a private investigator.

Seconds later I was crowding nervously inside the apartment behind him, only to run right into his back when he came to an abrupt stop. I didn't have to ask why. It was evident. We gazed around the apartment in respectful silence. The view overlooking the lake was pretty spectacular—and unrestricted, given there were no drapes over the windows. Moonlight flooded the dark rooms, showing us there was no furniture either. The apartment was totally empty.

"Are you sure you got the right apartment?" I whispered.

"I'm sure," he said grimly, not bothering to whisper.

"Maybe she moved."

"You think?"

"Unless she suddenly got an urge to do major redecorating. Where are you going?"

"To have a look around."

"At what? The empty walls? Or are you shopping for a new apartment?"

"She could have left something behind."

"With our luck, it'll be a body," I muttered under my breath, feeling increasingly apprehensive.

The apartment was big and it was mostly dark despite the full moon glinting off Lake Erie. Brandon produced a tiny penlight flashlight that he used to probe the kitchen drawers and cupboards and every closet we came to. It appeared Nicole Wickley had cleared out everything including the cobwebs.

No bodies of any sort appeared.

"Can we go now?" I asked, trying not to whine in my need to get out of there.

"No reason to hang around, I guess. She won't be coming back, but I wonder when she moved out."

"Does it matter? Isn't the where she went more important?"

He shot me one of those inscrutable looks of his, turned off the flashlight and let us out. But when I would have started back down the hall, he shook his head and moved to the door across from Nicole's and rapped firmly.

"What are you—"

The man who answered was huge. Maybe the Browns' whole defensive line, if I'd learned my football terminology correctly. The bottle of beer clutched in one hand was practically swallowed from sight by those meaty fingers. He wore a black tank top that showed off bulging muscles on his forearms and black shorts that showed off beefy legs. I swallowed hard, sliding closer to Brandon. Brandon didn't appear the least bit disconcerted—or intimidated.

That was okay. I decided I'd be intimidated for both of us.

"Hi, sorry to bother you. My wife and I were looking for Nicole Wickley."

I was a wife now?

"She lives across the hall from you."

"Not anymore," the man said, only slurring his words slightly. "She moved out."

He turned his head and called to someone in the room at his back.

"When did Nicky move, Carla?"

"Coupla days ago," a high-pitched female voice called back.

"You wouldn't happen to have a forwarding address or a phone number for her, would you?" Brandon asked.

The woman who appeared beside the man looked like a child at first glance. She was extremely petite with a literal mane of black hair that tumbled past her waist. She was dressed in a clinging black leotard and nothing else. In her hand, an identical bottle of beer looked much too large for her tiny fingers.

I felt a giggle rise inside me and contained it with an effort. The first bottle was too small. The second bottle was too big. Was a normal-size person going to appear next?

"I think she went to New York," the woman called Carla was saying. "I heard her tell the manager she got a job on some soap. He was ticked 'cause she brought in movers with no notice or anything. She didn't care. Nicky's such a snob. Oops. I guess I shouldn't have said that if you're friends of hers. Come on, Donny, the wax is almost ready for us."

Without another word Donny closed the door. I met Brandon's expression. I couldn't help it. The giggle erupted. By the time we reached the elevators we were convulsed with laughter.

"What do you think…?"

"The wax? Please…" he held up his hand. "I'm trying not to think about what they were going to do with that wax."

And we were off again. I was wiping at tears when we reached the lobby. If anyone else had gotten on that elevator, they'd have thought we were nuts. It wasn't so much that they were such an odd couple— *though they were!*—it was just that we needed a release after the tension of the past few days. Every time we thought of that wax—well, it was enough to start us off all over again.

We had it under control by the time we got back to his borrowed minivan.

"Now what?" I asked.

"We need more information on Nicole Wickley."

"I left my computer at the shop," I said.

"The shop it is then."

George the cat was delighted to welcome company. He wound himself under our feet until Brandon picked him up just so he didn't trip over the little pest.

"What happened to your other cat?"

"Mrs. Crispen took her back home," I said, not wanting to explain.

I led the way to the office without turning on any lights. I didn't want the diligent Lakewood police force to come knocking and ask what we were doing in there at this hour of the night. I shut the office door, turned on the light and turned on the computer.

"It'll be easier if we both sit in the visitor chairs so that we can see the screen at the same time," I told him.

I should have thought first about how cozy that would make things. With the door shut, the closet-size room took on an intimacy I wasn't ready for. Brandon smelled good. I'd noticed it earlier, but I'd been able to ignore it when I could put distance between us or there were other people around. Now there was nothing else to focus on. He smelled good, he looked good—

I didn't see him put the cat down, but while we waited for the computer to boot, he leaned over, lifted my face and kissed me full on the mouth.

Every fiber of my body felt the sudden rush of desire that left me unable to do the simplest things— like breathe or think. I burned like a wild thing when he released me and sat back.

"What was that for?" Amazing how steady my voice came out when I was quivering gelatin inside.

"I figured we'd better get it out of the way first. I've been wanting to kiss you all night and this is just a little too intimate, don't you think? I decided we'd better take the edge off the hormones."

"The edge—"

"Mine if not yours. Do you mind if I...?"

He reached over, pulled the computer toward him and typed in a search command while I sat there speechless. My brain was still stuck on his wanting to kiss me all night.

"Bingo. She has a Web page."

He shoved the computer screen back so I could see the display, as well—as if my eyes could actually focus on anything else yet. But they did—a bit blankly at first, but finally I saw Nicole Wickley. Pages of Nicole Wickley. She was in various poses and costumes in scenes from plays and acting jobs she had done over the years. My sluggish brain came back on line as I realized what I was looking at.

"The wigs!" I said suddenly, leaning forward. The kiss was anything but forgotten, however I managed to shelve it for the moment as I looked at Brandon to see if he was seeing what I was.

"I told you there were no wig stands in her bedroom." I felt triumphant, vindicated. "Didn't I tell you there should have been some?"

"What are you talking about?"

"That's Elaine Russo!"

His eyes narrowed. He angled the screen in his direction and studied the picture of the brunette in a blond wig.

"I think you're right."

"You know I'm right. How can you sit there looking so calm?"

George leaped onto the desk and curled on the edge closest to Brandon. Brandon reached out to stroke the animal's head absently. The cat purred loudly in contentment.

"If I start yelling, I'll upset the cat," he said.

"Nicole Wickley's been posing as Elaine Russo!"

"Or Nicole Wickley and Elaine Russo are the same person."

I swallowed an instant denial and thought about that. "Is that possible?"

"Why not? What do we know about Elaine Russo?"

"Nothing except that she likes to see her name in the paper, is a poor tipper and isn't generally well liked."

"Sort of sounds like what that couple implied about Nicole Wickley, wouldn't you say? Let's see what the computer can tell us about Elaine."

A simple search of her name in the computer told us surprisingly little. She served on several charitable organizations. Her picture had made the society pages of *The Plain Dealer* more than once, but other than that, she didn't seem to exist. We brought up several of the newspaper pictures and tried for comparisons to Nicole's Web page. Unfortunately the pictures were too small and too grainy to tell us much.

"Could be Nicole but it's hard to be sure."

"Why isn't there a wedding announcement?" I asked.

"Maybe the Russos didn't get married in Cleveland. Or they didn't put an announcement in the paper. Not everyone does, you know."

"Or they aren't really married."

He stopped petting George to look at me.

"Brandon, I don't think these pictures are of the same woman."

He sat back. "Nicole Wickley is the Elaine Russo I met."

"I agree. But there weren't any wigs in Elaine's bedroom."

"Okay, explain these wigs to me again."

"I found a strand of long blond hair from a wig in her otherwise spotless car the night I was tailing her. It was a hot night like tonight. I'm pretty sure the Jaguar had just been cleaned. No one wears a wig if they don't have to on a night like that. If Elaine Russo is a blonde, she doesn't need to wear a blond wig. If she's a brunette and does wear wigs, she'd have some in her house. Say Elaine and Nicole are the same person. And say as Nicole she keeps a separate apartment for her acting persona. Do you really think she wouldn't have kept some stuff at the house that overlapped, like a wig or two? We didn't see anything at all—not even stage makeup. That simply doesn't make sense."

He tapped his finger against the desktop. George batted at his finger.

"I'll tell you something else that bothers me," he continued. "Whether Elaine and Nicole are the same person or not, why did she keep a .38 tucked up under the seat of her Jag the night she met you? I can see her wanting to carry a gun for protection, but why not carry it in her purse?"

Brandon straightened up so fast that George jumped down from the desk, startled. Immediately the cat set to grooming himself, as if to prove it didn't matter to him if the crazy humans were acting weird.

"She never mentioned having a gun," he said.

"Seems to be a lot of things she didn't mention. I can run an in-depth computer search on Elaine and Nicole, but it will take time."

"How much time?"

"Depends. A couple of hours, maybe less."

He shook his head. "It can wait until morning. You really think we've got two different women here?"

"Yes."

"Because of the gun?"

"Because of the wigs and the gun."

Brandon fell silent as he studied the picture of Nicole Wickley in the blond wig, then flipped to the picture of Elaine Russo at a society gathering.

"All right, we have two different women. In a way it makes perfect sense. If Russo knew Elaine called me, he wouldn't want her meeting me, but if I never heard from her again after her initial contact, he could be sure I wouldn't rest until I found out why."

"So he hired Nicole to pose as Elaine. That doesn't bode well for Elaine."

"No," Brandon agreed.

"I wonder when Russo started seeing Nicole Wickley."

Brandon looked at me with approval. "It's always possible the two of them were already seeing each other when this happened."

"You think he picked a local actress who just happens to look remarkably like his wife to have an affair with?" I sneered.

"Some men actually prefer a certain type."

Implying that Brandon didn't? I wasn't sure I wanted to know the answer to that question. I was nothing like his pretty blonde and I'd be tasting his lips all night as it was.

"Nicole is fairly well known locally," I told him. "She does those Jerry's Cars ads on television."

His eyes lit. "Better and better. What do you want to bet Elaine's friends and Albert's friends have commented on how much they look alike? I bet it won't take much digging to find out."

"We'd have to find out who their friends were, first."

"You have pictures of Elaine's friends, don't you? It's a start."

"Hold it. You think Nicole met Elaine's friends the night I followed her? I don't think so. I'd certainly know if someone came to me pretending to be my friend Sharon or Lorna or someone I knew well."

Brandon sat back in his chair. "Well, I doubt if Nicole met a group of her own friends while pretending to be Elaine. She had to have met a group of Elaine's friends."

"That's nuts."

"Risky, certainly, but what if it was a group of women Elaine only saw infrequently, say, on a committee? And what if Nicole told them she'd just had plastic surgery or some cosmetic procedure, maybe BOTOX injections or something like that? She didn't spend much time with them. And if she didn't spend much time with them on a regular basis and they expected to meet her at a prearranged place and time and she showed up with maybe a health-related story about her appearance, would they really know it wasn't her?"

I mulled that over.

"Don't forget Nicole is an actress," he added. "She plays roles all the time."

"I still think I'd know the difference, but I guess it would depend on what she said and how good she is. But it still seems unlikely."

"I agree. However let's assume she's very good and these weren't close friends."

"But why would she take that risk?"

Brandon's gaze narrowed thoughtfully.

"If we're right and Nicole is posing as Elaine, I'm guessing she and Russo found out about this dinner meeting at the last minute. Rather than raise questions by not showing up at all, Nicole went with some excuse for a discrepancy in her appearance, met them and used another excuse not to stay and hoped for the best."

I felt cold. There was only one reason I could think of for Nicole Wickley to take such a huge risk.

"They killed her, didn't they? They killed her and set us up," I said, feeling my outrage building.

"It's starting to look that way," he agreed calmly. "That would explain why Nicole kept me so busy on the way to Pennsylvania that night. She knew you were following us. You were supposed to photograph us going into that hotel room."

"Why?" I asked, trying to get it straight in my head.

He tapped the edge of the desk unconsciously as he considered the situation. "So as Elaine, Nicole could show up in Albert's office the next afternoon and create a public scene, remember? Everyone who was there certainly does. Nicole made it clear I was having an affair with Elaine."

"Ohmygod, so when her body turned up, the first person the police were going to look at—"

"Well, maybe the second. The husband would still be the first, but I'm sure he'd already set the frame a bit tighter."

"Wait a minute, wait a minute! Then why would Russo warn me off? Why try to run you off the road? That doesn't make sense."

Brandon shook his head, but for once his normally bright eyes had a dark expression I'd never seen before.

"Oh, yeah, in some convoluted fashion I think it does. We just have to put all the pieces together. You see, they don't want you involved because I don't think I'm supposed to be alive when they find Elaine Russo's body."

Chapter Ten

I was furious that he could be so nonchalant over such a supposition and we were still debating that issue when we finally left the store a good while later, having resolved nothing at all. My aunt had driven Binky back to my apartment, so Brandon had to drive me home. I was considering whether to invite him up or not when I suddenly remembered I was supposed to stop by and check on Mrs. Keene's house.

"Sorry, but I did promise."

"That's okay. It's late enough that our rose-and-candy-bearing burglar should have been and gone a long time ago by now."

Turned out he'd been there all right. When we circled the house, checking, we found the screen door ajar on the back porch. The back door was unlocked. To my complete shock, Brandon produced a gun from a leg holster I hadn't even suspected he was wearing.

"What are you doing?"

"Be quiet," he breathed in my ear. "Wait here!"

He went in through the back door like some

movie-star hero while my insides iced over. I waited as long as I could, then I crept inside after him. Mrs. Keene had left the hall light on. Or someone had. A dozen red roses sat in a crystal vase on the center of her kitchen table. Propped on one of her old kitchen chairs was a giant pink-and-white panda bear with a huge yellow bow around its neck. In front of the bear on the table was another gift-wrapped two-pound box of Malley's chocolates. There was no note.

I wasn't sure what I felt. Giddy. A little scared. Amused. Sort of sick when I thought about the young guy we'd seen running away. What was going on here? Brandon came back down the hall putting his gun away.

"Don't you know the meaning of the word *wait?*" he demanded.

"I didn't come charging after you, did I?"

He looked disgruntled as he straightened his pant leg.

"The house is clear. You'd better call her."

"It could wait until morning."

He gave me one of those looks Aunt Lacy is so fond of and I pulled my cell phone out of my purse. I had to dig for the number I'd written down when I'd spoken to Mrs. Keene earlier. Despite the hour, which felt late, Mrs. Keene sounded alert and chipper and not at all dismayed that I was calling her. She was clearly excited rather than upset when I told her what we'd found.

"A teddy bear, you say? And more chocolates? Oh,

my. No, Ellie, I told you he'd be back. Well, they aren't good for my waistline, but I do love the light-chocolate creams. Now, Dee, I told you I don't want you calling the police. Besides, he didn't break in. I never lock my back door. Everyone knows that. I'll be right there. Ellie's house is over here on Arden. It won't take me long to get home at this hour."

I disconnected and offered Brandon a rueful shrug. "She doesn't want us to call the police. She never locks her back door. Everyone knows that. She's on her way."

Brandon closed his eyes.

"This would be sort of sweet if he wasn't young enough to be her grandson."

Brandon opened his eyes. "You think this is sweet?"

"Well, it's like he's courting her or something. I mean, flowers and candy. And a teddy bear?"

"Sweet."

"You know, I've never heard anyone put quite so much sour into that word before."

For several long, long seconds he didn't say anything at all. And then he did.

"Come here."

And I'd never heard anyone put so much suggestion into those two words before, either. The entire atmosphere in the room changed. It was just a kitchen, but suddenly it wasn't. The room dissolved until there was just Brandon and me and a melting gaze that promised all sorts of dangerous, exciting things.

Every molecule of my body had been on some sort of male-female alert since the moment I'd met this man. Now, as his gaze skimmed my body, I felt as though he'd touched me at several heated points. My insides were actually fluttering with a wildness that affected my breathing just short of outright panting. My lips hungrily remembered his earlier kiss, and even while I told myself it wasn't wise, I crossed the room to *here*. Heck, wild horses and baying wolves couldn't have kept me from going to *here*.

He made a sound low in his throat that was almost a chuckle and sounded suspiciously of masculine satisfaction as he slid his arms around me and pulled me against all that lean, muscled firmness.

"You're something else, you know that, D.B. Hayes?"

It felt as if something inside me would snap if this delicious tension went on much longer.

"Are you going to stand there talking until Mrs. Keene comes home or are you going to kiss me?" I demanded.

His lips curved. "Oh, I'm definitely going to kiss you. I prefer a little sass to *sweet*."

And before I could tell him to get on with it already, he did.

I already knew he knew where the noses went, but he also knew where the tongue went, as well—and how to use it in ways that made me wet and hotter than I'd ever been in my life. Who knew the ear could be an erogenous zone? Certainly none of the guys I'd ever dated.

I'm not sure when Brandon pressed me back up against the refrigerator, but suddenly I felt the cool metal door against my back as my dress rode up my thighs and he deliberately inserted his leg between mine. The feeling was highly erotic. His pant leg pressed against my bare skin while his mouth worked its way down the curve of my neck.

I became aware that one hand was gently cupping my breast through my dress and bra, lightly pinching my erect nipple, and I didn't mind a bit. In fact, I was doing my best to arch and give him better access. I pulled his face to mine and kissed him back, feeling the press of his arousal against my thigh.

Suddenly he jerked his head up. His body tensed, listening hard. To my whimpering dismay, he stepped back, straightening his clothes.

"Mrs. Keene's home," he said gruffly.

"Tell her to go away," I muttered fiercely.

His chuckle sounded as rocky as I felt. "Better make yourself presentable. I'll stall her."

While I stood there, grateful for the refrigerator's support, he bent and retrieved something from the floor. Handing me a white orchid, he kissed the tip of my nose.

"And, Dee, so you know? You kiss like one sexy adult."

I was pretty sure that wasn't meant to be an insult, but I couldn't quite get my brain to function at the moment. I could feel my hair tumbling about my face. On legs of rubber I made my way to the hall bathroom off the kitchen and stared at the stranger's face in the mirror there. My lips were puffy and swollen, my eyelids half closed. The eye shadow was gone without a trace, as was the lipstick, of course, but my cheeks were a bright, vivid shade of scarlet. The rest of the orchids hung limply to one side of my head. My hair was back to its usual tangled lack of style.

A small bruise was forming on my neck where Brandon had applied a little too much passion. I hadn't had a hickey since high school. I couldn't believe he'd given me one now. Even worse, I couldn't believe the sight excited me.

How far had I been willing to let him go tonight?

The answer was scary. I was twenty-four—almost twenty-five years old. Did I really still believe in Prince Charming and happily ever after? And if I did, was I stupid enough to think Brandon was going to step into a pair of tights and a plumed hat? Not likely.

So, could I overcome years of indoctrination and fall into bed and have great sex with a man I'd just met? A man who was my professional rival? A man who left women panting in his wake just by smiling at them? A man who was driving me around town in his date's minivan? I was really, really afraid the answer to those questions might be yes.

The two of them were just entering the kitchen when I came out of the bathroom. Mrs. Keene looked like a child on Christmas morning. Even in the dim light I saw her face glowing in delight. It didn't seem to bother her a bit that the person—a young man—had illegally entered her home while she wasn't there to leave the tribute.

It took all Brandon's considerable charm to get her to stop cooing over the stuffed bear and check out the house and be sure nothing was missing. According to her, nothing was.

"Isn't it exciting, Dee? I have a secret admirer."

"Mrs. Keene, he's a young man."

She gave a girlish giggle. "I know. Isn't that just too charming? I wonder what he'll bring me tomorrow?"

Nothing we could say would change her mind about notifying the police. When we finally got back in the minivan, Brandon started the engine but didn't put the car in gear.

"I'm going to call Dex," he said.

"She doesn't want us to call the police."

"We won't make an official report, but he ought to know what's going on. What if there's been a pattern like this somewhere else? This could be some pervert's MO."

"For what purpose? I mean, he already got inside her house. What does she have that anyone would want?"

"I don't know." He pulled out his cell phone. "But I don't—"

"What's wrong?" I could tell from his abrupt silence and the way he stared at his phone that something was wrong. He glanced at his watch, then at me. I didn't know what time it was, but I knew it was late.

"Someone tried to call me an hour ago. I had the phone set to vibrate. I didn't feel it go off."

Probably because we were setting off our own vibrations an hour ago, but I didn't need to remind him of that.

"Call them back."

"They called from my apartment, Dee. No one should have been inside my apartment."

"One of your family? You should call them."

"My dad has a key, so does my sister-in-law, but it's really late. If it wasn't one of them, I'll wake them and worry them for nothing."

And if it had been... I felt the same sense of urgency I saw in his eyes. "We should go to your place."

"I'll take you home first."

"Don't waste time. Besides, you might need help."

We were on the same wavelength. He looked at me with dark eyes. "You've got a gun?"

"Not with me, but I can create a mean distraction."

He almost smiled. "That you can."

We practically broke the sound barrier going across the bridge into Rocky River. If we'd passed one cop car, we'd have been busted for sure, but the roads were empty. Based on all the blinking yellow traffic lights, it was much later than I'd dreamed.

Brandon had a ground-floor apartment in a small complex off Detroit Road, not far from his office. We swept through the parking lot slowly with our lights off. Nothing looked odd or out of place. The night was filled with the usual sounds.

Inside the building he checked his front door for booby traps—something I wouldn't even have thought to do—while I stood there and tried not to shiver. He went in with his weapon drawn, and I hoped none of his neighbors would happen along and call the cops on us.

I kept expecting to hear shots. The silence was actually scary. And I had reason to be scared.

Brandon had briefed me on the layout. A one-bedroom unit much along the lines of mine with a living/dining room area, a kitchen, bathroom and bedroom. I knew about how long it should have taken to sweep the entire place. When he didn't come out after three minutes, I went in.

A large brown sectional couch took up most of the living room. There was a shirt thrown over the end of the couch. A pair of scuffed tennis shoes sat where they'd been toed off beneath a pine coffee table that was home to several soda cans, beer bottles, newspapers and the remains of what appeared to be Chinese carryout.

A good-size pine wall unit housed his TV and stereo. Two arching metal floor lamps came up and over either end of the sectional to provide lighting. The dining area had a small pine table and four chairs. The table held mail and papers and a coffee cup. That was the extent of the visible furniture. The small coat closet stood open, a tennis racket spilling out.

I already knew neatness wasn't one of his virtues, so the clutter didn't bother me. Brandon's darkly forbidding expression, however, did. It sent spears of icy fear straight to my nerve endings as he appeared outside his bedroom door.

He put his finger over his lips, motioning me to silence when I would have asked him what was wrong. My fear multiplied as he all but shoved me out into the hall and closed the apartment door quietly behind us.

When I opened my mouth to give voice to my fear, he shook his head. Silently I followed him back to the van, my nerves screaming.

"What's going on?" I demanded as soon as I climbed in and he started the engine.

"Which is closer—your place or your dad's?"

"My apartment. Will you please tell me what's going on?"

"Delvecchi's on my bed. He's got a hole through the back of his head."

"Ohmygod!"

"Give me the address."

"What?"

"Give me your damn address! We need to get you away from here!"

"Are you crazy? We have to call the police!"

"After I get you out of here!"

"Look, I appreciate your noble need for self-sac-
rifice—"

"Don't you get it? It's another setup. How are we
going to explain this to the cops?"

"We tell them the truth!"

"Dee…"

He struggled for words, closed his eyes and took
a deep breath before opening them and looking at
me again.

"I *was* a cop, remember? My father was a cop.
Will you trust me on this? Please. I need to take you
home. Here's the story you tell, and you stick to it
no matter who asks, no matter what they say, no
matter how you think it will help me to tell the truth.
We went to dinner. We went to the play. We went to
the flower shop to check something on your computer. It is no one's business what we were checking. It's private and none of their affair. Stick to that!
Then we swung by Mrs. Keene's house. After that I
drove you straight back to your place. We sat in your
parking lot and talked for a little while. Then you
went inside. You never looked at a clock. You have
no idea what time it was. That's all you know. Can
you do that? Can you stay with that story?"

I was scared. Stomach-clenchingly, mind-numb-
ingly scared silly. The intensity was sheeting off him
in waves and I understood. This was our alibi. *His*
alibi.

"I can stick." I wanted to throw up.

"Thanks. What's the address?"

I gave it to him and he drove even more quickly back into Lakewood than we'd left.

"Brandon, why didn't someone hear the shot?"

"I'm guessing a silencer. But it is a Friday night. Lots of people would be out and about."

"Someone must have seen something."

"We can hope."

He didn't sound like he had much. By the time I let myself into my apartment, I had a bad case of the shakes, because it had occurred to me that if Albert Russo had left a dead Hogan Delvecchi in Brandon's bedroom, he just might have left a dead Elaine Russo in mine. Part of me was glad that hadn't occurred to Brandon, as well. The other part wished it had, because he didn't come inside with me and I did not want to go in there alone.

The living area looked exactly as I had left it. I inched open the bedroom door with all the bravado I usually reserve for water bugs and other cockroaches. The bed was blissfully empty. I began to breathe once more. Mama cat looked up from the closet, where her babies cuddled close. I sat down on the floor beside her and gave in to the pressing urge to cry.

Admittedly it wasn't very professional, but I felt too full of too many emotions not to give vent to some sort of release. My tears didn't last long. I picked up one of the little gray kittens and petted its small head. The multicolored one squirmed its way

over to my knee, so I picked it up, as well. There wa
something soothing about holding the tiny kitten
and I began telling mama cat about my day, worry
ing about what was happening at Brandon's apart
ment.

I consoled Mama and myself with the knowledge
that Brandon knew what he was doing. Even so, why
was Hogan Delvecchi dead on Brandon's bed? Who
had called to tell him so? Was Albert Russo trying
to frame him for the murder? And where were Ni
cole Wickley and the real Elaine Russo? Was Elaine
dead or not?

When the telephone rang, it woke me from a deep
sleep. For one long, hazy minute I didn't remember
getting undressed or falling into bed. It didn't feel
as if I had been there very long. My eyes were gritty
and unfocused as I reached blindly for the persistent
instrument.

"Hello?"

"Dee? Are you sick?"

"Aunt Lacy? What time is it?"

"It's ten-fifteen. Were you asleep?"

"Ten-fifteen?" I sat up, wide awake.

"Dee, I think you need to get down here. You have
some people waiting here to see you."

"The police?"

Aunt Lacy made an unhappy sound that could
have been assent.

"It's okay, Aunt Lacy. Let me throw some clothes
on and I'll be right there."

I decided no matter who it was, they could wait long enough for me to take a quick shower and wash the sleep from my eyes. Then, of course, I had to clean the litter box and feed Mama. Since I was going to face the police at some point, it seemed prudent to look as young and innocent as humanly possible, so I pulled a soft-lime sundress from the closet and pulled my hair on top of my head into a loose ponytail. Leaving last night's earrings in place, I grabbed my sandals and a caffeinated cola from the refrigerator and headed out the door.

The store looked like we were holding a rummage sale. I had to park halfway down the block and go in through the back just to get inside. I caught Trudy's eyes and she gestured toward the office, where a uniformed officer stood talking with Aunt Lacy. He turned in profile and I relaxed.

"Hey, Allen," I greeted.

Allen Longsworth turned toward me. A stocky man with thinning brown hair and a sharp widow's peak, he'd dated a friend of mine off and on through much of high school. We'd had several classes together and even sat near each other in English class our junior year.

"Hey, Dee. How's it going?"

"Pretty good. I didn't know you joined the police force."

"Last year," he said, looking almost embarrassed. "Uh, Dee, this is Detective Martin from the Rocky River police force. He'd like to ask you a couple of questions."

"Sure thing. Hi, Detective. Nice to meet you."

"Ms. Hayes. Is there someplace we could go to talk that's a little more private?"

"I'll shoo everyone out of here, Detective," my aunt promised. "You can use the office, Dee."

"Thanks, Aunt Lacy. Sorry I overslept this morning. Late night last night. Gentlemen, come on in. Go ahead and close the door. It's a little cozy in here, but we'll fit."

I walked around the desk with a calm that should have won me an Emmy at the very least and settled carefully in the truculent chair behind the desk. Detective Martin took a seat, but Allen remained standing in front of the closed door. Keeping me in or others out? I didn't like either thought.

"How may I help you?"

"Would you tell me where you were last night?"

"Okay, I figure this is an official inquiry, so sure, but may I ask why?"

"We're trying to verify an alibi, Ms. Hayes."

"Brandon needs an alibi? Oh, this is rich. You do know he's my competition, right?"

Detective Martin did not appear to have a sense of humor. I figured it was okay if a little of my unease showed through, but I was supposed to be a professional so I tried to act like one. I stayed with the script as directed. I named the restaurant and told them what play we'd gone to see. I even mentioned that there was a substitute actress in for the lead so they'd know we'd actually attended. I did not mention Nicole Wickley's apartment building and I tried to skim over the fact that we'd stopped here at the store to use my computer. I fully expected the detective to jump on that. He didn't disappoint me.

"You came here after the play to use your computer? Pardon me if that seems strange, but why would you do that?"

I tried to look embarrassed. "A question came up during the play. We, uh, wanted to do some research."

"What sort of research?"

I arched my eyebrows. It was only my reputation, after all. Let him think what he wanted. I saw Allen looking at me speculatively and knew he was thinking along the lines I was trying to promote.

"I really don't see the relevance to that question, Detective Martin," I told him. "You didn't ask me the specifics of what we had for dinner. I had pasta Alfredo, if it matters. The point is, if any of the local patrol officers were making their rounds and paying attention, they certainly saw the van Brandon was driving parked in the lot out back. We weren't trying to hide or anything. On the other hand, we didn't turn on a lot of lights to draw attention, either."

The detective didn't push any further. He did, however, want to know why we had gone to see my father's next-door neighbor so late. I was prepared for that.

"Detective Martin, as you're well aware, I'm a licensed private investigator. I know I don't look like

one and I know a lot of police officers don't have much
respect for what I do, but I take my job seriously. Mrs.
Keene is my client. If she wants you to know why we
were there at that hour, she'll tell you. Brandon was
only with me because I had promised to stop by at
some point last night and it had gotten late. He didn't
want me going back there after he dropped me at
home, all right? We left her house—"

"What time was that?"

"I don't know, to tell you the truth. I wasn't wearing
a watch last night. I didn't put one on this morning, either, you'll notice. I tend to forget my watch. It's a fail-
ing of mine. So is being on time. I know it was late
because the traffic lights were flashing yellow when
Brandon drove me home. We sat and talked outside my
apartment for a while. Then I went in and played with
the kittens and went to bed. Would you like to know
the number and color markings on the kittens?"

"And you never looked at a clock at any point?"
he asked, ignoring the kitten remark.

"Believe it or not, no, I didn't." At least that was
the complete truth. "If I'd known Brandon was going
to need an alibi, I'd have made a point of noting
times, but it was a date, not a job. I'm sure even at
your advanced age you remember dating, Detective.
We had an enjoyable evening out, like any other pair
of mature adults. Now, I've been a good, cooperative
little witness, so in the interests of professional courtesy, you want to tell me what this is all about?"

Detective Martin managed his scowl. I had the

distinct impression he didn't quite know what to make of me and I was doing my best to foster his confusion. I looked innocent, hopefully sounded intelligent if a bit scatterbrained and I'd seemed relatively forthcoming.

"A man was shot and killed in Mr. Kirkpatrick's apartment sometime last night. Mr. Kirkpatrick discovered the body when he returned home."

I tried to let just the right amount of surprise flash in my eyes. It wouldn't do to overact here.

"Who was killed?"

"You don't seem shocked, Ms. Hayes."

"Shock is for winning the lottery or finding exactly the right color shoes to go with the dress you're going to wear to your best friend's wedding. I'm a private investigator, Detective Martin, just like Brandon. I didn't figure you were looking for an alibi because he forgot to take the trash out."

"Do you know what cases he's been working on lately?"

"Hardly. I believe I mentioned we're competitors?"

"Yet you're dating."

"That's personal. Have you seen the man?" I rolled my eyes and raised my brows expressively. I caught Allen grinning.

"I won't take up any more of your time then," he said, getting to his feet.

"Not going to tell me who was killed?"

"I can't release that information pending notification of the next of kin."

Somehow the idea of Hogan Delvecchi having a next of kin made his death more real. The officer set a business card on the desk.

"Someone will be in touch with you to follow up and take an official statement."

"It'll be the same statement I just gave you."

He gave a terse nod and strode out the door past Allen. Allen offered me a goodbye nod, looking sympathetic. The crush of people out front had diminished significantly, but Trudy and my aunt were still busy, for which I was grateful. I needed a few minutes to pull myself together. I returned to the office and collapsed on the chair, nearly ending up on the floor in the process.

I cursed the chair and my sleep-fogged brain as I strained to think. I'd done what Brandon had ordered, but it wouldn't last. How could it? As soon as the police started investigating Hogan Delvecchi, they'd be back. It wouldn't take them long to find out he'd been here in Flower World only a couple of days ago.

This, I realized, was why Brandon hadn't wanted them to find me in his apartment last night. The situation was going to get complicated. Anything I said was only going to dig his hole a little deeper—or our hole, once they realized the truth.

What was Brandon's expression? Kimchi. We were in deep kimchi.

There was a brisk tap on the door. I raised my head from where I'd buried it in my arms on the desk and found Aunt Lacy regarding me with eyes creased with worry.

"What happened last night?" she demanded.

I lifted my head all the way off the desk. "Nothing," I told her truthfully.

She stared at my neck. I felt the blush start somewhere around my navel and work its way up from there. I'd forgotten all about the hickey. Oh, heck. No wonder Detective Martin hadn't pushed about what we'd been doing here in the office. Well, I'd been trying to foster that very impression, hadn't I?

"We have several orders that have to get out this afternoon. Are you free to help, or should we call Florence?"

Florence Olesky was a friend of Trudy's who helped out whenever we were shorthanded. I was sorely tempted to tell her to call the other woman, but while I was still trying to work through the situation in my head, it helped to have something to do with my hands. It also, I realized, helped to talk to Aunt Lacy and Trudy—or would have except for the pursed-lipped disapproval so clear on Aunt Lacy's features.

I found I resented that. She was fine with me being a detective as long as I dabbled and didn't have a "real" case. Not that I was getting paid for this case, but that didn't matter. What counted was that what I was doing was important—and dangerous. So Aunt Lacy did not approve and she was making her view clear.

Bearing in mind what Brandon had told me, I did not tell them everything about last night. Basically I stayed with what I had told Detective Martin, leaving out our stop at Nicole's apartment. Aunt Lacy's attitude made it easy to skim details.

"Exactly why did you come back here?" she demanded.

I tried to ignore the censure in her tone. "My computer was here. We ran a check on Nicole Wickley and guess what? She's the woman we both know as Elaine Russo."

"What happened to Elaine Russo?" Trudy asked.

"That's what I'd like the two of you to help me find out."

Trudy raised a single eyebrow but looked pleased, while Aunt Lacy's lips thinned to nothing.

"I think you should forget about all of this before someone gets hurt."

"Too late. Delvecchi's dead and they want to tag Brandon for his murder."

Her expression flattened. "That horrible man who was here is dead?"

Oops. "Forget I said that."

"*He's* the man Brandon killed?"

I faced my aunt feeling more angry than I could ever remember being in my entire life.

"Brandon did not kill anyone! He was with *me*

when Delvecchi was killed. If they try him for that murder, they'll come after me, as well, because we *were* together."

"In a biblical sense?" she sniffed.

"Lacy!"

I dropped the mutilated daisy on the table and stared at my aunt. She didn't lower her eyes. The bell out front rang, indicating a customer.

"Think what you like," I said.

In three strides I crossed to the office, snatched up my purse and headed for the back door. Trudy blocked my way. Aunt Lacy had gone up front to deal with the customer.

"She didn't mean it, Dee."

I was shaking. "She meant it. This isn't going to work, Trudy. I knew the situation was questionable from the start."

"She loves you."

"Love isn't the issue here. I don't have the time or energy right now for her feelings about my work."

"She's just upset."

"Tough. So am I."

"Dee, please. Let me help."

I wanted to storm on out and tell her I didn't need her help, but that was a gut reaction and unfair. I wasn't mad at Trudy. I wasn't even mad at Aunt Lacy. I knew my family didn't approve of my being a private investigator. I'd thought at least Aunt Lacy respected my right to choose my own lifestyle. I'd always respected hers.

"You want to help? Get me whatever information you can on the four principals involved. Elaine Russo and Nicole Wickley. Who are their friends? Where were Albert and Elaine married? How long ago? Where does Elaine come from? What do we know about Russo? He's not homegrown. When did he first show up in Cleveland? Who backed him? Who's behind him now? When did he start seeing Nicole Wickley? That last one is especially pertinent. How long has Delvecchi worked for Russo? In general, whatever the gossip mill has, I need to know."

"I'll get what I can. Where are you going?"

"To call in every favor I can. If Elaine left town, there'll be a money trail I can follow. Susan Arrensky works for the same bank Russo uses. I'm going to find out how grateful she is for my help with her divorce case."

"Dee, wait and talk to your aunt," she pleaded.

"Later. I've had very little sleep and I'm upset. You'd better call Florence to come in and give you a hand for a while. I'm going to be pretty busy until all this gets resolved."

SUSAN ARRENSKY WAS DELIGHTED to see me until I told her what I wanted. I'd gotten there right before the bank closed at noon, but she'd ushered me into her office anyhow. She got up in a hurry and closed the glass door.

"Dee, you know I can't give you someone else's account information."

"I don't want specific information. I only want to know if there's been activity." I leaned in close and brought my voice down to little more than a whisper. "Susan, this is between you and me and only because I know you so well. It's going to be a police matter soon enough. This information doesn't leave this room. I'm trusting you."

Susan leaned toward me, her eyes wide.

"I have reason to believe Elaine Russo was murdered."

"No," she breathed.

"You can help me check by looking to see if there's been any activity in her accounts in the past few days. That's all I'm asking. Will you help?"

I watched her think about that. "A favor for a favor?"

It was my turn to hesitate.

"Lyle threatened to destroy my grandmother's loving cup."

I was already shaking my head. I knew what was coming even before she had the words out of her mouth.

"You get the cup away from him for me, I'll get you the information."

"I could lose my license!"

"*I* could go to jail! Do we have a deal?"

I closed my eyes. "Deal."

Susan turned back to her computer. "You wouldn't happen to have her social-security number, would you?"

"Better." I pulled out the copy I'd made of Russo's check to me.

"You're right. This is better."

She punched a few keys and studied the screen Her brows knit. "Wait here a minute, okay?"

That didn't bode well and it gave me time to stew over what came next. How was I going to steal the ugly loving cup away from Lyle Arrensky without getting arrested for illegal entry, or worse, pulverized by one of his hamlike fists?

Susan was gone long enough to add to my nerves. I was actually thinking about getting up and leaving when she returned with a peculiar expression on her face.

"Your check was drawn to an account held solely by Albert Russo. Elaine had her own accounts."

"Past tense?"

Susan shifted uncomfortably. "I could get in a lot of trouble for even answering that question, but yes. She closed out her checking and savings accounts last Friday."

"Are you sure it was Elaine Russo?"

"What do you mean?"

"It wasn't someone posing as her?"

Her mouth fell open. I should have kept that bit to myself. I stood and faced her. "Susan, when the cops come or you talk to your dad, we never had this conversation."

She grabbed my arm. "You won't forget the loving cup?"

"I won't forget." If I lived to be a thousand, I'd never forget that ugly loving cup. My life seemed in-

exorably tied to that stupid loving cup—and Lyle Arrensky.

I stepped outside the bank and my cell phone
rang. Caller ID said it was a pay phone so I answered cautiously. Brandon's voice, mixed with
static, filled my ear.

"Can you spare a lift?"

"Where are you?"

"Rocky River Police Station."

"I can be there in fifteen minutes."

"Ten would be better."

"I don't think getting a ticket would be advisable
right now, but I'll see what I can do."

Traffic was bad. It took closer to eighteen minutes.
He was standing outside in the hot sun looking rum-
pled and tired to the bone. He was still dressed in last
night's suit, sans tie, with the shirt unbuttoned at the
collar and the jacket slung over his shoulder. He
needed a shave and his hair was badly finger-combed
and he still looked better than any man had a right to
look. Just seeing him produced a tingle low in my
belly that sent all my female hormones dancing and
prancing in anticipation.

He surprised me further by giving me a quick kiss
as he folded himself inside Binky and sank back
with a sigh.

"Rough morning?" I asked.

"I've had better. How about you?"

"About the same. They sent a Detective Martin
over to the shop. He was very polite."

"You didn't—"

"Tell anyone anything beyond the script we agreed to," I assured him. "I have, however, managed to unearth one interesting tidbit. Elaine Russo—or maybe Nicole Wickley posing as Elaine Russo—walked in and cleaned out Elaine Russo's checking and savings accounts last Friday."

His head whipped toward me. Satisfied with the reaction, I put the car in gear and started driving.

"I think it would be interesting to see if either one of them booked a flight out of town since then. What do you think?"

"I think I'm in desperate need of a shower, some clean clothes, a decent meal and a full night's sleep before I'm going to be capable of coherent thought," he said slowly. "My unit's now a crime scene. Think your father would mind if I used his place again? We could stop and pick up some clothes at the mall on the way over."

"No problem. I can swing by Westgate Shopping Center. Uh, Brandon, we have a tail."

"Yeah. I'm not surprised. They want me to know I'm being watched. They think I killed him. Still think your father won't mind?"

Since I was still smarting over my aunt's disapproval, I was more than ready to tackle my dad if he raised an objection, but I didn't think he would. Dad's generally pretty easygoing about most things. Of course, I'd never brought a murder suspect home for dinner before.

"Come to think about it," Brandon added, "do you mind?"

"No." Maybe I said that a little too sharply, because he frowned at me. "I sort of let the police think we went back to Flower World to, uh, make out last night."

His lips curved.

"Well, what did you tell them?" I asked.

"That it was none of their business."

He gave me the sort of heated look that would have steered Binky right off the road if I hadn't stopped for a red light.

Deep kimchi. Very deep kimchi.

And the curve of his lips became a grin, as if he knew exactly what I was thinking.

"Mind if I borrow your cell phone?" he asked. "I never got to recharge mine last night and the battery died."

I indicated my purse with a wave of my hand. Words were a little beyond me at the moment.

"Hey there, Fred, it's Brandon. Uh-huh. I know. Sorry about that. Listen, gorgeous…"

My head swiveled. The driver of the brown Chevy leaned on her horn as I swerved into her lane as I started through the light.

"…I've got a favor to ask," he continued unperturbed.

I forced my gaze back to the road. My attention, however, was totally focused on the conversation taking place beside me.

"Ah, chicky, you wound me to the core. Of course it's you I love above all others. How about lunch next week and five big ones to ease the pain of our separation? Uh-huh. Yep, it's that important. Trust me, my love, I'm between the proverbial rock and a hard place at the moment. No. I need it all. Names, dates, how they paid— Uh-huh. Right. Hold on a sec."

He began rummaging through my purse as I turned into the shopping center without causing a wreck. After fishing for a second he pulled out a pen with a duck cap on the end. I'd forgotten the stupid pen was in there.

"Go ahead, Fred."

He began writing on his arm.

"Got it. You're a beautiful person. See you Tuesday. 'Bye."

I pulled into a parking space, turned off the engine and regarded him steadily.

"Care to explain?"

"Might be more fun to let you sit there and stew."

I tapped the steering wheel. "Think so?"

"Uh, maybe not. It just cost me five hundred dollars and lunch on Tuesday, but I got it," he said. "Do you realize at the rate the cost of bribes keeps going up no client is going to be able to afford us?"

"We don't have a client."

"Good thing. We'd play hell collecting on this bill."

"What exactly is the *it* you just got?"

"Your entrance into the master database at Cleveland Hopkins Airport to see who booked tickets on flights going in and out of there in the past twenty-four hours, both domestic and international."

I tried not to look impressed. "My entrance."

"While I'm taking a shower, you can see whose name pops up."

He unfolded himself from Binky's interior and headed for the mall entrance. I had to run to keep up with him.

"You're not joking."

"I don't joke about five hundred dollars. Alfreda Tikku was a friend of my brother's. Now she's mine."

"Expensive friend."

"Worth every dollar."

I mulled that over as we went into the men's department. One of the fundamental differences between males and females is the way they shop for clothing. Most women I know try on several outfits after looking over everything on offer. After that they still may not buy anything at all. The men I know go in, look at the size, pull the item off the rack and their shopping experience is over. We were in and out in under thirty minutes and then only because we had to wait for someone to ring up the sale.

We made a second stop at the pharmacy for toilet articles and then we were back in Binky and on our way into Lakewood, our tail still glued in place. I resisted the urge to wave.

I'd left my laptop at the store, but Dad has a home office in the third bedroom upstairs. I felt a little guilty about using his computer to run the illegal hack, but since I'd been given the password, I figured it would be all right.

We had to go right past the grocery store, so I stopped for dinner fixings. My stomach was rumbling and Brandon said he hadn't eaten anything resembling real food and I figured a meal was the least I owed my Dad since I was dumping a houseguest on him without notice.

I was making cookies and deviled eggs to go with the tossed salad, baked beans and ham when Dad strolled in the door. Brandon had gone upstairs to take a shower. I'd heard him on the telephone when I was on the computer, but I wasn't trusting my hormones anywhere near Brandon and a bed.

"Hi, sweetie. What brought about this sudden surge of domesticity?"

"Hi, Dad. Brandon's borrowing the shower and my old room for the night if that's okay."

"Problem?"

"Uh-huh. Dead man in his bedroom."

My father raised his eyebrows, grunted and headed up the stairs. I figured I'd let Brandon handle the rest of the explanations.

They came down together a short time later talking tools. I decided that was a good sign.

"Hungry?" I asked, setting the meat on the table.

"Starved," Brandon agreed.

He looked tired but better than when he'd gone upstairs.

"Pull up a chair and dig in," my father told him. "We don't stand on ceremony around here."

"I didn't know you could cook," Brandon teased me.

"I can't. That's why we're having ham and other things that only have to be heated or baked."

"Don't let her kid you. She can do anything she puts her mind to," my father said, piling his plate high. "She's just like her mother."

The unexpected compliment caught me at the back of the throat with a surge of raw emotion. Dad isn't one to toss out compliments. I blinked back the sting of tears and looked down at my plate, quickly clearing my throat.

"Better taste the food first," I said gruffly, giving Dad's hand a grateful pat. He took my fingers and gave them a quick squeeze in return.

"What did you find with the computer search?" Brandon asked.

I looked up quickly.

"Hey, I figure your dad has a right to know the sort of mess I dragged you into."

"Oh? You're taking credit for it all now?" I demanded. "Did you recommend me to Mr. Russo in the first place?"

Dad forked a bite of beans and sat back to chew with obvious relish.

"Are we going to argue over this?"

"She argues over most things," Dad pointed out.

"Keep out of this. For your information and edification, Mr. Kirkpatrick, Elaine Russo did not book any airline tickets out of Cleveland. However, Nicole Wickley was supposed to have been on a flight to New York City last night."

"She didn't show?"

"Nope."

He frowned as he cut into a piece of ham on his plate.

"It gets better. *She* didn't purchase the ticket. Hogan Delvecchi bought it using his personal credit card."

Brandon stopped chewing midbite.

"But wait for it. I'm not finished," I told him feeling a flush of satisfaction. "I did a little exploring. That site ties in with several other networks. While Elaine Russo never purchased tickets out of Cleveland, she—or Nicole posing as her—did purchase a ticket to fly to Reno, Nevada, this morning. The flight wasn't direct, but it originated in—drum roll please—"

"New York City," Brandon said, setting his fork down with a soft snick.

"Exactly."

"She never claimed her seat either?"

"Nope."

"So which one is dead?" my father asked.

Chapter Eleven

We were still debating that issue after we finished the dinner dishes and sat down to join my father over coffee and cookies. My cell phone trilled. I grimaced when I saw who was calling and inclined my head toward next door.

"I could dump the phone in the garbage and tell her I lost it."

"No!" my father said forcefully. "She can see your car. I do not want that woman coming over here on the pretext of looking for you. I'll never get rid of her."

"Good point." I answered the phone. "D.B. Hayes."

"Dee," Mrs. Keene shrilled. "He's here! He's right outside in my driveway!"

"What? Do not open the door! I'll be right there!" I disconnected, jumping to my feet so fast, the chair toppled. "Mrs. Keene's mystery lover is in her driveway right now," I told Brandon.

"Do you have a gun?"

"Not here."

"Come on. At least the cop on duty should be useful for something."

We were out the back door, leaving my father sitting there with a cookie halfway to his mouth.

Racing across the lawn, we spotted a young man walking onto the front porch as brazen as anything. He saw us charging toward him and immediately changed his mind. Wide-eyed, he yelped and sprinted back down the steps. At the same time, Mrs. Keene opened her front door and began screaming at me. Brandon yelled for the kid to hold it right there. The kid was doing no such thing.

I glimpsed the cop in the unmarked car get on the radio, no doubt requesting backup. I saved my lungs for running.

The youth saw he'd never make his car ahead of Brandon and changed direction, sprinting across the grass instead. Unfortunately pudgy old Mr. Ball was out for his evening constitutional with Peanut and Brittle. The small Chows began yapping in high excitement at all the commotion. Their leads tangled as they danced around the helpless man. Two girls on bicycles paused to watch.

Brandon launched himself through the air in a flying tackle. That was too much for the dogs as well as Mr. Ball. He landed on the ground with a cry, dropping the leashes. The plainclothes officer ran toward us shouting something. The girls dropped their bikes to help and the dogs took off yipping, leashes trailing. Mrs. Keene continued screaming something in her high, shrill, excited voice as neighbors began appearing on porches.

I stopped running to pick up something our youthful would-be Romeo had dropped on the ground. The package was wrapped in silver foil with a tiny red bow around what looked suspiciously like a jewelry box to me.

Sirens wailed in the distance. Mr. Ball wailed much closer to hand—something about his hip. Brandon hauled the struggling young man to his feet. One of the Chows clung firmly to the leg of Brandon's new jeans. The other had run over to the plainclothes police officer and stood there yipping furiously at him. The hapless officer had drawn his weapon, but he didn't look as if he knew who to shoot first.

As soon as the gun appeared, the poor girls began to scream right along with Mr. Ball. He alternated between yells of pain and begging the man not to shoot his excited animals.

And Mrs. Keene bustled onto the scene dressed in one of her filmy, overly bright multicolored caftans, wildly waving her arms and generally adding to the din. Privately I hoped no one had thought to capture the moment on video.

I had visions of turning on the television one night and seeing myself on one of those television shows that buys outrageous moments.

By the time the Lakewood police arrived we had drawn quite a crowd. I noticed my dad had gone inside and pulled the shades on all the windows. No doubt by now he was in the basement with the saw going, trying hard to pretend he didn't know any of us. I have to admit I was sort of tempted to slink away and join him.

It took a while to get it all sorted out. They needed an ambulance for Mr. Ball, who was too shaken to tell if he was seriously injured or not. But we finally ended up in Mrs. Keene's living room eating from one of the boxes of Malley's candies and politely ignoring the gingersnaps she'd made that afternoon.

Her youthful stalker turned out to be a pimple-faced nineteen-year-old by the name of Jeremy Smith. He claimed his uncle was Kerwin Dogsmore. *Judge* Kerwin Dogsmore. Who just happened to be a fellow parishioner at Mrs. Keene's church.

"Uncle Kerwin's got this, like, crush on Mrs. Keene. He thought it would be cool to pay me to deliver stuff for him on accounta Uncle Kerwin's in a wheelchair since he got hurt in that motorcycle crash. He figured she might not pay attention to him in the chair since he couldn't court her like he wanted. I thought it was sorta dopey, but he pays good. Only, then these two started chasing me and I was afraid Mrs. Keene was going to call the cops. Uncle Kerwin said he'd take care of any trouble, so I thought it'd be okay, but this dude's sorta scary, you know? It is okay, isn't it?"

"Of course it is, dear boy," Mrs. Keene gushed.

The three officers looked at one another, then at Mrs. Keene. "You don't want to press any charges?"

"Absolutely not! You heard the dear boy."

"What about you?" the female officer asked the dear boy.

"Me?" Jeremy's voice rose an octave. "Heck no. I just want to get out of here. I've got a date tonight."

"How about you?" they asked Brandon. "Did the dog actually bite you?"

"No. He just grabbed the pant leg. We're fine. What about the old man?"

"The paramedics took him in to get checked out. His blood pressure was up pretty high."

"What about the dogs?" I asked.

"The little girls offered to take them home to his wife for him," the male uniformed officer said.

"So no one was hurt," the female officer said, "and no one wants to press any charges, right?"

"Right," Brandon agreed.

"Then I guess we're out of here," the male uniform said. "You want to write this one up?"

"Not me. You're primary," the female officer stated. "I was backup and I'm pulling a double shift in the morning."

They were still arguing as they left with the plain-clothes officer from Rocky River. I handed the wrapped package to Jeremy.

"You dropped this. We'll see you later, Mrs. Keene."

"Oh. You can stay, dear," she said to me.

"No. I really can't. Thanks anyhow. It looks like you won't be needing my help any longer."

"I guess not," she burbled. "Can you imagine? Judge Dogsmore and me?"

I was trying hard not to imagine, but a motorcycle-riding judge and colorful Mrs. Keene did sort of seem to have something in common.

"Now, you send me the rest of your bill," she admonished.

"We're fine, Mrs. Keene."

"We are most certainly not, but we'll talk about it later. Sit down, Jeremy."

"But—"

"Sit!"

I almost felt sorry for the kid. Almost. Brandon and I made our escape.

"Nothing like a little Saturday evening excitement to take your mind off your troubles," he said.

"Are you okay?"

"Other than feeling foolish, I'm fine. Good thing I went with jeans instead of slacks. Little Peanut put a hole clean through these suckers. Or was he Brittle?"

"Who knows? Even Mr. Ball can't tell them apart. We have to go around to the back. Dad's trying to pretend he doesn't know us."

"Can't say I blame him. You do have a knack."

"Hey! Are you trying to blame this on me?"

"Mrs. Keene wasn't my case."

"Maybe not, but I wasn't the one who made the flying tackle, remember?"

"I remember lots of things."

And he stopped me on the back porch, pushed me against the wall and proceeded to kiss me into a black hole of total oblivion right there in front of God and any of my dad's nosy neighbors who happened to be outside still watching to see what other sort of mischief I might get into. We gave them quite an eyeful. That man could kiss!

"Let's move this inside," he said when he came up for air.

And have my father see me melt on his kitchen floor?

"I have to get home. You need sleep."

"I'd sleep better with you."

"Not in my father's house you wouldn't."

His grin was rakish.

"We could go to your place."

I liked that idea. I liked that idea a whole lot until I remembered Mama and her six kittens and the explanations that would have to accompany them. I laid my hand on his chest. I could feel his heart hammering beneath my palm. Or maybe that was my heart hammering. I couldn't tell.

"You need to rest. I need to rest. We'll regroup in the morning."

"Is that a new term for it?"

"Elevate your mind. We are not going to have sex."

"Ever?"

He nibbled on my ear.

"Stop that."

"I could change your mind."

No question about it.

"I am going home. We have work to do. A murder to solve."

"And then?" he breathed against my neck, planting tiny kisses along the sensitive skin there.

I shivered. I'm not sure where I got the strength, but I pushed myself clear, stepped inside, grabbed my purse from the counter and yelled good-night down to my dad. Brandon flattened me against the refrigerator and gave me one more kiss that involved tongues and heavy breathing before he let me go.

I staggered outside with my eyes half closed and my knees so weak, I wasn't sure I'd be able to drive. Somehow I pulled out onto the street and even managed a weak wave at the policeman still parked two doors down. As I headed home I wondered how much longer I was going to remain a virgin.

That thought followed me down into sleep and woke with me in the morning. I told mama cat my concerns as I took a bit of extra care getting ready for work and played with her kittens. Then I remembered I didn't have to hurry in to work. It was Sunday. Besides which, I'd told Trudy to call in Florence and I knew it was going to have to be a permanent arrangement.

I didn't want to think about that. Sooner or later I'd have to deal, but later was definitely preferable. What I did have to do today was go and retrieve the stupid loving cup for Susan Arrensky.

I considered calling Brandon. His skill with locks

would be a plus. On the other hand, he was in enough trouble. I didn't think the cop following him around would take kindly to our breaking and entering a private residence.

I didn't either but I didn't see much choice.

Parking Binky several doors away on the street, I strolled up to the Arrensky house, ignoring the morning heat, and surveyed the sagging front porch. I wondered what the odds were that Lyle might have forgotten to lock the window with the ripped screen. It would be a simple matter to pop the screen and slip inside if he hadn't set the window latch. Of course, half the neighborhood seemed to be outside at the moment. Kids were running up and down playing while adults who were obviously coming from church were standing around talking to those who were tending their yards with garden hoses and sprinklers.

The more I studied the house, the more I realized my timing couldn't be worse. I should come back after dark. Three in the morning sounded about right. With luck Lyle would be passed out by then and probably wouldn't even hear me if I had to break a window. Also on the plus side, his neighbors would all be in bed asleep. I liked that plan.

I turned to head back to Binky when a voice hailed me from the front porch of the house next door.

"Dee? Dee Hayes? Is that you?"

A heavyset woman so pregnant, she looked like an overinflated balloon, waved to me from her front porch swing. I stopped and stared, having no idea who she was.

"It's me. Penny! Penny Blumberger. Well, Nerwonski for the past three years. I thought that was you. You haven't changed a bit."

What a shame. She certainly had. I didn't recognize her even when she stood up and tottered to the edge of the front steps. Penny had never been exactly thin, but she was well past chunky now as she stood there in a pair of valiant shorts and a sleeveless top straining its utmost to cover the mound of her vast belly.

"I haven't seen you since high school graduation. What are you doing in Birdtown? I heard you moved to New York."

I cast an uneasy eye at the Arrensky house as I crossed to Penny's sidewalk and moved to the bottom of her porch. Penny had a voice that carried halfway down the block. I was a little concerned Lyle might be home, even though there was no sign of life at the house next door. Letting him see me again did not seem like a smart idea. It was a safe bet he wasn't at church this morning and an equally safe bet that he wasn't at work. I wasn't even sure he still had a job. His work ethic had been one of the bones of contention in their marriage.

"How are you, Penny?"

"Pregnant again, as you can see. Twins this time."

"Twins," I said uneasily, eyeing the bulging stomach. "When are you due?"

"Today. I'm just waiting for Earl to get home so we can head to the hospital."

I tried to swallow and failed. "You're having the babies now?"

"Oh, well, I'm not in labor or anything, though I do have one hellacious backache. But the doctor decided to take them out before they get any bigger."

"On a Sunday?"

"Yeah. I wasn't too happy about that either, but he's leaving for a vacation this week and today was the only day he could fit me in."

"Uh, shouldn't you be sitting down or something?"

"Yeah. This heat is killing me," she said, waddling back over and plopping back down on the defenseless glider. "Earl took the other two over to my mom's this morning."

"You have two more kids?"

"Yep. Human guppy, that's me. I'm having the tubes tied this time, though. Enough is enough. Were you looking for Susan? She moved out, you know. Applying for a divorce. About time she dumped Lyle, the pig."

I couldn't argue that one. "Uh, yeah. She, uh, asked me to stop by and pick up something she left behind. You wouldn't happen to know if he's home or not, would you?"

"Oh, he's home."

Thank God I hadn't tried the window!

"Still sleeping it off would be my guess. He

doesn't get up until noon or later. He got a job working nights at that new taco place on Detroit. I think he does night-shift cleanup or something."

"Remind me never to eat there."

"Ain't it the truth? Hey, did Susan give you a key? 'Cause I've still got her spare out in the kitchen on the rack if you need one. You may as well take it and give it back to her for me. I don't want it now that she doesn't live there anymore."

Life couldn't be this simple. It was never this simple. There had to be a catch somewhere.

"I'd get it for you, but my back's killing me."

"That's fine. Stay put. I'll get it."

"Thanks. Kitchen's on the left. There's a whole rack of spare keys, just bring me the rack and I'll show you which one. I wish Earl would hurry up and get here."

So did I. "Thanks, Penny."

"Don't fall over my suitcase on your way in. It's right inside the door. And watch out for baby toys. I'm not much of a housekeeper."

Actually Penny had cleaning down to a science. If you don't do it, things grow and multiply. Simple science. I found her kitchen. The refrigerator was too big to bury, though there was enough stuff tacked to the outside that she'd given it a valiant try. I found the rack holding keys and threaded my way back to the front door with it, only to find Penny scrunched on the swing, her face screwed in pain.

"Call an ambulance!"

"What?"

"I'm in labor."

"You can't be in labor. Earl's on his way."

She panted, and I dropped the rack of keys beside her and pulled out my cell phone.

"I need an ambulance and I need it fast," I told the dispatcher, giving him the address in a voice three octaves higher than normal. "My friend's having twins on her front porch as we speak."

"All right, ma'am. Stay calm. Our ambulance is on another call at the moment."

"Well, get it back! Or send a fire truck! Send a police car! Send someone who knows how to deliver a litter of babies! Blood does not come out of crepe, you know!"

"Oh, God. My water broke," Penny wailed as liquid spewed forth, soaking her shorts and forming a puddle on the swing and the gray painted floor underneath.

"Her water just broke!"

"Ma'am, calm down."

"I will not calm down! She is having her babies right here on the front porch. You are a male. You are an idiot!"

"All males are idiots!" Penny agreed and then groaned.

I disconnected, trying to stem my panic. "I'll get some towels."

"And my suitcase! I'll need my suitcase."

"And your suitcase," I promised. "We'll take Binky."

I ran back in the house, tripped over a stroller and

nearly killed myself in my frantic search for a bathroom and some towels. It occurred to me she might want something larger than a bath towel, so I grabbed the sheet off her unmade bed, as well, and rushed back outside, grabbing the suitcase as an afterthought as I stumbled over it on my way out.

Penny had her eyes closed. Her head was thrown back and she was moaning.

"Okay. Hang on, Penny. I'll go get Binky and drive you to the hospital. I can have you there in no time."

A siren came screaming up the street. I offered up a quick prayer of thanks because I had no clue how to go about delivering a baby, let alone a litter of them, and I really didn't want to learn if other options were available.

The police car pulled in front of the house. I recognized the officer as the female one from last night. Lucky her. She'd said she was going to pull a double shift.

The lady across the street hurried over in her floppy sun hat and dirty gardening gloves, carrying a spade. Did she still think babies grew in cabbage patches? Was she planning to dig them out?

Okay, I was feeling a trifle hysterical, but Penny was having babies. People all over the neighborhood had stopped to watch. The cop was not going to be pleased. It was last night all over again.

In the distance I heard a second siren. A well-used green van pulled in the driveway with a thin, weedy-looking man behind the wheel.

"Earl, you stupid jackal, where have you been?" Penny shouted as he climbed out.

"I stopped to get gas. What's going on?"

"My water broke!"

Earl just stood there with a stupid expression on his face. The police officer beat him to the porch. She looked at me and did a double take.

"Weren't you—"

"Uh-huh. Last night. Afraid so. Penny and I went to school together."

"She's in labor?"

I nodded. "Her water broke and she's having twins. The hospital's already expecting her. That's her husband, Earl."

We looked at Earl, who was still standing there looking puzzled by all the commotion. An ambulance came screaming down the street. Penny let out a loud moan. I gathered up the keys and moved off the porch, out of the way.

The crowd had grown. It continued to swell as the paramedics hurried over to us, finally spurring Earl into motion. The police officer joined me, requesting her neighbors move back.

I looked toward the Arrensky house. Lyle Arrensky was standing on the front porch in a pair of faded red boxers sprinkled with pink doves that had probably once been white. He was scratching his hairy belly as he watched all the commotion. As if karmically drawn, our eyes met and held.

"You!"

He pointed straight at me. Feeling the cop's eyes turn to me, as well, I looked over my shoulder as if searching for the person he was pointing at. He started down his front stairs. I moved closer to the cop.

"He looks dangerous. Is he allowed to run around out here dressed like that in front of all these little kids?"

She gave me a suspicious look and moved to intercept his lurching momentum. I eased back into the crowd. Penny was groaning in earnest now in between hollering at Earl and the two paramedics. Time to leave. I could return the rest of her keys at another time.

Lyle started yelling at the cop. Penny was yelling at Earl. The neighbors were all talking. Somewhere a dog started barking. I climbed into Binky and drove down the street without a backward glance.

I stopped at the doughnut shop on Madison and picked up a dozen assorted since I didn't know what Brandon liked. Then I headed over to my dad's place. As soon as I hit the kitchen I knew the house was empty. There was no note, nothing to tell me where they'd gone.

Fuming, I ate two of the doughnuts while I tried to decide what to do next. Probably I should get back on my computer and do the sort of research I was good at. We needed more information on all of the players. But whatever gossip Trudy had picked up would probably help more than any computer search.

I wasn't angry with my aunt, though her comment still stung, but I knew things would never be the same between us again, so I dialed her number with some trepidation.

I'd never intended working out of the flower shop to be anything but a temporary situation. I'd accepted Aunt Lacy's offer so I could save money to open my own office, figuring it would take me a year or two, max. Now I wondered if that had just been a dream. I hadn't liked working for the big New York outfit, but maybe I should consider applying to work for one of the smaller local P.I. firms.

Like Brandon's?

I pushed that thought aside as her phone began to ring. When the answering machine picked up, I frowned and looked at the clock over the kitchen sink. They should have been back from church by now. Where was everyone?

Sometimes they went over to the shop on Sundays to clean and redo the window display. Seeing no help for it, I took another doughnut and a can of soda from the refrigerator and headed over to Flower World.

I parked out back as usual. Trudy's car was there. I steeled myself, scooped up the rack of keys and strode inside the air-conditioned back room of the flower shop. It was another sultry day and the early afternoon sun had turned Binky into a sauna hot enough that I fervently wished I'd skipped the doughnuts.

"Trudy?" I called out. There was no answer, so I

went into the office, dumped the rack of keys on the desk and eyed the telephone. I was miffed that Brandon hadn't called me yet, but I resisted the temptation to pick up the receiver and try his office. I was bound to hear from him soon. Better to wait and let him call me. I didn't want to look too anxious after that kiss last night.

I went out front, calling Trudy and my aunt. There was no one there. Frowning, I went back to the workroom. Trudy's purse wasn't sitting in its usual place. They'd probably walked down the street to have brunch at one of the small restaurants nearby. That was fine with me.

I went back to the office and started sorting through the rack of keys. It was easy enough to put aside the keys that were car keys or too small or oddly shaped to be house keys. When I was finished I had five possibilities. Those I tucked into the pocket of my white slacks.

I looked at the clock, feeling antsy. Then I stared at the phone, willing it to ring. Finally, feeling foolish, I picked it up and dialed Brandon's cell phone. It rang straight to his voice mail, of course. He couldn't charge it since he couldn't get into his apartment to get his charger.

I had to look up his office number. His voice answered after two rings, sounding deep and professional. I started speaking before I realized I was talking to a machine. Feeling stupid, I waited for the beep and left him a quick message asking him to give me a call when he got the chance.

Where the heck was he? In case he and my dad had gone out for something to eat, I tried my Dad's cell phone number, as well. When my dad's voice mail came on, I hung up without leaving a message.

Since I had nothing else to do, I got online and decided to check out the airlines again. I was going through the lists when there was a tentative knock on the office door. I glanced up to see Aunt Lacy standing there. I'd never heard her come in.

"You have visitors," she said without inflection.

"On Sunday? Tell them to come back."

"I did. They have."

With that cryptic remark, she disappeared. The next face I saw was Mickey's. He looked smaller and younger than ever before.

"Mickey."

I didn't have time for Mickey and his missing cat this afternoon. I really didn't. I was about to tell him so as diplomatically as possible when I caught sight of a blond woman at his back. The protest lodged in my throat. The last time I'd seen the blonde, she'd been behind the wheel of the blue minivan Brandon had driven on our date.

"It's okay, Mom. This is D.B. Hayes," Mickey said.

The blonde came all the way into view. Cool, stunningly attractive, she was dressed in a perfectly fitting sundress of white and mint green. She looked suave and sophisticated and about seven years older than me.

"Dee, this is my mom."

She came forward with one slim hand outstretched. Her perfect nails were tinted a light peach. I decided then and there to hate her, wishing I could hide my short, unpolished nails and the healing scratches on my hand.

"Ms. Hayes, I'm Julie Kirkpatrick."

Chapter Twelve

Air rushed from my lungs. I gaped at her, trying to get my brain to stop tripping over her last two words.

"You—you're…"

"Brandon's sister-in-law," she said in a soft voice.

Sister-in-law. She was his sister-in-law. Of course she was. Mickey had told me his father had been killed. Why hadn't I put it together much sooner?

"May we come in?"

"I thought you were his girlfriend," I blurted out.

She smiled briefly without humor. Mickey, on the other hand, thought that was a hoot and giggled merrily. He walked in and plunked down on one of the visitor's chairs. Instantly George the cat appeared out of nowhere and made a beeline for the boy.

"Hey there, George. How ya' doin', boy?"

It was eerie. I could almost hear Brandon saying that. Mickey produced a bit of string from a pocket and began to dangle it in front of the cat.

I looked at Julie. There were dark circles under her eyes. She was watching her son with a sad, almost

wistful look that tugged at me. I forced myself to
gather my scattered wits and stood, gesturing her inside.

"I'm sorry. I don't always act like an idiot. Please,
have a seat."

"Wow. That's a lot of keys," Mickey said, eyeing
the rack on the desk.

"Yes, it is." I closed the door behind Julie, then
hesitated. "May I get you something to drink or—"

This time her smile was genuine. She had a
lovely·smile.

"We're fine. We just had a soda down the street.
We came by earlier but the store was closed and your
aunt said you hadn't come by yet, but she thought
you might."

"Then the police showed up," Mickey put in, looking up with troubled eyes, "so we scrammed."

"The police showed up?"

He nodded, wide eyed. "They arrested Uncle
Brandon!"

"What!"

Julie Kirkpatrick shook her head. "We don't know
that they arrested him yet, Mickey. They're asking
him questions," she soothed, but the hand she used
to push back a strand of natural blond hair was trembling ever so slightly.

"Grandpa said they're going to arrest him."

"Whoa. Wait a minute. Let's slow down here," I
demanded. "Brandon was here and the police came
and took him away for more questioning?"

"Yes," she agreed, not quite wringing her hands but clenching them together until it looked like those beautifully polished nails were drawing blood. "It looks like they're going to charge him with murder."

I glanced pointedly at Mickey.

"It's okay, Ms. Hayes, I don't keep secrets from my son."

"Dee," I said, sounding as weak as I felt. I moved back around the desk to sit down.

"Dee," she agreed. "For one thing, keeping a secret from Mickey is impossible. For another, we only have each other so we don't keep secrets."

"Except I tried to about Mr. Sam," Mickey said, looking down at his shoes, clearly unhappy over that memory. "I should'a told you when he got out."

"Yes, you should have, but everyone's allowed to make a mistake, Mickey. I tell you when I make one," his mother said.

"Yes, ma'am."

"The other night, when he thought Brandon was coming for dinner, Mickey confessed that he hired you to find Mr. Sam. I've been so preoccupied lately, I didn't even realize the cat was missing. Mickey takes good care of him and I've been pulling a lot of overtime lately…. Well, the bottom line is I never realized the old boy had gotten out and I should have. Mickey had worked himself into quite a state by the time I got home."

"We tried to find the cat," I started to explain.

"I know, but there's no way on earth you could

have. By chance I learned that one of my neighbors had discovered him locked in her potting shed days ago. She thought he was a stray and took him inside. She's been caring for him ever since."

"You never asked your neighbors if they'd seen him?" I asked Mickey.

He shrugged his thin shoulders.

Silently I berated myself for being an idiot. I hadn't thought to ask him such a simple, logical question. What sort of investigator did that make me? And then it hit me.

"Wait a minute! Are you telling me Mr. Sam is Brandon's cat?" I'd spent days searching for my arch nemesis's cat when I don't even like cats?

Julie looked from her son to me. "Well, technically it belonged to his fiancée but she dumped the cat when she dumped him."

Brandon had had a fiancée?

"Brandon was okay with it. He likes Mr. Sam, but he thought because he was gone so much of the day that Mickey would be better company for the cat. In a way you could say Brandon dumped him on me. Ironically my neighbor planned to keep him because her cat died recently and Mr. Sam's such a lovable old guy. So of course there was no way you could have found him."

"Lovable. Right." I shook my head and opened the desk drawer. The crumpled wad of bills was still there. I shoved them across the desk at Mickey.

"That's the money I paid you to find Mr. Sam."

"And I failed."

"But you tried," Julie protested.

"Trying isn't good enough. Go buy your Glimmer Man game." To Julie I said, "Let's get back to the reason you came here today."

She hesitated. Finally she nodded at Mickey, who scooped up the money. "Thank you. I don't know what's going on between you and Brandon…"

I was pretty sure the collar of my sleeveless blouse covered the hickey, so I worked at trying not to blush.

"…but I want to hire you to help him."

"Forget it. You don't have to hire me to help Brandon. My neck and my reputation, not to mention my investigator's license, are on the line every bit as much as his right now. We were together the other night. Working on a case," I added hastily. "I can and will swear to that in a court of law. Neither one of us killed anyone. And fortunately for us, I'm pretty sure we have an independent witness who can also attest to the fact that we were someplace else at the time Delvecchi was killed."

Julie drew in a hiss of air at the name.

"Blast. I keep forgetting they haven't released that yet. I'd like to tell you to go home and not to worry, but frankly you should worry all you like. I'm certainly going to. What I can promise you is that I'm going to be doing all I can to unravel this mess."

"But what about the gun?"

I stared at her blankly. "What gun?"

"The gun they took from Brandon's apartment

when they searched it. The one they said was used to kill Delvecchi."

My hands gripped the edge of the desk while my stomach did a quick somersault.

Her eyes widened. "You didn't know. They found the murder weapon hidden inside the air-conditioning vent in the floor in his dining room."

Mickey looked up as I swore.

"You aren't supposed to say that."

"No. I'm not," I agreed faintly.

Julie looked as scared as I felt.

"You said there's an independent witness."

I dropped my hands below the edge of the desk, out of sight. They were shaking and I didn't want to scare either one of them any more than they already were.

"There is, depending on what time Delvecchi was shot."

"I don't think they have the coroner's report back yet."

"No, I don't imagine they do."

I tried to slow my breathing and think. We had an awful lot of time we couldn't account for that night even with our visit to Nicole's apartment. We basically only had each other. As alibis went, that wasn't good.

Julie shuddered. "This is all connected to what happened to Seth, isn't it?"

"I don't know," I told her honestly. "Maybe."

"I knew he should have left it alone. I told Brandon to drop the investigation."

"How could he? Seth was his brother."

"Even if it gets him killed, too?"

"Julie, Brandon's an investigator. It's what he does."

She stared hard at me. "You sound just like him."

"I'll take that as a compliment. If someone had killed one of my brothers, I'd do whatever it took to get justice. And I'm not even all that close to my brothers."

"I want justice, too! I just don't want to see any-one else killed."

"I understand." And I did. She was scared. So was I. Lots more now than I had been half an hour ago. "Look, Brandon said your father-in-law is retired police. Maybe he can help."

"I called Harry this morning. He was going to talk to some people."

"Good. That's good. In the meantime, so will I." I reached for a business card. "This is my cell phone number. You can reach me at any time, providing I'm not in jail."

"Let me give you my number, as well," she of-fered, writing it on the pad of paper I passed over to her.

Our eyes locked as our hands met. Hers were fraught with worry and fear as they assessed me.

"Thank you, Dee."

"Thank me after I do something. I'll be in touch."

I liked this woman, I realized. Despite her perfect hair and nails, she was someone I could relate to. She was scared, but she was tough. She'd handle whatever she had to handle.

I knew as soon as Julie and Mickey left, my aunt and Trudy would descend demanding details. I was right. They came in as I was packing up my computer.

"What are you doing?" Aunt Lacy demanded.

"I'm going incommunicado for a couple of days," I told her. "Someone is trying to frame us for murder."

"Nonsense."

"Tell it to the person who killed Delvecchi and hid the murder weapon in Brandon's apartment. I told you we were together and we were. This could get sticky. One of us needs to remain free to prove it."

"This is not a movie, Diana Barbara."

"Believe it or not, I had noticed that, Aunt Lacy. Trudy, were you able to get me any information?"

"I'm sorry, Dee. I didn't realize there was a rush."

I looked hard at her. Her skin reddened and I realized Aunt Lacy had told her not to help. I felt a surge of temper and squashed it flat. Anger would serve no purpose. I picked up the rack of keys, my computer and my purse.

"I am not going to stand here and watch you ruin your life," Aunt Lacy said angrily.

"Then have a seat. It will probably play better from that view anyhow. It would be real nice if one of you would call the pound about Mama and her kittens. I won't be able to care for them for a while."

"Dee, you come back here!"

I brushed past a stunned Trudy and headed for the back entrance. As I steered Binky onto Bell Avenue, I saw the police cruiser pull in front of the shop. It had been that close.

I was scared. Deep-down, want-my-mommy scared. I was also in as close to a blind rage as I have ever been. Albert Russo and his girlfriend could not be allowed to manipulate people's lives and get away with it. There had to be a scale of justice somewhere, and I was going to jump up and down until that scale started tipping in the right direction.

Binky had a tendency to stand out in a crowd, so the first order of business was driving over to see Ted Osher. Even though it was Sunday, I knew I'd find him at the closed garage. He and the owner have a deal. He can work on his own projects there whenever he wants in his spare time.

I parked out back and let myself in through the side door. As usual Ted was buried under a car hood, up to his armpits in engine parts. A radio at his back was blasting away. I tapped him on the shoulder and he looked up reluctantly, not even startled. His eyes lit in pleased surprise when he saw it was me, but his expression instantly changed to one of speculation as he came out from the bowels of the car.

"What did you do to it this time?"

I gave him my usual response to this question—a glare. "Can we talk outside?"

He knew I hated the noise and the fumes of the garage. At the moment the heat was making me sick to my stomach despite the fans he had running. I didn't wait to see if he followed. I strode to where Binky sat looking oddly forlorn amid the mostly larger, shinier, newer cars parked there and patted his engine fondly.

"What's wrong with the car?" Ted demanded.

"Other than drinking a quart of oil every five minutes, not a thing. I need a favor."

Ted's a muscular guy with brown hair and sweet puppy-dog brown eyes. He cleans up nicely after a gallon or two of soap and water. He's a terrific mechanic and a nice guy, but looking at him, I realized why I was still a virgin. He didn't produce that tingle I got low in my belly whenever Brandon gave me that same sort of look. Ted was just a nice guy I was fond of.

"I need to leave Binky here and borrow a car."

"Why?"

I sighed. He deserved to know the truth. "Because the police want to talk to me about a murder and I don't feel like getting arrested right now."

He rubbed at his jaw, leaving another smear of grease behind.

"If you don't want to tell me the reason, just say so."

I deepened the sigh.

"How long do you need the car?"

"A day or so should be enough. By then it will either all be over or—"

"I'll read about you in the news, right? Never mind. I can let you have this 1961 Austin-Healey Sprite roadster I'm restoring."

He gestured, and I eyed the miniature car he'd indicated in disbelief.

"Where do you put the key to wind it up?"

"Hey! You drive a VW Bug!"

"Binky isn't green."

Not just green. Brilliant, electric, in-your-eye, lemon-lime, here-I-am-stick-out-your-tongue-and-barf green.

"It runs."

I shook my head. "Do large dogs play fetch with it?"

"Do you need a car or not?"

I groaned. "I need a car. I'm not sure that qualifies."

"Everything important works. It just needs a top."

"There's no top?" I squeaked.

"It's not supposed to rain for a couple of days. I'll get the keys." He paused. "Are you still mad at me?"

"You give me a car that looks like this, don't you think I'm the one who should be asking that question?"

Teeth flashed in his grease-smeared face.

"Do you need a date for Lorna's wedding on Saturday?"

I thought about Brandon and shook my head.

"Billy, right? I knew I should have called you last week."

I didn't disillusion him, but I felt strange. It was sad to realize a part of my life had just ended. While nothing permanent was likely to come of my relationship with Brandon, I knew in that moment I wouldn't be dating Ted anymore. It wouldn't be fair to either one of us to continue on the way we had been. We could never be what the other one needed no matter how hard we tried.

I think Ted sensed some of what I was thinking because he looked at me with a funny expression when he came back outside and exchanged keys with me.

"Be careful, Dee," he said.

"You're a good friend, Ted. I won't destroy your latest masterpiece, don't worry. I'll bring back your little green frog as soon as I can."

The grin flashed, a little sad this time, and he nodded.

"Hey! Wait a minute," I called in panic as I studied the car. "Where's the trunk? There's no trunk!"

"The front seat backrest is hinged. See? There's storage space."

"For a toothbrush!"

"It's for driving around town, Dee. Or it was, back in the fifties and sixties. Just don't push it too hard. It's only got a top speed of seventy-five miles per hour."

"Terrific."

"Well, you aren't planning to race him, are you?"

"No." And I wouldn't be trying to outrun any police cars in this matchbox-size car, either.

Instead of going straight back into work, he waited while I transferred the laptop, the keys and my purse to the car. Binky was small, but somehow Frog, as I'd decided to call him, seemed so much smaller—and lower to the ground. I kept feeling as though I should be pedaling or something. I managed a wave as I drove off with only a minimum of grinding gears.

Now all I had to do was figure out where to go next. Neither Rocky River nor Lakewood had big enough police forces to cover my apartment 24-7, so going there seemed safe enough. They wouldn't be looking for me to drive up in something as brightly gaudy as Frog. Hopefully I'd see the police before they saw me.

Still, I parked down the street from my apartment just to be safe. There was no sign of any unmarked cruisers, and I didn't run into anyone as I hurried up to my apartment.

No doubt going there was an idiotic thing to do. I was cursing myself for ten kinds of a fool as I made my way inside the building. I did not want to go in there with every fiber of my being, but I needed clothing and my cell phone charger—and my gun.

People were getting killed around me. I didn't want to be one of them. I think I'm allergic to the idea of dead people. Not that having a gun would protect me. But just maybe it might make someone think twice about shooting if they knew I could shoot back.

Yeah. Right. If they'd ever seen me on a practice range, they'd have a fit of the giggles. And if my heart beat any harder, something would rupture. My hand shook so badly, it took me three tries to get the key in the lock.

"It's about time!" The woman standing in my kitchen doorway said impatiently.

A tiny scream erupted before I could stop it. I couldn't help it. All that suppressed tension had to go somewhere, so I screamed and dropped my keys.

"What are you doing? Stop screaming! Shut the door! Do you want your neighbors to come running?"

The woman strode forward with total arrogance and yanked me inside, closing the door at my back.

"What are you doing here?" I managed to demand of the woman I had followed to the shopping center and across state lines into Pennsylvania with Brandon. I was shaking all over in reaction, but Nicole Wickley was definitely not dead. She was standing in my apartment minus the blond wig and she looked far better as a brunette.

Her tailored, short-sleeved blouse and matching slacks in splashy bright red were the perfect color for her carefully made-up features. Her hair was piled carelessly on top of her head and still managed to look good. The lipstick and polish matched her outfit, as did her open-toed high-heeled shoes. A dainty black onyx teardrop hung from a silver chain around her neck. Matching drop earrings graced her ears. She looked expensively chic and as out of place in my apartment as any human could have looked. I disliked her on sight.

"I've been waiting for you," she said, making it sound like a serious hardship. "The police have been here twice."

I wasn't at all surprised.

"So, what are you doing here? And how did you get in?" I could not imagine my nosy superintendent letting her inside.

"You have lousy locks."

"I'll be sure and tell the management. You *are* Nicole Wickley, aren't you?" I asked, still trembling in reaction. I couldn't think of a single good reason for the woman to be standing in my apartment, but several disturbing ones were skittering through my brain.

"Of course I am!"

"There's no 'of course' about it. The last time I saw you, you were pretending to be Elaine Russo."

"I can explain."

"Good. The police will be very happy to hear that."

"We can't go to the police! He'll kill me!"

"Who will?"

"Al," she said as though it was perfectly obvious. "Why do you think I'm here?"

I shook my head. "I haven't a clue."

"I thought you were a hotshot detective. I have to admit you don't look like much, and this apartment…"

She waved an elegant hand to encompass my pink drapes, green couch and orange cat tree.

"You really could use a decorator, you know. But you certainly have got Al's shorts in a twist."

The slights to my apartment evaporated under the sudden thunder of my heartbeat. "Al being Albert Russo?" I asked.

"Who else?"

Who else indeed? I wanted to sit down—or maybe throw up. What the heck, I could manage to do both. It wasn't bad enough I had Cleveland's biggest gangster mad at me, now I had his shorts in a twist. There was something to make me feel good.

"Look, do you have anything to drink in this place? I couldn't find a thing except diet soda."

She'd been going through my kitchen?

"I don't have any alcohol, if that's what you were looking for."

She pouted. "Isn't that just my lousy luck?"

I didn't know about hers, but *lousy* certainly summed up my luck of late. On jelly-rigged legs I walked to the refrigerator and pulled out a bottle of diet cola. Opening it, I offered it to her. She frowned and reluctantly took it from me, careful not to actually touch me.

Great. She thought I had cooties. I was feeling better by the minute. I let her get her own glass. She seemed to know where they were. I unscrewed the lid on a second bottle and skipped the glass. Taking a long swallow, I regarded her. It was past time to get a handle on this situation.

"Okay, let's start from the beginning. Why are you here?"

"I want to hire you and Brandon Kirkpatrick."

I choked on my soda. She took a dainty sip of hers, then crossed to the dining room table, opened an expensive designer purse I hadn't even noticed sitting there, pulled out a wad of bills large enough to boggle my mind and peeled off ten one-hundred-dollar bills, handing them to me as if they meant nothing.

"Will this do as a retainer?"

Somehow I kept my face impassive. "That depends. Exactly what do you want to hire me—us—to do?"

"Keep me alive long enough to get out of town."

"You had a plane ticket to New York," I pointed out.

Her eyes widened in surprise. "You know about that?"

"I am a private investigator," I reminded her.

Nicole shrugged. "Yeah, well, I was supposed to have a ticket there, courtesy of Al, but that didn't exactly pan out."

"What do you mean?" I asked, watching her closely.

"Even if he'd given me the ticket, like he promised, when everything started going wrong I realized if I went to the airport, I was as good as dead."

"Hold it. Let's start at the beginning, all right?"

She brushed that off with a wave of her perfectly manicured hand.

"Do we need to do this now? The police could come back here any minute, you know. Why do they keep coming here, anyhow?"

I smiled without humor. "They think I had something to do with the murder of Hogan Delvecchi."

Chapter Thirteen

"Delvecchi's dead? Oh, God, Al really is going to kill me! We have to get out of here!"

"Relax. This is the last place your boyfriend is apt to come."

"That's what I thought when I came here, but if Delvecchi's dead... You didn't kill him, did you?"

I was glad I wasn't swallowing when she asked that question.

"Hardly."

The light on my answering machine was blinking a summons, probably from Detective Martin. I ignored it and tried to ignore my instinct, which was screaming at me to grab my stuff and go. The question was, go where? I needed to know what the heck was going on before something else happened.

"Let's go in the bedroom. You can talk to me while I pack a few things."

"You have *cats* in there!"

She made them sound like poisonous snakes. I

forgot I wasn't a cat person and smiled with a lot of teeth. "Cute, aren't they?"

She drew back a step. "I don't like animals."

"That's okay. I'm sure it's mutual. As I was saying, we'll go in the bedroom and you can explain to me why Albert Russo wants you dead and why you've been pretending to be his wife."

"That's why he wants me dead."

"He doesn't know you were pretending to be his wife?"

"Of course he does. That's why he hired me in the first place."

I shook my head and I swear I heard my brain rattling.

"The bedroom," I said coldly. "Now."

I'm not sure which of us was more surprised, but she preceded me into the bedroom and I closed the door behind us.

"If the police come, we don't answer the door," I told her.

"What if they come inside?"

"We're only three stories up. We go out the window."

She stared at me like I was crazy. I was feeling pretty crazy at the moment. There was no way I was jumping three stories down, but she didn't have to know that.

"So you were simply working for Albert Russo. You weren't having an affair with him."

"Of course I was. That's why he hired me."

There went that rattling noise again. All my marbles must be escaping through the multiple holes in my head.

"Explain," I said, going to my closet and taking down my small overnight case. Mama glared at me. One of the baby kittens hissed. I apologized to all of them. Nicole stared at me as if she was having second thoughts about jumping through the window.

"What's there to explain?" she demanded. "Al came backstage one night after a performance. He said he'd seen me in those Jerry's commercials I've been doing and he wanted to meet me in person. I knew who he was, of course, so I played up to him. I mean, the man's as rich as Croesus and he's telling me what a fabulous actress I am and how I'm wasted in that two-bit production. Only a fool wouldn't eat that up, right?"

I'd put two T-shirts and some underwear into the case when I realized there was no way in heck it was going to fit in the minuscule storage space behind the driver's seat in Frog.

"Hold on a minute. I'll be right back." I went out to the kitchen, found a paper sack with handles one of the department stores had given me and returned.

"So you two started an affair and then he hired you. To do what?" I transferred the clothes to the sack and added a pair of slacks.

"To pretend to be his wife. See, everyone had told him I looked like her. I don't see it myself, other than our general size and shape, but I'm an actress, right? I know about makeup and costuming and I'm good with voices. So he tells me how he's got this prenup thing that says if either of them are unfaithful they can get a divorce right away and she isn't entitled to anything. He says he knows she's been having an affair with someone only he can't prove it. He wants my help getting some compromising pictures of her so he can divorce her."

Daintily she sat on the edge of my bed as if afraid of contamination.

"His wife's been trying to cause him some grief with this detective, so he figures to get them both back. I mean, it made sense, right? All I was supposed to do was call Fitzpatrick, arrange a meeting, let you follow us—only I don't know it's you personally, just that he hired another detective to take pictures of the two of us looking chummy. The next day I'm supposed to come to his office still pretending to be her and raise hell over the pictures. In return he said he'd set me up in an apartment in New York and get me an audition with this Broadway director he knows. If the guy agrees, Al would back this play with me in the starring role."

"All for a few pictures?" I asked skeptically.

Her eyes went huge as I pulled my nine-millimeter semiautomatic out from under the bottom of the mattress.

"Hey! It's the truth! I swear!"

I set the gun in the bag under my slacks and managed not to smile at her expression.

"So, okay, I knew there had to be more to it than

that," she continued quickly, "but hey, a starring role on Broadway? I mean, even if he only arranged an interview with the director and gave me a year's lease on the apartment, I figured it was worth it. Except at the last minute he tells me I've got to meet some women his wife was supposed to have dinner with that night. I mean, I'm good and everything, but nobody's *that* good. But he swears they don't know Elaine very well. All I had to do was tell them I just had a Novocain injection or something and I'm in a lot of pain and ask for a rain check."

"Why not have you call them and beg off?"

"It was too late when he found it on her schedule. He didn't know how to call them to cancel."

"Where did he tell you his wife was while you were pretending to be her?"

She watched nervously as I added two spare clips to the bag with the gun.

"He said she's supposed to be out of town visiting family. He swore she'd never know about any of this. I figured maybe she was off shacking up with her new guy and he was just ticked because he couldn't find them or something."

I couldn't believe she was serious. "You didn't think all of this was strange?"

"Hey, it's none of my business. You don't ask someone like Al a lot of questions, if you get my drift."

That much I could believe. Just thinking about those eyes of his made me want to shiver.

"Wait here a minute."

I went into the bathroom, scooped up a few toilet articles and returned. She was eyeing the cats in the closet with a frown. I wanted to tell her she'd get wrinkles that way, but she probably wouldn't care. She'd just get a face-lift anyhow.

"So why did you call Brandon to meet you at Russo's?"

"See, that's the thing. That's when I started getting scared. I mean, why would Al want me to give the guy something? It didn't make sense, but I'm still thinking, okay, he's willing to back a play with me in the lead role. This is my big break. In my line of work you do what you have to do or you don't get anywhere."

"Uh-huh. What was Al's explanation?"

For the first time her face took on a scared look.

"Al doesn't give explanations. They were moving my furniture out and Al called me on the cell phone and said there was one more thing. I was to call the detective and arrange to meet him at the house and give him some papers. Hogan Delvecchi would be there with my ticket. He'd tell me where the papers were and make sure everything went smooth. Afterward I could board the plane and go to New York, as scheduled."

Remembered fear flickered in her dark brown eyes. "Have you ever met Delvecchi?"

I nodded but suppressed an instant flare of sympathy.

"Oh, right. You're supposed to have killed him."

She eyed the brown sack with the gun nervously

"Look, I'm not going to pretend otherwise—i didn't feel right to me, you know? Especially when Al had Delvecchi pick me up at the last minute and drive me over there. Frankly that man gives me the willies." She swallowed. "I guess that should be pas tense now, huh?"

I nodded. She no longer looked quite so in con trol.

"See, Delvecchi told me to go upstairs after the de tective got there and the papers would be on the dresser in Elaine's bedroom. I had a real bad feeling but I figured, what could I do? I couldn't tell Al no and I sure as heck wasn't going to argue with Del vecchi. There was a chance Al was playing straigh with me, but it didn't feel good. You know what mean?"

I knew.

"So I did what he said. Only when I picked up the papers they were just copies of some junk he'd got ten off the Internet. I was really scared then and when I came back downstairs Delvecchi walked i with a gun and I was never so scared in all my life I knew he was going to kill me. I knew it! If you hadn't tossed that brick through the window—"

"Cell phone," I corrected.

"Whatever. You saved our lives. I had to boost car just to get away. I haven't done that since I wa a kid."

"Interesting childhood." I wanted to ask her where she'd grown up, but at the moment I had more pressing issues. "So why are you still here? Why didn't you drive to New York?"

Her features tightened. "Al had them ship my car along with my furniture. Only, see, it isn't in New York. I don't know where my stuff is. There's no apartment, no director waiting to interview me. It was all a lie. He planned to kill me."

Fear pinched her features. She might be an actress, but I doubted she was acting now. She was squeezing her hands together tightly enough to draw blood.

"So you went to the bank pretending to be Elaine, withdrew all the money in her accounts and booked a ticket from New York to Nevada in her name. How did you manage to pull that off, if you don't mind my asking?"

"What are you talking about? I didn't do any of those things. I dumped the car in a shopping center, called Perry to come and pick me up and I've been hiding at his place ever since, trying to figure out what to do."

"Who's Perry?"

"A part-time actor I know. Does it matter? I did some checking and found out Al had lied about everything and I realized I was dead if I didn't get out of town. I heard Al tell Delvecchi getting you involved had been a miscalculation on his part. I figured if you worried him, you could help me get away. You can, can't you?"

I was trying to assimilate everything she'd said. Maybe I was nuts to believe her, but I did. I thought she was too scared to be lying. Heck, I was scared, too. As for getting her away…

"Why don't you just go to the police and tell them?"

"Are you crazy? Al would kill me for sure."

"They can protect you."

"What are you? Some naive virgin or something? We're talking about Albert Russo here. He's got cops in his back pocket. He's friends with the mayor. The only way I'm going to survive this mess is to get away. I've got some money set aside, but I don't know how to disappear. Oh, hell, I made a mistake coming here. I figured you—"

"No you didn't. Sit back down," I told her sharply. "I just have to think this through. If you didn't take the money out of the bank, that means Elaine Russo is still alive. But that doesn't make any sense. Why would Russo go through this charade unless he was trying to make people believe she was alive when she wasn't?"

"Maybe he thought she was dead."

Out of the mouth of an actress.

"Except if Al wants somebody dead, they're dead," Nicole added. "Al doesn't fool around."

No. Al wouldn't fool around. I was in kimchi up to my neck and sinking fast and I didn't like the taste even a little bit. We couldn't stay here and I couldn't take her to my Dad's place or the flower shop. Even my aunt's place was out. It was bad enough when I only had the police looking for me. Now I had to worry about Albert Russo coming after me, because I was pretty sure Nicole was right. He'd want her dead whether Elaine was still alive or not.

Was Elaine alive? Or had he killed her after she'd gone to the bank and closed her accounts? And if she was alive, where was she hiding and why?

"All right, here's what we're going to do. I'm going to take you to stay with a woman I know. Russo will never find you there, I promise."

Besides, I sort of figured Nicole deserved to meet Mrs. Keene. Mrs. Keene would take her in. Mrs. Keene loves company.

"But I don't want to stay in Cleveland. I want to get away."

"I got that, but I need time to make some arrangements."

What arrangements, I hadn't a clue, but right now the important thing was to stash Nicole until I could talk to Brandon—assuming he wasn't under arrest for Delvecchi's murder.

"Do you have a car?" I asked her.

"No. I had Perry drop me off."

"Just out of curiosity, why can't you stay with Perry?"

"His wife's coming home tonight. She wouldn't like having me there."

Yeah. I could understand that. I changed Mama's water, added some food and cleaned the litter box, to Nicole's profound disgust. Then I hustled her outside. We didn't bump into anyone I knew and there were no police cars, marked or unmarked, loitering around.

To my surprise, Nicole thought Frog was cute. She didn't seem to mind riding around in the airy vehicle. I didn't see any cop cars loitering on my dad's street, but I pulled all the way up in the driveway to the garage out behind Mrs. Keene's house. She greeted us on the back porch with a wide smile.

"Dee, how lovely. You brought company. Come in. I just baked an apple pie."

"Thanks, Mrs. Keene. This is Nicole Wickley."

Nicole shot me an angry look, but Mrs. Keene immediately gushed a welcome.

"Oh, yes, I recognized her. You're that beautiful woman who does those annoying car commercials," she gushed. "Please come in. It's such a pleasure to meet you. You're far more attractive in person."

Nicole preened.

"Do come in," Mrs. Keene urged again.

We did. The house smelled of fresh-baked pie. Nicole sniffed appreciatively. Too bad I knew it wouldn't taste as good as it smelled.

"Dee, the police have been at your father's house today looking for you. Of course, I told them I hadn't seen you, but I was wondering if something was wrong."

"No, they just want to ask me some questions.

about something that happened on one of my cases. I'll get it straightened out shortly, but I was wondering if Nicole could spend the afternoon with you. I need to make some arrangements and she needs a place to hide from a stalker," I improvised. "Unfortunately her stalker isn't like yours. Her stalker is dangerous, so there is some serious risk involved."

"Oh, you poor dear. That's horrible! Don't you worry about a thing. You've come to the right place. Dee knows I'll keep you safe. Our Dee here is an excellent investigator. She'll help you just like she did me. She lives such an exciting life."

My cell phone rang before I could interrupt. Caller ID showed it was a pay phone. It didn't seem likely that the cops would call me from a pay phone, so I took a chance.

"Hello?"

"Dee?"

I'd never been so relieved to hear anyone's voice in my life. Brandon sounded exhausted.

"Where are you?" I demanded.

"Same place I was the last time I needed a ride."

"This is definitely one of those habits you need to break."

"Very funny. Can you come pick me up?"

Aware of my audience, I was careful of what I said. "Things are more complicated this time."

"You aren't alone," he said after a second's pause.

He was good. "That's right."

"Should I call Julie?"

"No. We really need to talk, but I'm avoiding your friends at the moment."

"I could catch a bus to Westgate Shopping Center. We could meet in the men's department, where we went last time."

"Alone?"

"Sans tail, got it. I'll head over there now."

"Great. I'll meet you there."

Relieved, I disconnected and smiled at the two women watching me. "I'm going to pick up Brandon," I assured Nicole.

"He's such a nice, helpful young man," Mrs. Keene put in. "He's her partner, you know."

I didn't bother to correct her. "You two stay here and I'll be back in an hour or so, all right?" To my astonishment, the actress nodded easy acceptance. Rattled, I turned back to my father's neighbor. "Uh, Mrs. Keene, don't mention Nicole's presence to *anyone,* all right?"

"Don't you worry, dear. I'll take good care of Miss Wickley. We'll have a bite of lunch and she can tell me all about her exciting career and all the famous people she knows."

Nicole sat down with all the grace of a queen and crossed her legs. Why, she was actually planning to enjoy this! I felt a flash of panic, but since I didn't know which one of them needed the warning, I smiled reassuringly and made a hasty exit.

As a normally law-abiding citizen, it felt wrong to be dodging the police, but I told myself as long as they didn't know I was dodging them it would be okay. I expected to have to wait for Brandon at the department store, but he must have caught a bus to Westgate almost immediately after we hung up. I was fingering an oxford shirt in the men's department when he came up behind me, took my arm and began escorting me through the store at a rapid pace.

"Keep walking. I'm not sure how well I lost my tail."

"The police want to talk to me," I said nervously.

"You haven't talked to them yet?"

"It didn't seem advisable until I talked to you."

He gave me a half grin. "Good thinking. Where's Binky?"

"I left him with Ted. I've got Frog."

"Frog?"

"You'll see."

He did. The moment he spotted Frog he muttered something under his breath that Mickey probably wouldn't have approved of.

"You couldn't have found something brighter? Maybe neon orange would have been more noticeable."

"Hey, he's small, and it's not my fault. I think Ted may be color-blind. Or else he gets some tremendous deal on paint."

"From an enemy? He's not painting Binky is he?"

The thought sent a shiver straight down my spine. "God, I hope not! Get in."

"How? I'm six-one."

I shrugged. "It didn't come with a shoehorn, sorry."

"You do realize if I climb in there with you, your father is going to consider us engaged."

"Very funny. Get in before someone notices us."

"Dee, no one in the world will miss us in this."

He muttered something else under his breath and proceeded to fold himself into the roadster.

"Put the top up," he ordered as I climbed in beside him.

"There isn't one."

He gave me a hard look.

"It's not my fault. This was all Ted had."

Briefly he closed his eyes. "Don't you dare tell me to duck."

I started the car and suppressed a grin. "Fine, but you could bow your head."

I got us moving with a minimal grinding of gears.

"Prayer does seem like a good idea. You do know how to drive a stick shift, right?"

"Binky's a shift," I reminded him. "Frog's gears stick. Quit complaining. I have things to tell you."

"I have a few things to tell you, as well."

"I already know about the gun. Julie and Mickey came to see me."

He swore.

"Mickey says we aren't allowed to say that. And we only have an hour."

"What happens in an hour?"

"We have to go back and pick up Nicole Wickley.

I stashed her with Mrs. Keene. She hired us to keep her alive and get her out of Cleveland."

I could feel Brandon staring at me, but I had to concentrate on my driving while struggling to keep the hair out of my eyes as we bounced out of the parking lot.

"You win," he said. "You talk first."

"I'm starving. Let's grab a sandwich at the drive-through. That way we can sit and talk in the parking lot and not be overheard."

"Because, of course, no one can overhear us talking in an open-air minicoupe painted a bright neon green that would draw the attention of a blind person." He closed his eyes. "I remember when life used to be simple. Back when all I had to deal with was drug pushers and perverts and cop haters."

"Yeah. Don't you just love being a P.I.?"

But he had a point, so we hit the drive-through at the nearest fast-food place and I took us down in the valley. There was an entrance conveniently close to Westgate and parking right there at the bottom of the hill. In the park we'd be just one more couple enjoying a late picnic lunch.

The valley is part of a chain of parks sometimes called the Emerald Necklace because it spans nearly a hundred miles of interconnecting roads through the Cleveland suburbs. There are always lots of people in the valley at any given time, so even though it's police patrolled, I didn't figure anyone would give us a second look.

I found a parking space near some empty cars and we sat and watched the muddy river tumbling past while we ate and defended our meal from the insect world. Even though I could see several expletives deleted, Brandon didn't interrupt as I gave him the gist of my day.

"Nicole's story is as screwy as everything else about this case," he said when I finished.

"When did Elaine first call you?" I asked.

"Last Thursday. Why?"

"Because according to my source, Elaine closed out her personal bank accounts on Friday."

Brandon nodded. "She was getting ready to run."

"Looks that way. So Russo must have killed her after that to keep her from talking to you again."

"Makes sense if she really did have some evidence that would have led the police to his front door."

I swallowed a French fry and watched him bite into his hamburger. "So why didn't she take this evidence to them? Why call you in the first place?"

"Fear. Unless she had firsthand evidence that would convict Russo of something, she had to know the police wouldn't put her into protective custody. I'm guessing she wanted to hand the stuff over to me and disappear."

"So Russo learns Elaine talked to you and kills her. He then has Nicole go through that elaborate charade to buy time?"

Brandon chewed thoughtfully and flicked aside an inquisitive fly. "Russo establishes a couple of things by having you take those pictures of the two of us. Proof that his wife is alive when she isn't and that she and I are having an affair. Anything I tell the police afterward is suspect after he has Nicole go to his office and throw that tantrum over the pictures."

"Okay, but Russo is still going to be a suspect in her murder even if he does kill both of you, isn't he?"

Brandon stared out over the water. I could tell that wasn't what he was seeing. He was thinking hard, trying to make the pieces fit.

"Not if the bodies don't turn up. If Elaine and I both suddenly disappear without a trace, the cops have a whole new situation," he mused. "Especially if it can be made to look like we ran off together. Remember the ticket from New York to Nevada? What do you want to bet Nicole was supposed to board that flight in Elaine's name?"

"She didn't say anything about that," I told him.

"Maybe she didn't know that was next."

"It was only one ticket," I pointed out. "What about you?"

His smile held no trace of humor. "Want to bet my car would have turned up in Nevada somewhere?"

I set down the French fry I'd lifted, no longer hungry.

"He was planning to kill you all along."

"That's why he had Nicole arrange to meet me at his house Thursday afternoon. I was supposed to die that day. Only you interfered."

I crumpled up the remains of my lunch and stuffed

them in the bag, suddenly feeling sick. "Delvecchi ran you off the road that morning," I protested slowly. "What if you'd been killed then?"

"So much the better. Elaine's car would have turned up in a parking lot in New York and it would have looked as though she disappeared from there. Maybe Nicole would have picked up her ticket for Nevada and flown there in her place. In fact, the more I think about it, the more I'm sure that was the original plan. Either I died or was injured in a car crash and Elaine took off without me and then I would have died or disappeared later. Remember, Nicole had told everyone she was moving to New York. No one would miss her right away. And when someone did, where would they start the search?"

"But it still all leads back to Russo eventually. It was common knowledge that he was seeing Nicole and people have commented on how much she looks like Elaine," I protested.

"Oh, the cops would have suspected Russo, all right, just like they suspect him of several other things, but where's the proof? If everyone is gone, all they've got is conjecture."

It made a horrible kind of sense that sent my insides roiling.

"But I screwed it up for them," I said more to myself than him.

Brandon's nod was sober. "You did. The minute you came to see me, Russo's plan fell apart. He never counted on the two of us hooking up. I noted your license plate Monday when I started following Nicole to the shopping center. The car looked out of place in Shaker Heights and you both were heading to the shopping center, so I automatically noted it. When she wasn't at the motel the following morning, I ran the plate and came up with your name. Then I remembered the woman who'd come inside Victor's and used the ladies' room and came up with—"

"Me."

"You," he agreed.

"Okay, but why kill Delvecchi in your bedroom?"

He took a minute to think about that before replying.

"Delvecchi failed twice to get rid of me. Russo now has two people running loose who are a considerable danger to him. Nicole, he can deal with. I'm a higher profile because cops know me. Russo can neutralize me or at least slow me down if the cops believe I killed Delvecchi. And Delvecchi has already shown he can't handle the job anymore."

"Whoa. Are you saying Russo himself killed Delvecchi? Or does he have another contract killer waiting in the wings? I know he's supposed to have gang ties and all that, but how easy is it to hire a killer?"

It seemed awfully chancy to me, but then, what did I know about people like the Russos? Or Nicole Wickley, for that matter.

"I don't see Delvecchi letting a stranger walk up behind him and shoot him in the head," Brandon

said slowly. "I do see Russo insisting on going with
Delvecchi to talk to me."

I thought about Russo's cold eyes and shuddered.
I didn't doubt for a minute the man was capable of
cold-blooded murder. "Nicole really is in danger."

"So are you. You're the one who made a hash of
his plans. That's why Nicole came to see you."

Lunch turned to stone in my stomach. He crumpled his food wrapper and shoved it in the bag.

"We need to have a talk with our new client."

"Shouldn't we go talk to the police?"

"Yes. As soon as we talk to Nicole, we'll call Dex
and tell him our theory. But I want to see what Nicole can tell us first."

I didn't. I wanted on the first flight out of the coun-
try. I was pretty sure Australia would be a nice place
to live. Instead we dumped our trash and headed for
Mrs. Keene's house.

I parked near the garage again and we walked to
the back door. When Mrs. Keene didn't answer right
away, Brandon twisted the handle and we walked inside. Lunch remains sat on the table. It was easy to
see which dishes belonged to Nicole. Nothing else
appeared out of place, but the house had an empty,
deserted feel that was tangible.

Brandon moved toward the hall, motioning for
me to wait. Obviously he didn't have a gun, but I
wasn't worried. I knew he wasn't going to find anyone.

While Brandon searched the house, I went back

outside to the garage. Mrs. Keene's car was gone, a fact I pointed out as soon as Brandon joined me.

"There's no sign of any trouble in the house," he told me.

I nodded. "Do you think they just went somewhere?"

"Didn't you tell them to stay put?"

"Of course I did, but Nicole had a wad of cash on her. Maybe she conned Mrs. Keene into taking her to the airport. Maybe she decided we weren't her best bet after all, retainer or no retainer."

"And maybe someone encouraged them to leave."

I didn't want to believe that. If it was true, I'd just put a harmless old woman in real danger.

Chapter Fourteen

We decided to wait around in case they had just run to the store or something. But while we waited, Brandon called his friend Dex and laid out our suspicions for the officer. Even from the one-sided conversation I was able to hear, I could tell his friend was less than happy. So was Brandon when he hung up.

"Dex is going to talk to some people and get back to us."

"What does that mean?"

Brandon looked angry. "If he can convince his captain we're right, and his captain can convince the powers that be, they'll go and ask Russo a few questions. In the meantime I'm supposed to tell you that Detective Martin wants to talk to you again."

"What are we going to do?"

Before he could respond, my cell phone rang. The number that came up showed the call was from another cell phone. I figured it didn't matter at this point if it was Officer Martin. In fact, I was thinking it might be a good idea to find myself surrounded by police officers.

"D.B. Hayes," I said briskly.

"Ms. Hayes, this is Albert Russo. I was wondering if we might talk."

My stomach did a quick flip, threatening the lunch I'd just eaten. I mouthed his identity to Brandon, who instantly moved closer. I held the phone out a short ways, hoping he could hear, too.

"Go ahead, Mr. Russo."

"Actually I'd like to meet with you in person."

Brandon shook his head violently.

"I'm outside your office, but I see the flower shop is closed. I'll wait for you to get here."

And he disconnected. I looked at Brandon. He was already reaching for my cell phone, punching in new numbers.

"Dex, Brandon... Yes, I know it's Sunday. I'm sorry, it was supposed to be your day off. Never mind talking to your captain, there isn't time. Russo's at Flower World. Dee and I are on our way over there to meet him."

"Are you crazy?" I demanded. He ignored me.

"We need backup... No! He'd spot an army and we've got no proof of anything... Yeah. That's what I'm hoping. I know it's a risk, but what choice do we have?... There's no time for a wire. Dee, do you have a tape recorder?"

"Not on me."

"We're on our own.... No. I know the layout. I'm

thinking Dee should go in alone. One of us can hide in the bathroom, the other can hide in the back room. If she leaves the office door open, we should be able to hear whatever is said."

"You're out of your mind!"

He squeezed my shoulder. "Right. We'll have to keep him from taking her anyplace. He won't kill her there, but if she can keep him talking, it should prove interesting to see what scheme he has in mind next… Uh-huh. Fifteen minutes."

I was shaking all over. "You're insane," I told him as he hung up. "Russo wants to kill us."

"He's going to want to find out how much you know and who you told, first."

"You make me feel so much better."

"You have to do this, Dee. It's the best chance we have. Do you have a gun? No, of course you don't."

"Actually I do," I said, trying not to let him see me shake. "It's out in the car."

"Great!"

"No, it isn't. What am I going to do with a gun?"

He grinned. "For me. I'm going to back you up. Dex is joining us. No one will hurt you, I promise."

"From your lips to God's ear."

"What?"

"One of Trudy's sayings."

He smiled then, one of those slow, sweet smiles that would have left me weak at the knees if they hadn't already turned gelatinous. Before I knew what he intended, he cupped my chin and kissed me with slow, deliberate thoroughness.

"I will not let anything happen to you," he said firmly. "I swear it."

My mind tumbled in chaos. I couldn't seem to think. I was scared past all reason, but somehow the fact that Brandon was so steady helped to steady me.

I knew I was going to do what he wanted because he was right. We needed to know what Russo was planning next. Our lives depended on this.

He folded down Frog's seat and had to work to pull out the small bag, which had become lodged in the narrow space. A lace bra spilled out.

"Very pretty."

"Pervert," I said, taking both the bra and the blouse that came next from his fingers. "I'll find the gun."

"Got it," he said. "Where's the clip?"

"There should be three of them in there."

After a bit more rummaging, he found them, inserted one and stuck the gun in his waistband. Then he stopped. "Would you rather…?"

"No! I don't like guns. And I have pepper spray in my purse."

"Better than nothing. Okay. Let's go. Drop me a street away and, whatever you do, don't get in a car with him."

"I'm not entirely stupid," I protested.

"You aren't the least bit stupid," he assured me. "Just be careful. Go in the back way and leave the door unlocked."

The shaking started once I dropped him off. Par
of me wanted to keep driving and to heck with Al
bert Russo and Brandon. The other part was insatia
bly curious. What did Russo want with me
now—besides the obvious?

He was parked out back in a long black Cadillac
and he was alone. I parked closer to the door and
headed straight there without acknowledging him.
kept one hand in my purse on the pepper spray. If he
thought I was carrying a gun, so much the better.
was glad Aunt Lacy and Trudy weren't still here.

"Thank you for meeting me so promptly," he said
stepping inside as I held the door open for him.

"It sounded like an order to me," I told him tersely
leading the way to my office. "Have a seat and tell
me what I can do for you."

I was proud of how businesslike I sounded. I wa
quaking inside, but I was darned if I was going to let
him know it. George appeared, brushing up against
my leg. Russo gave the cat a scowl.

"I dislike animals."

"George belongs to my aunt." I made no move to
chase the cat out but moved around the desk and care
fully sat down. I glimpsed a movement in the hall a
Russo's back. Reinforcements had arrived. George
immediately jumped into my lap, distracting both o
us. Russo's jaw tightened and those cold eyes grew icy

"Perhaps coming here was a mistake."

"What is it you want, Mr. Russo?" I asked, em
boldened with the knowledge Brandon was out there

"I want you to find my wife."

I had to force my mouth closed. It was almost past my lips to ask him which wife.

"I thought you were applying for a divorce," I said instead.

"That is my intention, however I need to find her first." He studied me the way he would an insect. I was really glad for the comfort George's small weight gave me. He purred as I stroked his head.

"Ms. Hayes, I am going to tell you something I have not told anyone else. I believe my wife killed my associate, Hogan Delvecchi."

Okay, he had me. I couldn't think of a thing to say to that.

"My wife was not having an affair with Mr. Kirk-patrick, as you already know. But as much as it pains me to admit this, she was having an affair with Mr. Delvecchi."

And the worst part was that even knowing what I did, I believed him. Or at least, I believed that he believed his wife had been having an affair with Delvecchi. There was an edge of anger in those words that sent a visible chill up my arms.

"Hogan Delvecchi is dead." And Russo had now handed me the perfect motive for both murders.

His lips pursed. "Yes. Mr. Kirkpatrick is being questioned by the police for his murder, I believe."

"We both know Brandon is innocent," I said harshly. "Do you have any proof?"

"That Elaine murdered Delvecchi? No. But if you

check with your police sources, I believe you will find that they discovered a woman had been staying at his home. I'm certain if you tell them it was Elaine they'll be able to prove it."

Was it possible? Could Elaine be alive, and not dead like we'd thought?

"Why don't you tell them yourself?"

"My wife has some business papers I would like to retrieve before they fall into the wrong hands. To that end, I would like you to find her first. I am prepared to pay you quite well, Ms. Hayes."

He started to reach for his pocket and I stopped him. Only because I knew Brandon was in position outside the door did I feel it was safe to risk my neck.

"You're talking about the papers Elaine told Brandon she had that would tie you to his brother's murder?" He stilled. "No, thank you, Mr. Russo. I know all about Nicole Wickley posing as your wife. I've already given that information to the police."

George leaped off my lap and ran out the door, startling both of us. Albert Russo recovered quickly. His cold eyes bored a hole straight through me with the intensity of his stare.

"You surprise me once again, Ms. Hayes. I don't generally underestimate people as seriously as I underestimated you. Your looks are…deceptive. Have you spoken with Ms. Wickley?"

"Yes, as a matter of fact. Before you spirited her away."

"I have no idea what you're talking about."

There was no way he could have feigned that blank look of surprise. And it quickly turned to an expression of calculation that lasted mere seconds.

"I believe this conversation is pointless."

He started to rise. My hand closed over the pepper spray and my mouth went dry.

"A gun is unnecessary," he said coldly, coming to his feet and eyeing my hand still inside my purse. "You are in no danger from me. However I can't promise the same immunity from my wife. If she believes you are helping me, she will kill you just as she did Hogan Delvecchi. I believe Ms. Wickley is in the same peril. Please pass that information along to her if you see her again."

I swallowed past my fear. "Everything is coming unraveled, Mr. Russo. No matter what you do now, the police are going to be investigating you."

"I believe you. I will go home and speak with my attorney at once. Take care, Ms. Hayes. I think it would be a shame if you don't live long enough to grow into your potential."

He turned and strode out the door. I hurried to stand, and the stupid chair rolled back, toppling me against the wall.

Brandon charged into the room a second later, my gun in his hand. He looked angry as he helped me to my feet.

"Jeez, you take chances."

I felt shaky, like someone who knew they'd just had a very close call. "He doesn't have Nicole."

"I heard."

"Where's your friend Dex?"

"He moved outside ahead of Russo when we realized he was leaving. He'll follow him to see where he goes."

"Good."

The sound of gunshots splintered the Sunday afternoon quiet. We raced to the back door, nearly tripping over George, only to face Russo, who came rushing back inside with a gun in his left hand. Blood ran down the side of his face.

"You filthy little bitch. You set me up!" he yelled shrilly.

His cold eyes were wild with hate. Brandon had shoved my gun in his waistband when he had helped me up. Now he reached for it, but he never had a chance. Russo fired.

With the sound ringing in my ears, I didn't stop to think. An empty pail we use to store flowers in while working on arrangements was sitting within reach. I heaved it at his head. As a distraction, it worked perfectly. A second bullet ripped through the pail, shattering a pair of ceramic vases on the shelf behind me.

Brandon was moving before he could take aim again. He slammed into Russo's chest with his head. Russo went back against the doorjamb with stunning force. Still, he brought his gun hand down against Brandon's shoulder.

Rage lent me a fierce recklessness. I don't like guns, I don't like being shot at and I really didn't like

Albert Russo. I ran forward and wrenched his bony wrist up and back as hard as I could. The gun fired once more. The sound was deafening. I refused to release my crushing hold. I barely noticed Brandon hitting him. Then hands pulled at me, yanking me clear. A large, scary-looking man with a ponytail and an unkempt beard yanked the gun free of Russo's hand. His own weapon was out and it was a whole lot bigger than Russo's nine millimeter.

I stepped back and let Brandon and the stranger toss Albert Russo against the workstation to get handcuffs on him. Sirens screamed their approach. Through the open back door I saw a crumpled pile of rags on the asphalt beside the black Cadillac. The rags moved feebly. I sprinted in that direction without conscious thought.

The rags proved to be a blond woman who could only be Elaine Russo. She was straining to reach a .38 revolver a few yards away from her blood-soaked body.

"Stay still," I told her, bending to retrieve the gun. "An ambulance is on the way."

She looked up at me with hate-filled eyes. "Go to hell."

I took a sharp step back and decided to let the EMTs and the police deal with Elaine Russo.

In short order the parking lot and the flower shop filled with people in uniforms. George escaped and I scooped him up, holding him close against my chest.

I was horrified to discover Brandon had taken a bullet across his forearm. He was actually lucky Russo had been such a terrible shot. The man had been standing only a few feet away, yet the bullet had only left a nasty gouge. He'd done a much better job on the wife, who'd been lying in wait for him beside his car.

Brandon's friend Dex had seen the whole thing. He'd left the shop, intent on getting to his own car in time to follow Russo. By the time he'd spotted Elaine open fire on her husband it had been too late. Russo had returned fire with a vengeance and headed back toward the flower shop, certain I had set him up for her attack.

I had to lock poor George in the office to keep him out from underfoot while the police went over the crime scene. Elaine Russo was rushed into surgery. A defiantly mute Albert Russo was also taken to Lakewood Hospital for treatment of a head wound. She'd managed to graze him, at least.

Brandon refused transportation to the hospital and was treated by the EMTs there at the flower shop.

I answered the same questions from multiple people, including Lieutenant Martin, who'd finally arrived with another plainclothes officer I'd never seen before. By then I was growing pretty frantic.

"Look, these other people won't listen to me, but you have to look for Mrs. Keene and Nicole Wickley!"

"Relax, Ms. Hayes. They are both safe," Detective Martin assured me. "Mrs. Keene took Ms. Wickley to see Judge Dogsmore this afternoon. After hearing her tale, he called me. We placed Ms. Wickley in protective custody this evening. I've just come from there. Ms. Wickley has confirmed what you told us about her part in this. Like you, she believed Mrs. Russo was dead. We already have confirmation that the real Elaine Russo had been staying with Delvecchi this week from several neighbors who saw them together. We're not as incompetent as the public believes, Ms. Hayes."

For the first time I began to relax.

"Good. I'm not either," I told him. "Brandon and I don't think Elaine killed Delvecchi, despite what Russo said."

Other than mild surprise, nothing showed on his face. He waited silently for me to continue.

"It makes no sense," I said, picking my words with care. "Why would Elaine try to frame Brandon? Albert Russo had a motive, she didn't. Russo would have been searching for Elaine, especially if she does have papers that tie him to Seth Kirkpatrick's murder. Ask Delvecchi's neighbors if someone else asked about the woman staying with him before you did. Brandon, Delvecchi and Elaine were dangerous to Albert Russo. Brandon thinks he ordered Delvecchi to go with him to talk to Brandon. I think he's right."

"You think Russo shot him?"

"Wouldn't the angle of the bullet be different if Albert was the shooter rather than Elaine? I know they are both tall, but I think Albert's left-handed. At least, that's the hand he was using to hold the gun when he came inside the shop tonight."

His expression was tinged with admiration. "You're right, Ms. Hayes, the angle does make a difference."

"I think Elaine was using Delvecchi. You won't be able to prove this, but I'm betting she planned to have Delvecchi kill Albert Russo and make it look like suicide or an accident. If there's a prenuptial contract, the only way she could inherit was if he died."

"Even if you're right, we won't be able to prove that unless Mrs. Russo confesses."

"I know."

"I'll need you to come to the station tomorrow and make a formal statement. It's late and Mr. Kirkpatrick is waiting to take you home. Thank you for your cooperation."

"Russo should have heeded his own advice and watched out for his wife," I said as Brandon led me over to a large, dark-colored SUV. "Whose car is this?"

"Dex's. I'll get it back to him tomorrow. Frog is trapped in the parking lot until the police finish for the night. You nearly gave me a heart attack, you know. What did you think you were doing, charging a gun like that?"

"Who had time to think?" I protested.

He swore.

"I'm telling Mickey," I warned him.

I closed my eyes, feeling exhausted. When I opened them again, we were pulling into my father's driveway. Dad should have been in bed hours ago, but the house blazed with light. He met us at the door and drew me into a fierce bear hug, kissing my forehead. Coming from a man who is not given to outward displays of emotion, it brought tears to my eyes as I hugged him back.

"Thanks for bringing her home, Brandon."

"You're welcome, sir."

"Why couldn't you marry and settle down like your brothers?" he demanded gruffly, letting me go.

"I like being a private investigator."

"You need to call Lacy and Trudy."

"In the morning," I promised. There was no way I could face that daunting task at the moment.

"All right, honey. I can see you're out on your feet. I'll let them know you're both home safe."

It wasn't until morning that the word *both* penetrated my fuzzy brain. If Brandon wasn't careful, they'd have us married and raising kids in a house down the street in no time. He had no idea how ruthless my family could be when it came to matchmaking and me.

I'd been wrong on all counts. Brandon did fit on the couch and I could sleep in a house with him under the same roof.

Despite a headache, I showered and dressed quickly

and found Brandon at the kitchen table reading the newspaper.

"Good morning," I greeted. "How's your arm?"

"Sore. We made the front page. Not a bad shot of you, either. You look cute."

"Let me see that!"

He was right. Standing next to him, I did look cute. I hate looking cute. Especially when he looked so handsome and coolly professional despite the blood on his arm and the bruise on his face.

"The police want to talk to us. And some of the media is offering to pay for an exclusive."

"How much?"

"Very funny."

"Did he kill her?" I asked.

"Elaine? Not so far. She made it through surgery, but neither one of them is talking. They found the evidence Elaine originally offered to give me. Apparently Russo had Seth's notebook and the tape he made of their conversation together. Seth was working on tying Russo to some serious graft that was going on at city hall. The mayor will be relieved to know his name wasn't mentioned, but Dex wasn't more specific about it than that."

"Dex being the big, scary-looking guy with the beard?"

"That's Dex. And changing the subject completely, I like the dress."

"What dress?"

He nodded toward the dining room. Draped over

a chair was a shimmery dress in ice-blue I'd never seen before. Or so I thought until I picked it up. The only familiar part was the bodice, with its rich array of colors. Kai had removed the cap sleeves and turned the gown into a delicate Empire waist, much lovelier than the original dress had been.

"Your aunt said Kai got an A on her project so she doesn't need the dress anymore. She thought you might like to have it back. Is that what you're going to wear on Saturday?"

I'd forgotten all about Lorna's wedding.

"Aunt Lacy was here?"

"While you were in the shower. She said she'd talk to you later. I can't wait to see you in that dress."

I set it down, feeling the heat of his gaze.

"I need caffeine."

He gave me a knowing smile and stepped back to allow me to enter the kitchen again.

"Ted says Binky will be ready by this afternoon."

I stopped in the act of opening the refrigerator. "What do you mean *ready?*"

"He says you're going to love the color. I told him I couldn't picture Binky in purple with white and green racing stripes, but—"

"You're kidding!" I felt faint. "You'd better be kidding. You are kidding, aren't you?"

"Hey, I'm just the messenger."

I thought about Binky and I thought about Ted and I couldn't tell if Brandon was teasing or not.

"What did you do with my gun? This is justifiable grounds for a homicide. No court will convict me."

"Speaking of courts, we need to let Detective Martin know we're on our way before he sends a car for us. And we won't be needing Frog. I returned Dex's SUV and he ran me over to pick up the Honda. You are *not* to name my car. So, as soon as you have something to eat…"

I pulled a can of diet cola from the refrigerator. "Breakfast. Let's go. And do not even think about lecturing me this morning."

He held up his hands. "Wouldn't dream of it."

I was the one who felt like I was dreaming this morning. I pulled the tab, took a swallow and waited for the caffeine to reach my bloodstream. "We need to stop in Birdtown first."

"I never heard of Birdtown."

"It's a local term for a block of streets all named after birds. I have to pick something up."

"All right."

We locked up and headed for the Arrensky house.

"I've been thinking," Brandon said after a few minutes. "We work pretty well together, wouldn't you say?"

I tried to calm the insane tripping of my pulse as I studied his impassive features. He was such a hunk.

"You mean, as investigators?" I asked.

He shot me a quick glance. "Yeah. How would you feel about forming a partnership?"

"What sort of partnership?" I asked cautiously.

"Kirkpatrick and Hayes Investigative Services?"

What had I expected? I squashed the other fleeting thought and faced him. "Hayes and Kirkpatrick," I countered. "Pull up in that driveway over there and hold on to that thought."

The street was quiet except for a girl on a bike at the far corner with a poodle nipping at her heels. Not another soul was in sight this gloomy Monday morning.

"I'll be right back," I told Brandon.

It wasn't three in the morning, there were people out and about and Lyle could be home. I found I didn't care. I strode up to the front door and inserted the first key. No good. The second key didn't work either. Before I could try the third key, the door jerked open and Lyle Arrensky stood there in a pair of white boxer shorts spritzed with yellow smiley faces.

"You!"

"Yes, me!"

I put my hand on his bare chest and pushed hard. He was so surprised, he moved back, allowing me to stride past him into the living room. I emptied the loving cup of peanut shells by dumping them on the floor and started back the way I'd come.

"You can't come in here and take that!"

I pulled out my can of pepper spray and glared at him.

"As a duly authorized representative of your ex-wife, I am removing this piece of her personal property. You have a problem with that, call a cop."

His mouth fell open.

"Now get out of my way or I'll spray you in your squinty little eyes. And for crying out loud, put some pants on, Lyle," I ordered as I strode past him carrying the ugly loving cup. "You're an embarrassment to the neighborhood."

Brandon had followed me onto the porch, ready to act as backup if necessary. I hadn't seen him until he held the door open for me. The look of respectful admiration in his eyes gave me a buoyant feeling I couldn't describe. For the first time in my life I felt about six feet tall myself as I strode down the steps and over to his car.

"Now about that name," I said as he got in behind the wheel and started the ignition. "I'm the native Ohioan, so we go with Hayes and Kirkpatrick."

He grinned. One of those curl-your-toes grins that set my stomach quivering.

"I'm looking forward to this negotiation, partner."

I leaned back and smiled. "So am I."

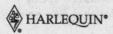

Emotional, compelling stories that capture the intensity of
living, loving and creating a family in today's world.

Modern, passionate reads that are powerful and provocative.

Romances that are sparked by danger and fueled by passion.

SILHOUETTE *Romance*

From today to forever, these love stories offer
today's woman fairytale romance.

Action-filled romances with strong, sexy, savvy women who save the day.

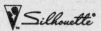

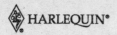

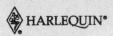

HARLEQUIN®

INTRIGUE°

presents the next installment of

The LANDRY BROTHERS

Protecting their own…by any means necessary!

FILM AT ELEVEN
BY KELSEY ROBERTS
(Harlequin Intrigue #855, available July 2005)

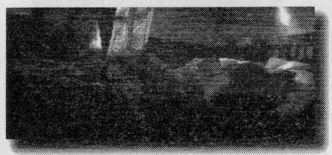

Dr. Molly Jameson's life was right on target…until
a stalker killed a woman on air, and vowed that either
Molly or news anchor Chandler Landry would be his
next victim. Would Molly and Chandler win their
desperate race against time to discover who
the madman was before he found them?

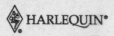

HARLEQUIN®

INTRIGUE®

ECLIPSE

**A gothic-inspired romance
from favorite Harlequin Intrigue author**

PATRICIA ROSEMOOR

GHOST HORSE

July 2005, #858

Hired to tutor his daughter for the summer, city girl Chloe Morgan kept
her real reason for coming to Graylord Pastures a secret from rugged
horse breeder Damian Graylord. After all, Chloe considered the dark,
brooding master of the house a suspect in the mysterious disappearance
of the previous teacher—and her best friend. Haunted by visions of a
ghost horse riding in the mist, Chloe believed the apparition was leading
her to the truth, but could anyone—or anything—protect her from
unexplained accidents and Damian's unbridled passion?

Available at your favorite retail outlet.

www.eHarlequin.com

HIGH